T0193151

FARSCAPE
FOREVER!

FARSCAPE FOREVER!

SEX, DRUGS AND KILLER MUPPETS

EDITED BY

GLENN YEFFETH

An imprint of BenBella Books, Inc.
Dallas, TX

"Frelling Fantastic" © 2005 by Justina Robson

"Theater of Faces" © 2005 by Michael Marano

"Down the Wormhole" © 2005 by Jeanne Cavelos

"Puppets, Sentient Blue Vegetables, Body Fluids and Love" © 2005 by Doranna Durgin

"Flatulence, Food and Fornication" © 2005 by Rick Klaw

"Looking Out for Number One" © 2005 by Patricia Bray

"Crackers Don't Matter" © 2005 by Jim Butcher

"Don't Make Me Tongue You" © 2005 by Martha Wells

"Dear John" © 2005 by Tee Morris

"The Big Brother" © 2005 by Amy Berner

"A Hitchhiking Pilot" © 2005 by Jean Rabe

"The Fall and Rise of Rygel XVI" © 2005 by Bill Spangler

"Zhaan: Plant, Priest, Archetype" © 2005 by Josepha Sherman

"My Imaginary Friend" © 2005 by Jody Lynn Nye

"Universe on a Budget" © 2005 by Roxanne Longstreet Conrad

"Starships Don't Just Happen" © 2005 by Thomas Easton

"Journey to the Feminine" © 2005 by Kelley Walters

"Realized Unrealities™" © 2005 by K. Stoddard Hayes

"*Farscape* Villains I've Known and Loved" © 2005 by P. N. Elrod

"Superior Villainy" © 2005 by Charlene Brusso

"Masks of Transformation" © 2005 by Kevin Andrew Murphy

Additional Materials © 2005 by BenBella Books

  Smart Pop is an imprint of BenBella Books, Inc.
10440 N. Central Expressway, Suite 800
Dallas, TX 75231
www.benbellabooks.com
Send feedback to feedback@benbellabooks.com

BenBella and Smart Pop are federally registered trademarks.

Printed in the United States of America
Library of Congress Cataloging-in-Publication Data
Farscape forever! : sex, drugs, and killer muppets / edited by Glenn Yeffeth.
    p. cm.
  ISBN 1-932100-61-X
  1. Farscape (Television program) I. Yeffeth, Glenn.

PN1992.77.F32F37 2005
791.45'72--dc22

2005012325

Cover design by Todd Michael Bushman
Cover photos copyright © Albert L. Ortega
Text design and composition by John Reinhardt Book Design

Special discounts for bulk sales are available. Please contact bulkorders@benbellabooks.com.

CONTENTS

FRELLING FANTASTIC

FARSCAPE, THE SHOW THAT BROUGHT BACK THE PLEASURE PRINCIPLE

JUSTINA ROBSON

Farscape is different. Every fan comes to that shock of realization at some point: "My God, they really are going to do that!" For me, I think, it was when Crichton was split in two, one of him going off with Aeryn and one staying on Moya. No merging of the two, no convenient death of one (at least not until much later, when it meant something). Farscape was not afraid to make its viewers uncomfortable; it was brilliantly, unrelentingly adult, despite the muppets. And the sex.... Farscape was adult about that as well. The brilliant Justina Robson talks about all this and more.

IN MY ORIGINAL PLAN for this essay I thought I'd write about the way that *Farscape* dealt with sex and humor, and how these things set it apart from other sf TV shows of recent times. I was going to say that it had reclaimed pleasure for the lives of the characters, and showed that it was possible to have fun, enjoy yourself, make a hash of your life and still take part in week-by-week sf drama. By contrast, the people in other shows, from *Star Trek* to *Babylon 5*, were leading lives focused almost entirely on Issues of Immediate Action or scientific and political

1

shenanigans, which filled up story lines on their own and left no room for any kind of normal human interaction. But then I began to think about space opera per se, and realized that *Farscape* was only following a long tradition of the riotous assemblage offered by horse operas, soap operas and sitcoms. It wasn't the subject matter that was different; it was the style of the show that allowed this stuff to emerge. That rather put a spanner in the works of my first plan, since I'd been about to attribute the best bits to Rockne S. O'Bannon and Brian Henson doing their part to drag screen sf into the heady zeitgeist of the early 1990s. But heck, I'll say that here, and then go on with Plan B.

In Plan B here, I'm going to angle this essay in my new direction, and say that it's the type of show, rather than any agenda or great fore-thought, that permitted this happy union of character, setting, sf cliché and ironic awareness to flourish and madly prosper. After that I'll men-tion something about why it seems to me that the pleasure principle was and is missing from a lot of sf, both on and off the small screen, and why it's important that *Farscape* brought it back. I probably won't be able to omit talking about those season three and four costume shifts (black leather, anyone?) and erotic stereotyping. This will no doubt lead to some mention of Orientalism, and sf as the genre of The Other. Finally, there will most likely be a concluding paragraph which will say some-thing like Hooray for *Farscape*! There are a lot of other subjects and features of *Farscape* to talk about and celebrate, but for the sake of this essay I'm going to call it quits at Hooray!

Just so that you know, because there really is no reason why you should know this beforehand, I'm writing here as a fan of the show who happens to also be a professional writer of novels and short stories in the science fiction and fantasy genres, and who sometimes reviews sf lit-erature in the British national press. What I have to say comes from that position. I would shore up my arguments with lots of quotations and references from other worthy writers and thinkers, but unfortunately I am too ignorant, so all this opinion is as much my own as I can make it. Where I can, I will point out anyone who had any good ideas that crop up during the discussion.

I first saw *Farscape* on its UK terrestrial TV debut and thought it could go either way: become either something truly dreadful or something rich and strange. It had all the hallmarks of terrible media sf: an overconfident American hero, obviously human "aliens" in squiffy Nazi uniforms running another version of the ancient and banal *Star Wars* Empire, cute robots, yet *more* aliens who were people in latex, a script that embraced cliché and muppets. The muppets were all new in this context. I hadn't seen muppets since *Fraggle Rock*. Now they were serious.

One thing stood between me and never watching it again. Two things: the acting and the dialogue. Three things: Ben Browder was number three. I fancy I sensed greatness. Or to be more academically specific, I greatly fancied him, and hoped he wouldn't go the grim way of the *Andromeda* cast, drowning in terminal banality, or be sucked into some political black hole like all the cool people in *Babylon 5*.

By episode two I was very heartened by the fact that the hero, John Crichton, appeared to have at least as much trouble believing any of it as I did, and that he relentlessly refused to give up his conviction of himself as a solid twenty-first-century American. He thought what I'd have thought, but with more composure and better looks. He made all the pop references I'd have wanted to make but would have been too busy cowering in a corner to actually say or think of until an hour after the moment had passed. The scriptwriters seemed to be borrowing as heavily from Douglas Adams as they were from *Doctor Who* and *Blake's 7*—two UK shows I grew up loving—so I thought that even if the series turned out to be crap, I could like it and watch it secretly if I had to.

Thankfully I was wrong about the crap part. After a couple of episodes wobbling about like a baby animal finding its feet, the show finally figured out how to walk and talk at the same time. The characters began to firm up and the dialogue got even more interesting, rather short and sharp, like something written by Lawrence Block.[1] It became obvious that *Farscape* was going to be very different from other sf shows in one very important and delightful aspect—it was going to be driven by the characters. They, in turn, were clearly being pulled by the two-horse team of actor and scriptwriter, and for once (I can't believe I'm sticking with this metaphor but I am), both were glad to go charging off in interesting directions.

This was quite a change, and one that I'd been waiting for ever since *Blake's 7* finished way back in 1981. *Blake's 7* was "a major science fiction TV series made by the BBC between 1977 and 1981. It surrounded the exploits of a group of interstellar terrorists and their efforts to inflict

---

[1] Lawrence Block is a prolific and popular writer best known for his crime stories. He also wrote a good book for people who want to be writers, called *Telling Lies for Fun and Profit*. His dialogue is usually to the point, and, like a lot of current TV show dialogue, or anything scripted a long time in advance, it demonstrates a clarity and wit rarely seen in real life.

serious damage on a vicious, corrupt and totalitarian galactic Federation."[2] But even *B7* had a mission goal—to destabilize the Federation. *Farscape* didn't pretend to such idealism. *Farscape*'s motley crew of ex-prisoners, like Lassie, simply wanted to go home. But they were lost. In space.

Other sf shows of the past and present were shaped by other kinds of agendas—agendas which tended to reflect the more active, positive traditions of U.S. culture between 1950 and 1990, in which the prevailing myth featured heroes who had strong goals and who succeeded through pluck, application and daring. *Star Trek* in its original series was set up to face us with the wonder of other worlds and possibilities, providing a weekly dip into the far reaches of the fantastic. It was almost pure adventure. In *Star Trek: The Next Generation* it developed a much greater sense of social conscience and global identity, a political dimension that tied it far more closely to contemporary human concerns. In *Star Trek: Deep Space Nine* those issues were pushed much harder as it became a show about minorities, faiths and the pressures of close-quarters living under threat. Finally, in *Star Trek: Voyager*, the franchise returned to its roots, though this time with a completely different coloration. Where *Star Trek* had looked to the future with awe and inspiration, *Voyager* was always looking over its shoulder, on the run from a much more hostile universe, lost and looking for home.

When it comes to other universes, the situation isn't much different. *Stargate* is basically a control fantasy, in which U.S. humans look out for Earth's interests and act like friendly policemen in a power struggle between (humanoid) aliens with very human issues, though this show has some interesting innovations I haven't time to talk of here. *Lexx* was, well, *Lexx* was a mess, like a teenager's bedroom hurtling around space getting into trouble and doing drugs. *Babylon 5* was a different kettle of fish altogether, but it maintained the themes of human survival among aliens of varying technological and biological prowess, negotiating their way in the universe and, like most of the other shows, was set inside a military and political operation. I could go on. I should probably talk about the energizing and liberating influence of *Hercules* and *Xena*, a tradition of fun and genre-bending that developed through *Buffy the Vampire Slayer* and then into *Farscape*, but that would take ages. I have to stick to this point about traditional sf formats for a minute, because of the huge influence that this type of show and movie has had on the

---

[2] For more information on B7 see this site, from which I clipped this neat definition: http://www.ee.surrey.ac.uk/Contrib/SciFi/Blakes7/

popular media image of sf and, by extension, science and all of the hallowed geekdom in which we live.

Military and political structures have one thing in common. They don't allow much individual room for self-expression—by definition, they can't. Their entire modus operandi is based upon the limitation of self for the good of much larger groups and their social and political ends. It's a great dramatic field, since we are all constantly in the difficult process of negotiating exactly such deals for ourselves. Because of these circumstances, although there are subplots and minor story lines involving personal development of major characters, those subplots and story lines can never be the driving forces of the show. The best they can hope for is to fuel a gripping plotline or two. Science fiction on TV has more or less demanded this format for practical and logical reasons—who else but the military and superpower governments of Earth would ever be able to fund and maintain a presence in space or a contact with other races (for which one should always read nations, by the way, since they are usually monocultures)? It's something of an imagination failure, and one which is starting to be addressed both by *Farscape* and by other "post-imperial" shows like *Firefly*.[3]

Farscape got around this problem by going back to some older kinds of stories, more like original *Trek* in feel, and by putting a set of mismatched and odd characters into a stolen boat and making them flee for their lives from virtually everybody else they could meet. Because it was not limited to political set pieces, military rules and series-plots, all of which have to maintain various kinds of status quo, it was able to exploit the best parts of different kinds of popular TV shows: sitcoms, soap operas, psychothrillers and romantic drama.

Farscape was a space opera, a genre based on the format of westerns, the romantic frontier horse operas of old.[4] These, in turn, are based in mythic structures of the Hero's Journey, as labeled by Joseph Campbell, such as you might find as far back as Homer's *The Iliad*. The shapes of fiction exhibited by these opera-types are universal in human storytelling, from the campfire yarn onward, and one such archetypal setup, arguably the most enjoyable of all, is the motley band of renegades on the run. (Better than the dreariness of the soap opera with all its domestic travails!)

---

[3] Interesting that both these shows got canned for similar reasons, namely failing viewing figures which led to funding withdrawals from advertisers. The forces of Capitalism and economic selection doomed them to extinction, leaving us with the enduring blandness of Uberpap, but that's another essay. In the immortal words of Homer Simpson, "Is there no place in this world for someone with an IQ of 105?!" Not in commercial television there isn't.

[4] *Firefly*, as noted previously, did this in an even more self-aware way, being literally a horse opera in space, replete with frontier towns and livestock.

Like *Firefly*, a series with which *Farscape* shared many of its popular elements, *Farscape* employed the sitcom tradition of the odd couple (a term and type drawn from an original play of the same name by Neil Simon in 1965). As its name suggests, odd couple situations feature two very different characters thrown together by circumstance, with frequently comic results. Here the couple was extended into the seven odd mates of the original crew (John, Zhaan, Ka'Dargo, Rygel, Aeryn, Pilot and Moya), who were later joined by another seven cast members at various times throughout the show's four seasons. Every one of the group came from a different species, united by their loathing of and need to escape from the Peacekeepers, the villains of the piece. No doubt other essayists will remark on the Peacekeepers' none-too-subtle resemblance to all other sf future empires and fascist dystopias; their particular twist was a poke at American foreign policy and the role of the United Nations, but it was a cheap and vaguely done exercise devoid of conviction, and I leave any more remarks about it at that.

Farscape also drew on much more recent literary traditions within science fiction, namely new space opera. New space opera is like space opera, but with modern political smarts chucked into a salad tossed from whatever the author thought was fabulous and cool and ripe for adventure.[5] Many of *Farscape*'s episodic plotlines came straight from the pulp tradition of the U.S. sf output of the middle of the twentieth century, but were thankfully given new twists, not least because a lot of those ideas had themselves already been preprocessed through other media until they achieved their present iconic status.

I'm thinking here about notions like Little Green Men, Flying Saucers, Men from Mars, Women from Venus, Abduction For Medical Experiments, Crop Circles, What Is This Mysterious Earth Kissing?[6] and other iconic situations. *Farscape* capitalized on this postmodern moment, following the road *The Simpsons* had paved, and created several shows which were themselves obvious homage.[7] It's also the first sf se-

---

[5] New space opera began in Britain about 1990. As with all space opera formats, its newness was generally five years behind the times. It was new because, until then, space opera had been true to the old pulp traditions of enshrining orthodox political outlooks and reinforcing conservative values, usually U.S. ones. New space opera despises that kind of oppressive cultural imperialism and is a phenomenon associated with the political Left because of that attitude.

[6] If this was never a painting by Roy Lichtenstein, it should have been.

[7] This is a common feature of many TV series and movies of the last ten years, where entire episodes are written as explicit pastiche, copies of or in relation to well-known programs, or incorporate celebrities and characters from real life and related mass media. It probably has a name, but I don't know what it is, though I expect it's related to music sampling and pop art. I'm going to call it Poptastic, for fun. Poptastic is a reference to *The Fast Show*, a British comedy series, which featured two DJs, Smashie and Nicey, who were spoofing on the kind of seventies and eighties DJ-ing styles of Radio 1 presenters in those decades. Hey, I almost made a useful reference!

ries (*Buffy* notwithstanding) which employs a modern and TV and culture-savvy hero, with whom the audience frequently sympathizes via shared media references. *Farscape* was highly Poptastic (see footnote 7), though never enough to derail what was frequently a reasonably good whack at some heavyweight moral and philosophical subjects, the sort which always tag along on sf plotlines.

For an example of this complicated layering, look at one early episode—"Thank God It's Friday, Again" (1-6). This installment depicted a successful struggle of workers' liberation against drug-induced slavery through the agency of Rygel's bowel activity—he peed nitroglycerine at a strategic moment and triggered a revolution. It also revisited another old sf trope (besides that of the Planet of the Oppressed), that of the Repulsive Yet Beneficent Parasite, to great effect when Crichton was made host to a disgusting intestinal worm. The worm, which unbelievably plowed into his guts via his navel, made him immune to the obedience drug that affected his comrades and friends. It was also in this episode that the relationships between the characters really started to gel and a completely natural bantering style emerged, a dynamic development that had every person contributing. This leads me on to what *Farscape* did that seemed new to me.

I think that there are two features of *Farscape* which mark it out from previous sf TV series as a watershed moment in sf viewing. These two features were important in the rapid development of its cult status. They also ensured that it would never rise to the stardom of the *Trek* franchise, mostly because of their effect on casual-entry[8] and family viewing. These were its complexity and its use of humor and sex. *Farscape* told outrageous stories (the ones you always longed to see from other shows, but never did) and took considerable risks.[9]

One major risk lay in the way it depicted sex and sexual activity, given its position in a moral and cultural climate of immense sexual hypocrisy. While the sex industry is colossal and the porn industry powers a great deal of technological development—almost as much as the military—and while we are all bombarded with extreme ideologies of what it is to be beautiful, desirable or even acceptable, the prevailing social rules and taboos on talking about sex and how it should be or-

---

[8] Viewers who switch on mid-series by accident or as a first-time viewer.

[9] When people talk about artistic risk they usually mean the risk of alienating your consumers by telling or showing them something they don't like or don't understand. There are other artistic risks also, such as trying out stories that may not deliver as you hope, so you have effectively wasted the viewer's time, or angered some orthodox authority with the power to stop your money and hence your career. Here I mean all of the above.

ganized in real life are extremely conservative. If they weren't then all the visual power and impact of sex as a tool of market forces would be kaput, but that's another essay. Here the important thing I want to note is that the portrayal of sex and pleasure in our culture here in the West has been freighted with guilt and confusion for an extremely long time. I initially wrote "since the Victorians," but it's much longer than that, probably since the arrival of Christianity into Europe and possibly since what Spinal Tap liked to call "the dawn of 'ist'ry." So this isn't to blame Christianity per se; there isn't a culture in the world that doesn't have some interesting attitudes and prohibitions concerning both sex and pleasure, most likely because they are two of our most powerful drives, exceeded only by survival.

Anyway, back to sf shows, which are extremely recent phenomena of our small corner of existence. Here those two subjects, sex and pleasure, have both been repressed by exclusion. People are often too busy with important other business, like exploring galaxies or shooting aliens or, heaven forefend, doing some science. Sex since the 1950s has often been given the sniggering teenage boy treatment (Captain Kirk and his Earth Kissing Lessons). Which isn't to say that the old Earth Kissing moments didn't have a certain erotic charge to the eyes of weary office workers and stay-at-home mothers after a hard day. However, whilst romance and sensuality might be on the menu of the occasional show for a full three seconds of screen time, they were never more than the icing on a much more important scientific or political or adventuresome cake.

Farscape, on the other hand, demonstrated pleasurable and fulfilling outcomes to both xenosex (pairings included D'Argo and Zhaan, John and Aeryn, Chiana and D'Argo, Zhaan and John if you count mindsex, and I could go on and on . . .) and crossbreeding,[10] and it also depicted pleasure taken in other activities, such as eating. Yes, these moments did occur within the context of much wider cultural meanings of sex and indulgence, but at least they were there and not something that always happened offscreen and somewhen else. *Farscape*'s characters seemed to actually have the lives of complete beings, and, like real and complete beings everywhere, they were also monumentally dysfunctional for much of the time, riddled with contradictions and problems from their pasts, lucky if they could formulate a plan for the next day, let alone the future beyond.

The pursuit of pleasure as an end in itself (as well as the need to es-

---

[10] Genetically unlikely but dramatically solid gold doorways into issues of race and gender.

cape death at the hands of tyrannical pursuers and to resolve the core conflicts of personality) was always plausible in this show. Rygel never hesitated to enjoy food. Zhaan denied herself nothing that was enjoyable, be it the photon bursts of a brilliant star, sharing orgasmic mind-melds with her friends or little moments of intimacy caught anytime, even when they were deeply surreal (for example in "They've Got a Secret" (1-10), in which D'Argo's story was revealed when he suffered a post-traumatic conversion and thought for a while that Zhaan was his long-lost wife, Lo'Laan). D'Argo took joy in combat and conquer. As for John Crichton and Aeryn Sun, they were, I think, the first pairing of genuine heterosexual chemistry in an sf show. For once, the awkward development of their relationship was not simply left to a few one-liners before the end of every episode. At last: fabulous adventure, fabulous situation, fabulous costumes and a pairing that paid off. We ought probably to be grateful that the show was canned right at the moment when they both jumped the shark[11] and committed to one another. After all, in dramatic terms, nothing gets old faster than true love returned.

But long before that happened there was all that business with the sadomasochistic theme in the costumes and other characters. S&M themes and situations became the calling card of big-screen movie sf throughout the 1990s. Here's a nice bit of explaining about BDSM (Bondage, Discipline, Sadism, Masochism) from Wikipedia:

> It is often agreed that [this] desire for dominance or submission is in fact the driving force behind sadomasochism, with the giving and receiving of pain acting only as an active stimulation to reinforce those feelings. This view is supported by the nature of sadomasochistic behavior. A masochist does not in general take pleasure in any arbitrary form of pain, only in pain received under the pretext of enforcing authority, and typically only that of a sexual nature. Likewise, a sadist usually only takes pleasure in pain that is inflicted for reasons of punishment and control, and most often for the indirect pleasure of the masochist. Many sadomasochistic activities involve only mild pain or discomfort. Often they are focused primarily on roleplay. (http://en.wikipedia.org/wiki/Sadomasochism)

BDSM had always featured in sf. As with all other forms of gaming and role-playing, it was used in stories that were either sexually explicit or completely implicit (an explicit example would be *Barbarella*,

---

[11] A phrase that denotes the moment when a story's central dramatic tension is resolved.

with Jane Fonda's eponymous character trapped in the Orgasmatron, and an implicit example *Terminator,* with the title robot choosing biker leathers and Ray-Bans as the outfit for killing) as ways of exploring the too-dangerous and absolutely criminal acts and motivations that underlie oppression and exploitation in the real world. By putting taboo and prohibited acts of doing or speaking into sublimated forms within drama, sometimes denoting them only by a single image, such as a strand of barbed wire or a pair of killer heels, the impulses and emotions which surround such acts can be examined, rather as if one has created a narrative "laboratory" in which lethal compounds can be experimented upon. And also, of course, their inclusion allows the story to make complex points about contemporary culture and issues. As for what the flourishing of BDSM motifs in American sf media output during the recent decades means in terms of the national psyche—I leave you to draw your own conclusions.

In *Farscape,* the evil empire of the Peacekeepers provided a good excuse to put pleasantly built actors and actresses into black uniforms and button them down firmly. But this trend didn't really hit its psychological stride in the show until the appearance of Scorpius. Scorpius was a living fetish—an alien who had mangled his own form, in an act of control and repression, to fit into the tightest black leather bondage suit this side of a dungeon. Scorpius, from name to sunken eyes, had everything that control fantasies are made of. He was a dungeon master, a torturer, a wit, a Machiavellian prince, a tragic antihero, an anorexic. I clapped my hands in girlish delight at his first appearance. At last! Here was straight-and-true handsome and all-American Crichton's perfect foil, the pale and vampiric moon to his down-home honest sun. The angels of archetype were shining that day, putting all of the repressed facets of Crichton's home culture on show. The gloves came off and the show changed at that moment, finding its real psychosexual feet—and they were wearing really huge black vinyl boots.

Scorpius, an instant gold mine in terms of his dramatic potential, was usefully exploited by both writers and costume department. His influence spread until he had become Crichton's torturer, nemesis, mentor, shadow, conscience and alter ego. Scorpius was so attractive he took up residence in Crichton's brain and tantalized him with promises of, and then failures to deliver, a father's love, both fulfilling and denying the major relationship that Crichton had lost at home. He was Aeryn Sun's one true rival. Allusions to Hamlet were never far away, and then the extreme and the ridiculous became sublime—none of this it's-all-over-in-two-episodes tosh where nobody changes no matter what happens to him or her. Crichton and Scorpius developed a relationship, shared secrets, became... closer than friends, and the plot warped around them.

By season three Scorpius' presence had seeded everyone's clothing with the BDSM look—black leather, long, tight, shiny vinyl, zips, buckles. This particular visual expression emphasized the sexual persona as a strong, vivid and dangerous force, one that had become a matter of personal politics. It promised charismatic power so explosive and powerful that it could only be kept in check by the toughest clothing available. It was a representation of the danger and darkness in all of us, expressed as a contemporary drag act: Satan as a frock. It was taken too far by the Scarrans (who look not unlike the gross malignant force of *Lord of the Rings* bad guy Sauron in their spiky insectoid armor plate). It was softened and reinvented by Grayza, a character from the Peacekeeper side who resembled a clone of Servalan from *Blake's 7*.

Grayza managed to find some fabric amid all the leather, but she didn't need clothes—she had pheromones that could seduce a wardrobe at fifty paces. By the time of her ascension into the status of Chief Architect of No-Good,[12] no trick of mind control had gone underexploited in the lengthy alien efforts to get into Crichton's wormhole secrets through his pants. How they all suffered. We could talk about the whole torture as metaphor for hormonal frustration thing, but that's rather obvious.

Let's move on to other kinds of pleasure beyond the torment of having your enemy living inside a chip in your head or losing the key to your handcuffs. *Farscape* also showed sex outside lasting relationships; sex that was good, bad or indifferent, and sex that was employed as a weapon. This happened a lot. Almost as often as in real life, but not quite—after all, it's meant to be entertainment.

There were also other interesting relationship angles which received uncommon outcomes in *Farscape*. The situation between Crichton and Crais is one example. At the beginning of the story, Crichton caused the accidental death of Crais' brother, and Crais swore (yawn) vengeance. He had several goes at killing John, all foiled, and then, as his involvement with pursuing John made him weak and a liability to the Peacekeepers, he started making deals with Crichton, Rygel and the others in order to ensure his survival. Finally Crais came to be the living com-

---

[12] I don't want to dwell on this icon of female sexual power in its guise as the whorish seductress because I'll get mad, so I'm skipping it here, but such women are rife in pulp sf and I'm heartily fed up with them all. Instead, think of Zhaan and Chiana, who are less like puppets of the male ego and the general demonization of the feminine.

panion/captain of Moya's offspring ship, Talyn, and eventually, having transformed his consciousness and that of his ship through story lines I can't include for length reasons, he died the warrior-hero's death in an act of selflessness.[13] This is more like a literary story line from a reasonably long epic saga than the common byline of an sf TV show, in which the usual outcome of such situations would have meant resolving the story line within a couple of episodes. And it was hugely satisfying.

Farscape's women also provided glimpses into various kinds of feminine expressions of desire, and they almost all initially disconform to the stereotypes approved of by mainstream American values, except in their uniform virtue of good looks. Aeryn was a military hard case with raw emotions and appetites she viewed almost as weaknesses. Zhaan was self-contained and at ease with taking pleasure (the ultimate in unacceptability, and also sadly lacking in dramatic chutzpah). Chiana was the rebellious teenager who would not listen to the voice of authority. Jool was loyal but bolshy and selfish. For once, although they engaged in sex and autoerotic moments, none of them were punished on its account. This violates the primary myth of the neo-Christian era—that original sin is equated with self-knowledge (of which sexual knowledge is an important part) and must be met with disapproval, ostracism and punishment. (For women, that is. Men have usually gotten away with it, but you don't need me to tell you that. Just read some books and watch some TV.)

Well, I never did talk about postcolonialism and the stereotyping of the Erotic Other, I see. The aim of doing so collided with a growing realization that the extent and complexity of the show wouldn't permit that kind of simple analysis without my having to write a load of dren that wouldn't add up to anything more than a few mean-spirited points about the fact that wretched postcolonial thinking could be weakly applied to almost all human pursuits and, thus, characters in *Farscape*. This would mean saying nothing of note when I could have said that the characters, story lines, issues and imagination in this show were absolutely frelling magic to watch and could leave material to satisfy analysts for years and years, not only on their capture of the uneasy zeitgeist but also through the turnabout they offered on what sf said the future could aspire to. I am not really such an analyst to want to do all that, except in the kind of conversation you have in the pub late at

---

[13] This is basically the same story as that of Spike in *Buffy the Vampire Slayer* but played out very differently in the detail.

night. I only dabble, and therefore the moment has come to bring this dabble to an end. Hooray for *Farscape*, a gem of modern science fiction. Don't read this. Watch that instead. It had acres of worthwhile thinking and experimentation in it, it was the first romance to score for ages in the genre, it employed all the best ancient stories, and it was good entertainment, too—the hardest trick of all.

Justina Robson is the author of three internationally critically acclaimed works of science fiction: Silver Screen, Mappa Mundi *and* Natural History. *Her next book is called* Living Next Door to the God of Love *and is out in late 2005. She occasionally reviews literary sf for the* Guardian *newspaper and the small press. Her short stories have appeared in the UK and U.S. She always wanted to be a writer and made it through years of practice writing TV and film fanfics, so this essay is by way of thanks to all the many happy viewing hours. For more information please go to www.justinarobson.com.*

THEATER OF FACES

HOW THE NONHUMANOIDS OF *FARSCAPE* CREATE A UNIQUE SF EXPERIENCE

MICHAEL MARANO

I can't nail down exactly when Rygel and Pilot stopped being muppets and started being characters to me—it just happened without my realizing it, some time in the midst of season one. At some point the muppets stopped making Farscape *less real and started making it more real. Michael Marano explains how.*

NATURALLY, WHEN I THINK OF PILOT on his home planet looking longingly at the stars in the episode "The Way We Weren't" (2-5), I think of a really ambitious Scottish guy who doesn't know that advice from witches needs to be taken with a grain of salt. And of course, when I think of Rygel looking at the ship on which he was tortured by that dickweed Durka at the start of "PK Tech Girl" (1-7), I think of a really hot Gypsy chick singing her lungs out to a dashing Spanish officer. I also think of a guy in a rubber suit knocking over models of Tokyo, how much I love an accumulation of green dryer lint named "Kermit" and a *Babylon 5* actor doing improv in the Sahara. In fact, when I think of any of the vast array of nonhumanoid (I guess "non-Sebaceanoid" is more applicable, but that's too hard to spell) beings that populate *Farscape*, I most often think

15

of innovations of live theater from the 1970s and the early 1980s...and the fact that I'm thinking of anything at all while watching *Farscape*—rather than marble-eyed drool-staring at the phosphor-dot teat-tube that weaned my brain—might be indicative of what makes *Farscape* so treacherously addictive for science fiction freaks like myself.

The renowned and boot-to-the-head-iconoclastic theater (and sometimes film) director Peter Brook famously said in his 1968 study of theater: "I can take any empty space and call it a bare stage."[1] Brook put this notion to an extreme test in 1972 when, through his Paris-based International Center of Theater Research, he took a collective of actors and theater persons—among them *Babylon 5*'s G'Kar himself, Andreas Katsulas, Helen Mirren of *Prime Suspect* and Elizabeth Swados, creator of the Broadway hit *Runaways*—on a journey through Africa to places without formal theater traditions in order to create improvisational theater in marketplaces and on street corners. Then, in 1981, Brook directed a still-controversial production of *Carmen* that boiled Bizet's opera down to a lean ninety minutes, eschewing formal scenery and instead using carpets and throw pillows to create settings, much to the dismay of opera purists who prefer their opera more...I dunno...*operatic*. Brook's reimagining of *Carmen*—which was staged without a full orchestra or crowd scenes and used a cast of only five principal actor/singers—was a stripping away of the grandiose excesses that Bizet imposed on the original bare-bones story by Prosper Mérimée. This was a fact that didn't register with opera buffs, who only seem to dig their productions cluttered and the spaces of their stages anything but empty. And you thought the fans of the original *Battlestar Galactica* were sticklers about "reimaginings." Thank God there wasn't a robot Daggit in Bizet's version.

The nonhumanoid aliens of *Farscape*, brilliantly crafted by Jim Henson's Creature Shop, are, at least partly, empty spaces like the ones Brook sought in Africa and created on the stage for his *Carmen*. The play of their features and their bodies is the play of theater; they push some of the same buttons that live theater does. Pilot, Rygel, the horse-headed Scarrans, Namtar and company are all incomplete creations to a certain extent, unlike Boris Karloff wearing Jack Pierce's makeup in *The Bride of Frankenstein* or Randy Cook's big dumb Cave Troll in *The Fellowship of the Ring*, neither of which could ever be called incomplete. The creatures of *Farscape* were not crafted and animated to seem *real* as the dinosaurs of *Jurassic Park* were crafted to seem real. (By the way, could I men-

---

[1] Peter Brook, *The Empty Space* (New York: Touchstone, 1996), 1.

tion for the record that the park in question is really *Cretaceous*?) For technicians and craftsmen to allow a fabricated creature some unreality is to grant it a certain *emptiness*. To the audience, these aliens feel truly "other" and thus succeed as unreal creations; George Lucas' walking, talking amphibious abortion Jar Jar Binks was allowed no unreality, and thus failed. (I'm still working on all the ways in which Peter Jackson's Gollum succeeds; even if and when Gollum is surpassed as an effects creation, he's going to be a milestone forever, in the way that stop-motion animator Willis O'Brien's King Kong and Ray Harryhausen's fencing skeletons from *Jason and the Argonauts* are.) This success lies in a kind of theater of faces, the filling of the partly empty space that is a character's face. Karloff's Monster, the hobbit-skewering Cave Troll and Jar Jar are more fully realized than are Pilot and Rygel; they are as a full-blown and traditional production of *Carmen* is unto Brook's production. I'll be focusing mainly on these two principals of *Farscape*, who through their intended unreality ultimately add to the reality of *Farscape*.

To nab phraseology from media critic Marshall McLuhan, Pilot and Rygel and the nonhumanoid aliens of *Farscape* are "cool" (they provide limited amounts of visual information), whereas other kinds of filmic creatures are "hot" (they provide the audience with dense visual information). To toss you an example, a caricature of a president in a political cartoon on the Op-Ed page of a newspaper is "cool," but a photograph of that same president on the front page is "hot." Both cartoon and photograph are "read" by the person who sees them, but they are read in different ways. "Cool" media are inclusive. "Hot" media are exclusive. If we're going to apply ideas of theater to these *Farscape* aliens, then we should think of them in terms of audience participation. The emptier the space, the greater the audience's involvement. More than effects, Pilot and Rygel and their latex compatriots are part of the *mise-en-scène* of *Farscape*. They, as aliens, are crucial to the crafting of the unreal worlds to which nice North Carolina native John Crichton must adapt; they help to collapse the TV viewers' participatory point of view with that of John Crichton.

Now, I know that at face value (no pun intended) what I'm saying seems obvious: "Neat-looking aliens make alien worlds look alien; now where's my Pulitzer?" But there's more to it than that. Pilot and Rygel aren't like the aliens of, say, *Pitch Black* (in which poor Claudia Black gets eaten) or *Alien*; in the case of both these movies, the otherworldly *mise-en-scène* had already been established through set design, sound design, costumes and so forth before the alien beings entered the narrative. In the case of the *Star Wars* cantina scene and its follow-up scene in Jabba's righteous party crib in *Return of the Jedi*, the arrays of Lucas' aliens, while in some cases not as technically sophisticated as the animatronic Pilot and Rygel, are complete. Viewers are supposed to see them and believe in them at face value (still no pun intended). There is nothing "empty" or theatrical about them, because they are purely cinematic creations: "hot" media. Pilot and Rygel and company don't merely inhabit the unreal world of *Farscape*; they force viewers to partly define that world. Pilot, Rygel and company, as "cool" media, are, in some ways, created by the audience, by the investment the audience brings to its reading of those characters; the audience contributes to the work done by the puppeteers and the voice actors. Thus, the characters' presence makes *Farscape* a deliciously unique experience among sf shows.

Think of the range that Pilot showed in the aforementioned episode "The Way We Weren't," Pilot's "origin" story, in which we saw in flashbacks how he was first joined to Moya. In that episode, Pilot expressed fury, desire, forgiveness, terror, pain. And think of the pomposity that Rygel conveyed in, say, "Throne for a Loss" (1-4), in which he forged an improvised scepter out of one of Moya's control crystals. The little helium-farter seemed to visibly swell before our eyes with puffed-up pride. Really . . . ask yourself this, and I don't mean this facetiously: could your average *Baywatch* actor or actress express the kind of emotional range these puppets do? My praising them is not meant to take anything away from the incredible vocal talents of Lani Tupu as Pilot and Jonathan Hardy as Rygel. But think of the way that Pilot and Rygel's faces take in your gaze as you watch them perform. They can take in your gaze because they are partly empty.

Pilot and Rygel's emptiness, functioning as part of the *mise-en-scène* of *Farscape*—as part of the definition of an unreal world—is in a way parallel to the emptiness of the *mise-en-scène* of a landmark production of *Macbeth*, staged in 1976 by Trevor Nunn. Nunn, then the youngest person to ever be artistic director of the Royal Shakespeare Company, created a production of *Macbeth* that, because of its inventiveness, emptiness and the levels of participation it demanded of its audience, has been called one of the great stagings of the play in the twentieth century. (So great is Nunn's personal vision that, according to Kenneth Branagh's autobiography *Beginning*, Nunn's name has become a verb; around the RSC to be "Trev'd" means to be swept up in Nunn's enthusiasm and charm, even when to do so goes against your intent or better judgment.[2])

---

[2] Kenneth Branagh, *Beginning* (New York: W. W. Norton & Company, 1989), 163.

In contrast to more bombastic productions of *Macbeth*, Nunn's 1976 version, his third staging of the play, was stark and empty, set against black backdrops with very few props. The costumes were plain; Lady Macbeth's wardrobe was a single plain black frock and a tea towel as a headdress. Members of the cast sat in a large circle onstage, even when technically "offstage," observing with and actually becoming the audience. Within the circle, the only brightly lit part of the stage, the drama played out. Cast members, in front of the audience, created the sound effects. Macbeth and Lady Macbeth, played by none other than Sir Ian McKellen and Dame Judi Dench, could be seen slathering their hands and daggers with stage blood mere feet away from the front row. This was a *Macbeth* without pageantry; it was so spare that it required those who saw it to invest imagination to flesh out the narrative.[3] There were no lofty castles full of tapestries and banners for the viewer to occupy vicariously. There were no sweeping battles with scores of spear-carriers by which to be thrilled. The audience was unbearably caught up in the psychology of Shakespeare's darkest play because its members were forced to *participate* in the play by visualizing the rise and fall of a king on what was basically a blank canvas. McKellen wrote of Nunn's interpretation: "There could be no more appropriate stage for these complex passions of the player king than a bare circle which can be Scotland, a blasted heath, Dunsinane Castle, a banqueting hall, an attic or a man's mind."[4]

The art of puppetry at the core of *Farscape*'s nonhumanoid creations is, much more than are other filmed special effects techniques, a theatrical art. (When was the last time you and your pals lined up to see a good *Bunraku* movie?) Principles of theater are applicable to the *Farscape* aliens, even though watching *Farscape* is nothing like watching live theater. Puppetry, as a theatrical art, requires and expects an investment from its audience that partly collapses performer and audience, a filling of the empty space. Brook said about his theatrical experiments in Africa: "The work that we're doing is related to audiences. We believe that no theater work can exist except through its relation to the people who are watching it—that the spectator is a participant. And so, consequently, the relation with the spectator is something that has to be studied,

---

[3] This production is currently available on VHS and DVD in the form of a 1979 broadcast of the play that aired on Thames TV in the UK.

4 From a broadside published to accompany the broadcast of 1979 RSC/Thames TV production of Nunn's Macbeth, available on McKellen's personal Web site at http://www.mckellen.com/writings/macbeth.htm.

felt, and learned."[5] (So fluid was the relationship between Brook's players and spectators that at one point the audience took over and crowded the actors off their improvised stage of a thrown red carpet.[6]) In
Farscape the TV audience animates each puppet nearly as much as the
puppeteer, because the performance of a puppet is dual-layered. Unlike
the performance of (fully) human actors, the performance of a puppet
is an *interpretation* of the movements a human actor would make. One
can look at Al Pacino as Shylock in Michael Radford's *The Merchant of
Venice* and marvel at how his movements and posture define his performance. To look at Pilot and Rygel "act" is to look at *representations*
of organic movement and posture. Pacino's movements are immediate.
Pilot and Rygel's are not; they are abstractions of movement, and on
some level, we in the audience are interpreting these movements as we
would an abstract painting. When we watch Rygel and Pilot perform,
we are meeting the *Farscape* puppeteers on a figurative red carpet. We
are noting the obviousness of Pilot and Rygel as much as Nunn's audiences noted the obviousness of his *Macbeth*.

Let me cite a few specific examples from Pilot and Rygel's *oeuvre*,
and how these relate to the viewer's participation in their performances.
Consider "Jeremiah Crichton" (1-14), in which the members of that
lost Hynerian-sponsored colony presented everyone's favorite Dominar with offerings of rare delicacies. Rygel looked at the goodies with
a Homer Simpson-esque junk food lust that was palpable. At least, we
viewers could recognize the look on his face as hunger. But ... how can a
rubber puppet know hunger? Consider the fan favorite "Crackers Don't
Matter" (2-4), in which that little freak T'raltixx talked to Pilot about
his shipmates on Moya. Pilot *visibly* lost patience with John, Aeryn and
company with a tilt of his head and furrowing of his brow. Loss of patience is an incredibly complicated emotional state for an actor to express. And yet we recognized it in Pilot, investing him with it because of
a few (seemingly) simple gestures.

Most special creature effects are devised to look real (as opposed to
"realistic," which is a matter of style, not quality of execution). Yet realness is not always an indication of success. By almost any standards of
believability, the CGI critter of Roland Emmerich's 1998 dud *Godzilla*
(dubbed GINO by fans: "Godzilla In Name Only") looks more real than

---

[5] Quoted in Margaret Croyden, *Conversations with Peter Brook, 1970-2000* (New York: Faber and
Faber, Inc., 2003), 92.

[6] For a fascinating account of Brook's travels in Africa, see John Heilpern's *Conference of the Birds*
(Indiana: Bobbs-Merril, 1978).

the lumbering man-in-a-rubber-suit incarnation of Godzilla that fans of Japanese monster flicks adore. Yet it is the rubber-suited Godzilla that is the far more successful creation. The rubber-suited Godzilla is a full-blown character. It communicates a sense of size, power and weight that the more "real" CGI Godzilla could not (I, for one, don't want realness in my giant four-hundred-foot irradiated dinosaurs). There's an awe that the old-school Godzilla can inspire; Emmerich's CGI Godzilla inspires a desire to knock it over and steal its lunch money. The *obviousness* of Pilot and company's artificiality give weight to their performances, and in turn to the worlds that make up *Farscape*.

More than just being empty spaces, Pilot and Rygel's faces are gateways as irresistible as the wormholes that sucked John across the galaxy. The aliens of *Farscape* feel more alien than do the ETs of almost any other sf show. Of the more than 650 hours of *Star Trek* produced, what percentage of the aliens in that universe feel truly *other*? For the most part, *Trek* aliens are bumpy-latex-forehead-wearing stand-ins for whatever social topic the *Trek* writers see fit to hyperbolize. The otherness of *Farscape*'s nonhumanoids can be startling—more effective in the establishment of an alien world than any CGI shot of a Federation ship entering the orbit of yet another Class M planet.

This otherness comes from a source far more profound than the keyboards of an effects house. It's an otherness that suggests an alien emotional reality, rather than an alienness defined by bumpy foreheads. There's a delight to the otherness of *Farscape*'s nonhumanoids that's rather like the delight early sf readers found in the work of Stanley G. Weinbaum, who in the 1930s was able to create alien life-forms and characters whose psychological reality felt distinctly nonhuman. H. P. Lovecraft said of Weinbaum: "Somehow, he had the imagination to envisage wholly alien situations and psychologies and entities, to devise consistent events from wholly alien motives and to refrain from the cheap dramatics in which almost all adventure-pulpists wallow."[7]

True, I mentioned earlier that it is we, the audience, who aid the performances of Pilot and Rygel through the act of watching them. Yet the stylization of their performances, even though they communicate emotions we can recognize, makes those emotions feel nonhuman. This discovery of alien psychology and emotional reality comes from our figurative sharing of Brook's red carpet with these nonhumanoids and their puppeteers, and their sharing it with us. Claudia Black said about her

---

[7] Lovecraft, cited in "The Wonder of Weinbaum" by Sam Moskowitz, in *A Martian Odyssey*, by Stanley G. Weinbaum (New York: Lancer Books, 1962).

many-armed costar: "There's something about the expression in Pilot's eyes, it's so articulated, the paint work and everything is so beautiful. Whenever he looked at me as a puppet, I was convinced I was looking at something real. Pilot would just look at me with these beautiful doey eyes, and I was gone."[8]

We, as participants in the animation of Pilot and Rygel, as investors of belief in these alien creatures, are granting them a sense of otherness that we create as much as do the puppeteers. There is no passive way to watch them perform, because their performances are partly ours. The "other" emotional reality that readers of Weinbaum found so delicious in the 1930s (I dare anyone to read Weinbaum's 1934 story "A Martian Odyssey" and not be charmed by his aliens) is dredged from the emotional, imaginary reality that lies deep in the minds of Farscape's audience.

As "cool" media—incomplete, artificial, partly empty stages—the nonhumanoid aliens of Farscape involve us in their universe in a visceral, primal way. The credibility they bring to that universe is partly our credibility, and not entirely the credibility of the effects technicians. The Star Trek universe, the Star Wars universe, the worlds of almost any other genre show or movie series do not ask for such an investment of imagination from their audiences. Even creatures so obvious as Star Trek's Horta and Star Wars' Jabba (in both his puppet and CGI incarnations) do not present their obviousness in the participatory way that Farscape's nonhumanoids do. The Horta and Jabba are "hot" creations. We do not invest belief in them, because as creatures divorced from traditions of live theater in a way that Farscape's aliens never could be, they do not demand or invite such an investment.

To apply this idea to another Henson creation: Kermit is a construction of green felt with two halves of a Ping-Pong ball for eyes, yet he's beloved by tens of millions. (Hell, if it weren't for Kermit on Sesame Street, I probably never would have learned to read well enough to enjoy the written science fiction that has so joyfully warped the brain of this Farscape fan.) Kermit, hunk of felt that he is, is brought to life by his audience to the point that its members are, in this context, almost costars with him in his "role"—much like Claudia Black is Pilot's costar. We act with Pilot and Rygel. There is an insertion of personal experience and vision, an energizing of belief that makes the nonhuman characters and the alien mise-en-scène real. In that it requires the participation of our imagination, Farscape, is to a certain extent like role-play. Just as surely

---

[8] Quoted from Farscape: The Peacekeeper Wars: The Battle Behind the Wars, short film included in 2005 Lions Gate DVD release of Farscape: The Peacekeeper Wars.

as unreal worlds are made real in the minds of Dungeons & Dragons players as they grip their twenty-sided dice, so does the role-play of investing belief into Pilot and Rygel's faces make unreality feel real.

Through Pilot and Rygel's faces, animatronic "actor" and audience are collapsed in the experience of watching *Farscape*. The show breaks the theatrical fourth wall and gives the viewer an immediacy born of the intimacy of shared role-play. This figurative role-play is possible only through the invitation of Pilot and Rygel's stylized facial expressions. There must be *space* for the viewer to occupy in order for such an invitation to have meaning. Empty spaces in a theater of faces allow science fiction geeks to experience a vision of the unreal unique within the genre. We do not merely watch *Farscape*; we partly occupy it.

As viewers who at least partly occupy the world of *Farscape* through the experience of shared performance, we participate in a small way in John Crichton's journey to the unreal worlds in which he finds himself. *Empathy*, that old bugaboo that has shown up as an sf plot contrivance from *Trek* to *Species*, refers to the feelings one invests in a work of art or craftsmanship. The empathy we invest into the nonhumanoids of *Farscape*, and the otherness we bring to them and to the worlds that otherness defines, allows us to feel empathy with John. He's our diagetic stand-in, our surrogate observer, as we follow him through the alien worlds that, through our shared performances with *Farscape*'s puppeteers, we have partly created. For an sf fan, *Farscape* provides a sense of wonder that's unique among filmed sf media. It engages us as no other show or film is willing to.

Michael Marano's "Mad Prof. Mike's Headbanger Movie Reviews" appear on the Public Radio Satellite Network program, Movie Magazine International *(www.shoestring. org). His criticism has appeared in publications such as the* Boston Phoenix, Science Fiction Weekly, MaximumRockNRoll *and* Gothic.Net. *His popular "MediaDrome" column appears in* Cemetery Dance. *His novel* Dawn Song *won the International Horror Guild and Bram Stoker awards, and his short stories have appeared in a few high-profile anthologies. His favorite* Farscape *episodes are the fan standards: "A Human Reaction" and "Crackers Don't Matter." Having seen and reviewed more than a thousand genre movies, he's unsuited for any other employment. Pity him.*

DOWN THE WORMHOLE

COGNITIVE DISLOCATION, ESCALATION, PYRRHIC VICTORY AND *FARSCAPE*

JEANNE CAVELOS

Conventional wisdom has it that the plots of television dramas could be boiled down to Problem-Complication-Resolution. *Brian Henson and company must not have gotten the memo.* Farscape *episodes can be boiled down to* Problem-Much Bigger Problem-Frelling Ridiculously Big Problem. *Unless they fall under the formula* Problem-Great Sex-Psychedelic Episode-Heartbreaking Tragedy. *Actually,* Farscape *never seemed to follow any formula, which is how it stayed surprising all the way through its run.*

IT'S NINE O'CLOCK ON FRIDAY, and for lack of anything better to do, you flip to that strange science fiction show, *Farscape*. It's the story of John Crichton, an astronaut whose spacecraft went through a wormhole and was spit out in some distant part of the universe, where he has adventures on a living ship with a group of argumentative aliens.

But what's this? Your TV seems to be showing the launch of a space shuttle, not a futuristic living ship. Do you have the wrong station? No, there's Crichton, but what is he doing in an old Earth spaceship?

Ah, it must be a flashback. Or a dream. Lots of TV shows have flash-backs and dreams—especially when they've run out of episode ideas. Indeed, Crichton seems to be reliving his old Farscape mission, the one in the pilot. There's his father in Mission Control. You've got it all worked out in your head. Crichton should wake up in his bed at any moment now.

An electromagnetic wave hits Crichton's ship; he's knocked uncon-scious. And then he does wake up.

But he's not on Moya. He's in a hospital on Earth.

And his dad is there.

"What the hell?" John says.

Your thought exactly. In fact, you realize this is often your thought when watching *Farscape*. You try to remember the previous episode. Did you miss some big new development last week? No, you distinctly remember watching it, and it ended with Crichton on Moya, as usual.

Crichton's dad asks how he feels.

"Hot. Dizzy. Kind of…feel like I've been hit by a house."

Again, not dissimilar to your feelings at this point.

Crichton's dad bends over for a hug. Crichton loves his father. This should be a comforting moment. Whatever strangeness is going on, to-gether they'll be able to figure it out and put everything to rights.

Crichton seizes his father and wrestles him to the floor, screaming, "I am not your son!"

Orderlies and nurses rush in and pull Crichton off as he yells hysteri-cally.

You spot Aeryn in the background with relief. She'll inject some rea-son into this craziness. But her hair looks weird, and she's wearing a white lab coat, and a stethoscope is wrapped around her neck.

Crichton calls to her, but as they hold him down on the bed most of his ravings are lost in a spray of saliva and insanity.

And we cut to the opening credits.

Thank God. You were about ready to start foaming at the mouth yourself. What the frell is going on?

It's just another Friday night of *Farscape*, the series that raises that immortal question, "Did the writers phone this script in from the insane asylum?" So many science fiction series limit strangeness and confusion for fear of alienating the viewer. They bend over backward to make the viewer feel comfortable and at home, and to provide sufficient explana-tions to stamp out any confusion. Expository dialogue is stuffed into the mouths of the characters. Spock explains to Kirk that they can't interfere in the planet's culture because of the Prime Directive (something they both already know), Data explains in a stream of technobabble why the problem they faced in this episode can now be solved, and in case you had a stroke during the commercial, the captain of the *Enterprise* recaps the important events in his captain's log. Mysteries or problems are generally revealed in small steps, so they don't overwhelm, with the characters pondering and discussing each new development, guiding the viewer through the mystery to the happy conclusion where all loose ends are resolved. While the problem may grow worse over the course of the episode, there is generally only a single problem, and most of the energy of the writers goes toward leading the characters to create a wise plan to solve it. The solution neatly restores the status quo, allowing the characters to go on as if nothing had really happened.

The writers of *Farscape* decided this was a load of dren. They realized that we science fiction fans had become sophisticated enough to handle some strangeness and confusion, and to figure out a lot on our own. They refused to move their plots forward in baby steps and pause for explanations each step of the way.

Casting off the heavy chains of exposition, *Farscape*'s plots instead throw us into the middle of the action and let us struggle to figure things out. The characters don't have time to hold our hands and explain. They're not on a leisurely mission to explore the galaxy; they're fighting for their lives and, in Crichton's case, fighting for sanity. Most of the time they don't understand what's going on themselves, and if they do, they aren't inclined to tell us about it. They'd rather argue, eat, have sex or get into more trouble. Mysteries and problems are piled on faster than you can say "Buckwheat," and often the characters are too preoccupied with their own issues to try to solve them. When they do try, their plans are half-assed at best, not all of the characters follow them, and they often only make things worse. Problems are not solved without cost; loose ends are not neatly tied. The result is exhilarating, confusing, suspenseful, insane, moving and, above all, entertaining.

Some of the most striking differences in plot between *Farscape* and other science fiction series come at the openings of the episodes. It's at the beginning of each episode that the strangeness and confusion strike us full-force. While other shows provide us with an intriguing little tease, *Farscape* bombards us with brain-twisting events, bizarre turns and alien images. It's like opening your front door and finding your cats holding a Victoria's Secret runway show on the ceiling—only stranger. Other shows prefer that you feel as if you've opened your front door and found your very own living room. They want you to feel at home spending time in their world. And who wouldn't feel at home sitting in the captain's chair on the *Enterprise*, in front of that huge viewscreen? It's just like sitting in your living room watching TV, but with a nicer chair and a larger screen!

Farscape doesn't want the viewers to feel at home. The characters live in a distant region of the universe, where things should feel overwhelmingly alien. More important, Crichton, our main character, is a stranger to this place. If we are to form a strong bond with Crichton, we need to see this strange, new world through his eyes, to feel the confusion and disorientation he feels. And that confusion and disorientation should only grow as his mental stability declines. The episode openings create this cognitive dislocation, immersing us in an alien, chaotic world. Our brains spin as frantically as John Crichton's, and considering that he spends much of the series going insane, that's pretty fast. It only takes a microt for the whirlwind of *Farscape* to sweep us like Alice down the wormhole. Which brings us back to our episode, "Won't Get Fooled Again" (2-15).

You pray that they'll explain it all when you come back from commercial. But why would they do that, when they can raise the weirdness quotient in a dizzying display of derring-do and sheer lunacy? It's not only thrilling; it serves as a brilliant method of reflecting our main character's descent to near madness. The episode unfolds as if Crichton's brain has been put in a blender on "puree." Before it ends, we get Scorpius as the hippest jazz drummer ever, Rygel in an S&M fantasy, tentacles as a lifestyle choice, a blue psychiatrist with a green card, *Hamlet* allusions, *Oedipus* allusions, *Wizard of Oz* allusions, Crais giving out phone sex numbers, D. K.'s wrists spurting blood, Crichton in a baby carriage, D'Argo proposing a ménage à trois and Aeryn exhibiting a freakish degree of tongue agility. As Crichton says, "I'm about as cognitively dislocated as it gets."

What is Crichton's strategy to get to the bottom of this strange situation? After subjecting this reality to such stringent tests as peeking into the ladies' room and ordering a pizza, he decides the best strategy is to get drunk and party. Only after playing with our minds for two-thirds of the episode do the writers finally reveal what's going on. A Scarran is feeding these delusions to Crichton to drive him insane. Yet the solution to the mystery comes from an unexpected source, and uncovers a more serious problem: the existence of Harvey, the neural clone Scorpius has implanted into Crichton's brain.

As happens so often on *Farscape*, problems breed more problems.

And no problem is solved without some cost to the characters. The extraction of this cost is what gives *Farscape* its intense and vital power. Without it, the crazy inventiveness, while entertaining, would ultimately be "sound and fury, signifying nothing." But *Farscape* has greater depths, as shown in this episode. Amidst the insanity, and the revelation of this new threat, the plot delivers an emotional hammerstrike: Crichton's dying mother wandering after him with her I.V., pleading that he stay with her this time as she dies. Just as we have shared Crichton's confusion, his dislocation, his enjoyment, his frustration and his insanity, now we share his pain. As Crichton curls into a fetal position, we experience the intense core of humanity in *Farscape*.

We're treated to another mind-blowing opening—literally—in "Out of Their Minds" (2-9). The episode begins with Moya's alarm blaring and Crichton hopping down the hall, putting on his boots, yelling, "I'm up, I'm up, I'm up!"

Aeryn reveals a strange ship is targeting them.

Okay, not such a crazy opening so far. Other shows might start with the appearance of a hostile vessel, though they'd do it a bit more slowly and without so much arguing.

Then Pilot reveals that Zhaan is on the enemy ship, and there it is again, the did-I-miss-something-last-week syndrome. The episode cuts to Zhaan talking to the birdlike alien Tak, and Tak claims that Talyn attacked him.

Your mind races with questions. Is it true? Did Talyn attack? And what the hezmana is Zhaan doing over there alone?

You try to reassure yourself. Surely the writers sent Zhaan over there to avert an attack. She'll convince them Moya and Talyn are innocent.

But within seconds, Tak fires on Moya. Sparks are shooting, blobs of energy are flying, and we're swept down the wormhole once again: Aeryn has been hurled into Rygel's body. Crichton is in Aeryn's body. And Rygel is in Crichton's body. Talk about cognitive dislocation. And we've only just gotten to the opening credits.

We've had characters swap identities in science fiction before. But those neat, clear exchanges, carefully explained, have very little in common with the insanity of this episode. This is not an exchange between two, but a round-robin between three, and two groups of three at that. For D'Argo is now in Pilot, and Chiana is in D'Argo, and Pilot is in Chiana. Yet again, the authors have managed to put us in the same mental state as the characters. Our heads are swimming trying to keep it all straight, and so are theirs.

How did this body swap happen? Where's our explanation? The characters have no idea, nor do they really care. They're too busy fending off the aliens, figuring out how to pee in their new bodies and enjoying the various organs that they didn't have before. The only real plan is Chiana's, and that's to abandon ship and run.

As often happens in *Farscape*, the characters' actions make things worse, adding new problems or exacerbating old ones, escalating the tension. They allow Tak onto Moya to convince him they are harmless, but that allows Tak to spew creeping acid vomit onto the ship. They solve the acid problem, but that only encourages Tak to fire on them again. When he does, you think that the attack must surely throw the characters back into their own bodies, for that's what would happen on any other science fiction show. But instead, they all switch to new bodies. Rygel is Crichton, Crichton is Aeryn, Aeryn is Rygel, Pilot is Chiana, and it's more than your brain can hold, more than any brain can hold, and you hear Chiana say something, but it's not Chiana, it used to be Pilot but now it's D'Argo, and what did he say?

It's one step beyond where any other show would go, and that step is a doozy. But the *Farscape* writers showed us again and again that the bulk of their energy wasn't focused on solving the problems for the characters; it was focused on making them worse. One of the best examples of this is in "The Flax" (1-13).

Aeryn is teaching Crichton how to fly a scout ship. The ship gets caught in an energy field, the Flax, and both are knocked out. The episode cuts back and forth between Crichton and Aeryn trying to save themselves, and D'Argo, Rygel and Zhaan trying to save them—in between pursuing their own private agendas and whims. We'll just follow Crichton and Aeryn, though the same plot principles are evident in the other half of the episode.

When the two awake, they discover the ship is damaged. This is where, on most shows, the cast would get out their cool flashing, beeping gizmos, start spouting technobabble and come up with a plan to fix the problem. On *Farscape*, though, the writers would rather cause more trouble. We learn that Aeryn doesn't know how to repair ships; Peacekeeper pilots aren't trained in repair. Their options limited, they try to break free from the Flax, but only damage the ship further. A fire breaks out, and though they manage to extinguish it, future fires remain a danger. So thus far, the characters have only made their situation worse.

Crichton and Aeryn don't feel assured that their comrades will come to the rescue, so they decide to try to fix the ship. They find that the atmospherics mix line is crushed; repairing it requires welding. Yet the crushed line is causing the oxygen level within the ship to rise, and welding in this situation will likely start a new fire. They come up with a solution! Yea! Maybe this show isn't so different from the rest after all.

They decide to depressurize the ship, releasing all the oxygen to space, weld the line and then repressurize. To do this, they'll need to wear spacesuits. They pull out the two spacesuits on the ship. You can taste victory already. They'll soon be back on Moya, arguing with each other as usual.

But wait. The helmet on one of the suits is cracked. Oops—there goes our solution.

Aeryn has two drugs with her that are specially made for Peacekeepers. One shot kills; the other can bring a Peacekeeper back from death. They come up with a new solution: John can wear the spacesuit and do the welding—he's the only one who knows how to weld anyway; Aeryn will go without a spacesuit, take the drug and die, and Crichton will revive her when the welding is complete.

The stakes have suddenly gotten much higher. Our characters don't just have to repair the ship; now Aeryn has to die.

After they fight about it, Crichton finally agrees. Aside from waiting around hoping to be rescued, it's their only other option.

New problem: the helmet is too small for Crichton. It only fits Aeryn.

They come up with yet another solution. Crichton must teach Aeryn how to weld, and he must be the one to die and—maybe—be revived. The drugs are for Peacekeepers, not humans. As Aeryn says, "We can't be sure it works until you're dead."

With that, Crichton decides to teach Aeryn CPR, and makes her promise not to leave him dead for more than four minutes.

At last, they execute the plan. Aeryn gives Crichton the kill shot, purges the oxygen and welds. When her four minutes run out, she stops welding and repressurizes the ship. Hmm. This is *Farscape*. Could their plan actually have worked?

New problem: the Flax shakes the ship, and Aeryn is knocked unconscious. When she finally awakes, she realizes . . .

New problem: more than four minutes have passed, and . . .

New problem: the vial holding the revival drug has broken.

Aeryn frantically performs CPR on Crichton and revives him. He's relieved that their crazy plan has worked. You're relieved, too. The writers made things pretty bad, but at least the characters have gotten through it.

New problem: Aeryn reveals that she didn't finish welding the line. The ship is still broken. And they have no more drugs for a second attempt. This is a death sentence for them both.

Most shows never reach this point; they don't want their characters to fail. That's why they don't dare pile the troubles so high. But *Farscape's* plots frequently escalate the conflict to the worst possible situation and let the characters fail. This is not a tame, friendly universe; these characters are not calm, competent professionals. They should fail, fairly often. And they do. That's what creates such strong suspense.

You wonder if the writers will come up with some convenient solution to save Aeryn and Crichton. They could activate the flip-flop override device, or remember a handy lifepod attached to the ship. But this is *Farscape*, and they don't.

On the upside, Crichton realizes that Aeryn must love him if she stopped welding to revive him. Expecting death shortly, they decide to have sex.

New problem: D'Argo comes to the rescue, interrupting them.

On *Farscape*, you can't even die in peace.

D'Argo's arrival is not some random, convenient event. To reach Crichton and Aeryn, he has given up a chance to find his home and his son. As in other episodes, problems are not solved without cost to the characters. And within the whirlwind of the plot, we are bound to the characters through their disorientation and pain.

This principle of unrelenting, high-risk conflict escalation gets taken to amazing extremes in some of *Farscape's* three-part stories. Having more time to tell a story often leads other writers to add filler and slow down the action to—shall I be kind?—a stately pace. Watch any film or miniseries produced by the Sci-Fi Channel, and you'll be gently lulled into a coma. Characters fill long scenes by spouting exposition, problems are repeated rather than escalated, and the search for a solution is dragged out until we lose all interest. But the writers of *Farscape* never took their plots off manic speed. They used their three-parters as opportunities to do ten times as much as they'd do in a single episode—to pile on more problems than ever, to create intersections of characters and plotlines that raise the stakes for our heroes and to exact greater costs and trigger major changes, sending the entire series spinning in a new direction.

The three-part "Liars, Guns and Money" (2-19, 2-20, 2-21) illustrates some of the best plotting *Farscape* has to offer. The story opens with the characters rescuing the reincarnated Stark. A reincarnation, on a normal science fiction series, would be the subject of an entire episode at least. Spock required a two-hour movie to go through the process of rebirth. Here, the writers allow Stark thirteen seconds of exposition to describe his travels while dead, how he reconstituted his body and how he came to be where they found him. Then he drops an entirely new plot on us: he has come up with a plan to rescue D'Argo's son, Jothee. A character actually has a plan! Of course, the character is Stark, his plan is insane, and the others can't agree on whether or not to follow it. Stark's plan, in a nutshell, is this: they will break into a shadow depository and steal enough money to buy Jothee, who is being sold in a lot of ten thousand slaves.

As the characters argue about the wisdom of the plan, D'Argo heads off alone to put the wheels in motion. This is one of many cases where characters go rogue or work at cross-purposes, creating yet more problems for each other and increasing the plot's unpredictability. D'Argo is captured by Natira, who runs the shadow depository, yet Stark reveals this is all part of his plan. If the others want D'Argo back alive, they have to go through with the rest of it.

So now they have two problems: rescue D'Argo and rescue Jothee. Lurking in the background is one additional problem, which has been growing for some time but is not yet serious enough to be an issue: dealing with Crichton's hallucinations of Scorpius.

Zhaan and Chiana execute the next stage of the plan, posing as shady operators with a deposit to make. By claiming that D'Argo works for them, they secure his release. Hey, is *Farscape* making things too easy on its characters?

Never fear. No sooner is the D'Argo problem solved than a new, even worse one appears: Scorpius. A huge amount of his wealth is stored at the depository. With Scorpius in the mix, the risks of the plan are greater and the stakes are higher. We're back to two problems: avoid Scorpius and rescue Jothee.

The plan almost seems to be working—Rygel, hiding inside Zhaan's giant safe deposit box, has broken out and switched the code so that when Zhaan withdraws her deposit, she gets Scorpius' container instead.

Then Crichton decides to go rogue. He sees the opportunity to sabotage Scorpius' cooling rods and takes it. Yet his hands won't spread the explosive onto the rods. He can't act against Scorpius. That pesky voice in Crichton's head has escalated into a full-blown handicap, right in the middle of a bank robbery.

Aeryn applies the explosive, and Zhaan heads for the exit with the container of ingots, but Scorpius catches on to them. All the doors are locked before Zhaan and Chiana can get out, and we reach a new high—four problems: save Zhaan and Chiana, fix Crichton's brain, escape Scorpius and rescue Jothee. At a time like this, the leadership of Stark, mastermind of the plan, is critical. Stark becomes hysterical and has to be tongued by D'Argo.

Zhaan and Chiana manage to escape, but when Scorpius confronts Crichton, Crichton's internal struggle reaches a crisis point. The sabotaged cooling rod incapacitates Scorpius, but Crichton is unable to kill him. All Crichton can do is crawl away.

We reach the denouement of part one thinking we've solved three of the four problems—amazing progress! Everyone is safe, they've escaped Scorpius, and they can use the ingots to buy Jothee. The only problem remaining is Crichton's tendency to converse with himself. Gee, this hardly seems like *Farscape*. Shouldn't things be worse?

But wait—at the very end, Scorpius' "ingots" transform into bug-like creatures and begin attacking the ship. The entire bank robbery has been in vain. We're not just back at square one; we're at square negative two. We not only have to rescue Jothee, we also have to stop Crichton's mental meltdown, not to mention save Moya! Now this is *Farscape*!

Part two starts not with the first steps toward a solution, but with a new problem. We discover that Scorpius traced Stark's data link during the break-in and stole from Stark the information about Jothee. Scorpius is now the proud owner of ten thousand slaves, including Jothee. Jothee is in more danger than he ever was before.

Stark's plan has only made things worse.

Crichton decides to take charge of this craziness and comes up with his own plan—one of the most complicated in the series. They'll gather different alien mercenaries with the skills necessary to free Jothee from the depository. As they do this, Zhaan struggles to keep Moya alive. She discovers that they can kill the bug-like creatures by burning, but they'll have to burn Moya too.

This scorched-Moya solution embodies *Farscape*'s practice of exacting a price for the solution of any problem. While other shows seek to solve problems and return to the status quo, there is no return to the status quo on *Farscape*. Every solution brings more problems and inflicts lasting damage on those involved. A price must always be paid. And the price is not always exacted by the villains; sometimes, the heroes exact a price from each other. When Crichton and Aeryn return to the burned Moya, Crichton says, "Our money did this?" To which Aeryn responds, "We did this."

They have succeeded in gathering all the mercenaries, but now they have no money to pay them. The problem count? Five: deal with a bunch of angry mercenaries, heal Moya, fix Crichton's brain, avoid Scorpius and rescue Jothee.

Crichton decides to kill three birds with one stone. He goes rogue and turns himself over to Scorpius in exchange for Jothee. Giving himself up is a unique way to end the problem of avoiding Scorpius. In addition, he figures that when Scorpius removes the chip from his brain and he dies, his problem will also be solved.

With Crichton now held captive in place of Jothee, it seems we've just replaced one hostage with another. But there are no even exchanges on *Farscape*, and indeed, the situation has just become much, much worse. Crichton's action has created a new problem, the most serious yet: the possibility that Scorpius will gain Crichton's wormhole knowledge and use it to kill billions and conquer the universe. While the conflict has been escalating throughout, with more problems and more lives in danger, suddenly the stakes have shot up as high as they can possibly go. Clearly, we end part two in far worse shape than we were when this whole escapade began. A plan to rescue a single person has turned into a desperate attempt to save the universe.

Note to self: don't listen to Stark.

In part three, we start to understand the extent of the costs of this plan. The 9,999 slaves in the same lot as Jothee are killed. Yet there is no turning back now. Stark manages to convince the mercenaries to attempt a rescue of Crichton, reminding them of the wealth in the depository. Talyn arrives, drawn by Moya's distress, but Crais refuses to help. He has committed himself and Talyn to peace.

Before heading down to the shadow depository to execute Stark's new, insane plan, several more crew members go rogue. D'Argo tells the mercenaries they should forget Stark's plan. Zhaan discovers their fire-belching mercenary couldn't toast a marshmallow, but doesn't tell anyone. Aeryn offers herself to Crais if he and Talyn will help. Characters following their own private agendas, characters trying to help others without telling them, characters facing private crises—these are real people with strengths and weaknesses, in way over their heads, succeeding and failing and running around like Durka with his head cut off.

The attempt to execute Stark's plan is filled with new problems and unexpected turns that bombard the viewer at a furious pace. One mercenary has his eye scooped out; two sacrifice themselves; a fourth betrays the group. Crichton learns that the process of removing the implant needn't result in his death, and his hope temporarily renewed, he convinces Natira to help him.

As the plotstorm builds around us, once again we find a quiet heart at its center, the heart that reveals the price paid by the real people pummeled by these forces. Surrounded by the enemy, Aeryn finds Crichton. He is finally breaking, losing his will and his mind. He tells her he's going back to Scorpius. She has to knock him unconscious to stop him.

Stark's plan in ruins—their second major failure in this story—the group climbs into one of the depository's storage containers for shelter while Aeryn has Talyn destroy the complex. Crude, but effective.

The end of the story finds Rygel reveling in all the treasures they salvaged from the depository. Everything seems all right. Jothee has been saved. But that one positive is countered by two negatives, two major problems that they didn't have when this all began. The stress of this experience has accelerated Crichton's deterioration, and Moya is seriously injured. More than that, because of their actions, thousands have been killed: slaves, mercenaries, depository employees and clients.

But the crowning cap on this story is our final glimpse of Crichton, tortured by the belief that he has killed Scorpius and unable to accomplish the simplest task. He lives in torment. After all that's been done to rescue him, he begs D'Argo to kill him.

This is one of *Farscape's* most powerful Pyrrhic victories. They have rescued Jothee, but the cost is horrific.

In an attempt to console the group, Bekhesh, the surviving mercenary, leaves with a heartfelt statement that only increases our discomfort with the way this has all turned out: "Thank you for teaching me to kill again."

Farscape's plots are the key to what makes this series distinctive, moving and powerful. Immersing us in the action and eschewing exposition, the plots throw us into a state of cognitive dislocation, wrenching us from our living rooms and tossing us down the wormhole in an experience that mirrors Crichton's, creating a strong, immediate bond between us and the character. Through high-speed, high-risk conflict escalation, they keep us off balance, building an unpredictable and exhilarating story and increasing the intensity of our journey, so that we cling to Crichton with ever-greater desperation. By allowing the characters to pursue conflicting agendas, to have flaws, to make mistakes and to fail, they not only increase suspense, they create real characters that we can believe in and identify with, turning our bond from one of necessity to one of deep emotional connection. And when the cost for the journey is exacted, we feel the losses as if they are our own. No other series carries this intense combination of disorientation and involvement, suspense and emotion.

Trusting us to use our brains and hold on tight, *Farscape* took us on a whirlwind journey of insanity, love, hate, despair and triumph—often all at the same time. In its boldness, invention and pure lunacy, it may never be matched. *Farscape* broke the rules of television science fiction and blazed a trail down the wormhole to a strange, exciting new land. We can only hope future writers in the field will follow this trail and carry us yet further into these exhilarating, uncharted territories.

Jeanne Cavelos began her professional life as an astrophysicist, working in the Astronaut Training Division at NASA's Johnson Space Center. After earning her MFA in creative writing, she moved into a career in publishing, becoming a senior editor at Bantam Doubleday Dell, where she created and launched the Abyss imprint of psychological horror, for which she won the World Fantasy Award, and ran the science fiction/fantasy publishing program. Jeanne left New York to pursue her own writing career. Her books include the best-selling The Passing of the Techno-Mages *trilogy (set in the Babylon 5 universe), the highly praised science books* The Science of Star Wars *and* The Science of The X-Files *and the anthology* The Many Faces of Van Helsing. *Her work has twice been nominated for the Bram Stoker Award. Jeanne is currently at work on a thriller about genetic manipulation, titled* Fatal Spiral. *Since she loves working with developing writers, Jeanne created and serves as director of Odyssey, an annual six-week summer workshop for writers of science fiction, fantasy and horror held at Saint Anselm College in Manchester, New Hampshire. Guest lecturers have included George R. R. Martin, Harlan Ellison, Terry Brooks, Jane Yolen and Dan Simmons. More information about Jeanne is on her Web site, www.jeannecavelos.com.*

PUPPETS, SENTIENT BLUE VEGETABLES, BODY FLUIDS AND LOVE
OR, HOW *FARSCAPE* SCREWED WITH ITS CHARACTERS

DORANNA DURGIN

Farscape *breaks every rule in television. So how the hell did it ever get made?*

A man walks into a bar.
   No, really.

Okay, let's say it's not quite a bar. Let's say it's a posh little place with the trendy name of Ratings, where flavored oxygenated sparkling water from Outer Kazootaville tops the menu and the napkins are undyed hemp, hand-embroidered with meaningful karmic characters. One discreet attendent moves smoothly from table to table, refreshing the aromatherapy oils tucked in amongst flowers notable for their spare, expert arrangement. A long sash angles over her head, half hippie, half trendy chic, and her layered skirts muffle the slight jingle of bells. A toe ring gleams, winking in and out from beneath the hem of the skirts.
   Atmospherically posh. Oh yes.

So. A man walks into what we'll call a bar and orders an exotic combination of freshly squeezed fruit juices blended in ice. A man who knows what he wants. A man who pays for facials and precision shaping of his silvered, thinning hair and who wears a suit so beautifully tailored that it almost hides the middle-aged slump of his body. He sits on a stool and snaps open an industry rag, his hand already reaching for and expecting to find the drink. He is not disappointed.

But he is bored. Not even the nearby mix of invigorating rosemary, mint and juniper essential oils makes his industry reading—the gossip, the speculation, the I-told-you-sos—seem stimulating. He lingers over an I-told-you-so.

So. There's already another man at this bar. A younger man, with his hair in a knockoff cut that's supposed to look as trendy as Ratings but instead crosses the line into grungy. The two-day beard doesn't help, nor does the tiny soul patch trying to hide in the growth. This man's got a laptop computer and a Wi-Fi connection, and he's scowling. He reaches for his iced chai and bumps the arm of his neighbor, and only then does he notice that he's no longer alone. "Excuse me," he says, and then there's the hint of a double take. Recognition. "Sorry, sir."

The bored man looks pleased at this recognition, and no longer quite as bored. "That's okay," he says. "You seem distracted."

And the young man hesitates, as though thinking whether he wants to have this conversation here, with this chance companion, or whether he should respond with a meaningless social nicety. But temptation and opportunity win out. "This assignment has me stumped."

"You're an entertainment writer." A statement of the obvious. The initials for *entertainment writer* are EW. Too amusing to ignore. And the man who makes the pronouncement—the man who garners such respect and feels he deserves it—this man has *Network Executive* written all over him. NetEx.

"Yes," says Ew. "Freelance. A little hungry right now. So I need this gig. But this show—*Farscape*—I'm just not getting it. The fans are ra-bid—"

"Loyal," says NetEx. "We like to think of all dedicated viewers as *loyal*."

Ew's response is hasty. "Yes, of course. Loyal fans. Enough of them so that once the show was canceled, the network allowed a miniseries finale."

NetEx nods. "Heard something about that."

Ew perks right up. "Are you familiar with the show, sir? Do you have any insights?" He spreads a sheaf of papers on the counter, between the iced fruit blend and the chai. They are seasonal episode guides—gleaned from the Web and sprinkled with neatly handwritten notes—and character sketches, complete with photos.

"I know all I need to know," NetEx says, but he puts down his industry rag and reaches for the printouts. "Astronaut shot through a worm-hole to Some Other Place, has adventures. Just a universal version of *Time Tunnel*. Yawn."

Ew opens his mouth to disagree with this casual assessment, but loses his nerve. Finally he manages, "It seemed more complex than that to me. Fresher."

"A show needs more than fresh. A good, viewer-grabbing show needs characters with whom the viewers can identify. Not aliens with alien motives and behavior. Not—" NetEx closes his mouth into a disapproving line and flips through the pages, stopping at a cast photo. An amphibious creature with a wide, expressive (and disapproving) mouth, imperious eyebrows and a flattened face with a high, tiny nose. The eyes, one must say, give the impression of a conniving creature. "Puppets. *Puppets*. Need I say more?"

Oh, but there's plenty more to say. Plenty to observe.

Take Rygel's smile.

The evil one.

The smile worth a thousand ineffective words, the one no mere human could reproduce—although a bemused and transplanted John Crichton recognized it as trouble regardless. Certainly he knew it shortly after his arrival when Rygel made an acquisitional snatch at Crichton's recorder.

JOHN: My equipment. It's mine.
(No fool he, drawing this line so bluntly. But Rygel is by no means deterred.)
RYGEL: Are you a sound sleeper? Hmmm?

And there it was. That smirk. The one that showed Rygel's complete satisfaction with the effect of his own words. The self-cognizant awareness of and pleasure in his devious intent. The corners of his mouth drawn up sharply, his mobile lips pressed together with satisfaction, the feathery brows quirked over half-lidded eyes. The expression that all of Moya's crew learned to regard with wary disgust.

(Rygel appears at the door of his cell quarters, holding a red crystal that he "borrowed" from Moya's vital circuitry. A red crystal he kept close at hand by swallowing it...and now he's in the position to return it. You do the math. Aeryn certainly does. Her hand hovers over the crystal, displaying her conflict. She wants it...and she wants nothing to do with it.)

RYGEL: I did wash it.

(Aeryn hesitates, then snatches the crystal and marches away—only
to freeze at Rygel's next words.)

RYGEL: Well...I think I did.

(Aeryn stiffens. Her shoulders square and she resolutely walks away.
She doesn't have to turn around to know the look on Rygel's
face....)

Yes. That smile. Have you seen it? Didn't it make you want to punt
the little obnoxious gasbag—Crichton's early description of Rygel, and
unexpectedly accurate at that—across the room? Effective, isn't it?

How better to portray a stumpy, aquatic little being than with a puppet? Or to present Pilot, the huge, gentle creature so central to the function of the living ship Moya? Multiple arms, a hard plated shell beetling
up over his head, expressive eyes and a mobile, lipless mouth containing not teeth, but a chitinous beak. Pilot was the result of imagination
allowed to play with all the tools a puppeteer has at his or her disposal.
His early scenes were all the more remarkable for the way his disgruntled disapproval—the lowered brow, the tightened mouth—came across
on static-y ship view screens. Ditto his ire when Moya was taken for
granted, pushed to the limits, in pain or otherwise abused. His outrage
in "Exodus from Genesis" (1-3) when an impatient D'Argo took a laser
prism saw to Moya's corridor to gain access to invading bugs—"How
dare you cut into Moya without warning!"—made us want to punt
D'Argo across—

Well, maybe not. D'Argo was hardly a puntable being. But you felt it,
didn't you? The deep response to Moya's startled pain? Pilot's personal
fury at the injury to his partner ship, so ably conveyed by brow and eyes
and expressive mouth?

Puppets. Need I say more? NetEx has asked.

Probably not, actually. The puppet actors themselves do the talking,
matching the human actors nuance for nuance, and evoking in us those
same reactions we generally reserve for living beings. A puppet is *there.*
A puppet talks back. A puppet becomes one of the cast, playing off
the drama and the intensity of the moment. *These* puppets transcended
what they were made of to become who they were.

"Over the top," declares NetEx.

"Oka-ay," says Ew, who has taken the photo of Rygel and studied it
with mixed reaction. "But people seem to love them."

NetEx waves a dismissive hand. "Nothing more than *Sesame Street* conditioning. People are trained to love puppets. It doesn't mean that puppets are a good storytelling tool for a serious dramatic endeavor."

Well, no one ever said *Farscape* was serious. NetEx has apparently not been privy to the wild twitch of Crichton's face when exposed to a Peacekeeper beacon. Or the effect of the entire cast arguing intently, ignoring their helium-raised voices in the presence of a nervous and gas-emitting Rygel. Or the more sly humor of the moment warrior D'Argo realized he was outgunned and had no defenses and threw the equivalent of a Luxan temper tantrum...and Zhaan transmitted it to the looming Sheyang ship, giving them significant pause and buying our heroes the time to rig a defense. There was even desert-dry humor mixed with drama, as in that same episode when Aeryn swooped to a swashbuckling rescue of Crichton and their temporary Peacekeeper tech ally, blowing the attacking Sheyang to explosive bits when her pulse rifle bolt and its natural fiery emissions collided. "Sorry for the mess," she said, with only the tiniest of smiles—and went back to what she'd been doing before the moment of crisis.

Don't deny it. If you saw it, you were smiling too.

But NetEx is oblivious to the fine comic timing of such moments; he jabs his finger at the out-of-context research, spearing the first handful of episodes. "And here's another thing," he says. "They really went wild with the aliens. Probably the puppet influence. How can viewers identify with such characters? They're used to safe aliens with forehead prostheses, not aliens with tentacles all over their heads, aliens with twisted mouths, aliens who are sentient blue vegetables, for God's sake! Look how many of these early aliens have different body language and bizarre voice inflection. Look at the way they move! At least they played it safe with the Monarch, and used the Delvian priest for her vocalizations. Then again, what am I saying? The sentient blue vegetable vocalizes through a psychic connection with an unimaginable brooding queen made up mainly of a giant ovipositor. What were they thinking?"

Ew gives a tentative scratch of his scruffy soul patch. Talk about an alien look. "Maybe...that the viewers could identify with Crichton's experience of those aliens?"

NetEx gives Ew a narrow-eyed look, as if he suspects the younger man is actually trying to think for himself. Can't have that. "Not," he said, "when you combine it with the behavior of these so-called shipmates. Self-centered, stubborn...and the flagrant, childish reliance on bodily emissions! Flaming piss, for God's sake!"

He says it like a man unused to saying the word "piss" at all, but as though he doesn't want to let on to the fact. "Just look at these notes. Was there ever a show with more of an obsession with bodily fluids? Even *The Exorcist* used less vomit than just the first season of *Farscape.* The Hynerian passes helium gas, belches copiously in every episode, spits thick greenish-brown slime and pees his way to safety at least once."

Well, yes. That's Rygel for you.

"At least the vomiting is spread more evenly around the crew," Ew offers, and then stops short as if realizing what he's said out loud.

Hey. Bodily emissions happen. Different beings are bound to have differing bodily emissions, from tears to sweat to excretion. One can coyly pretend otherwise, or one can take it in stride. More than that—*embrace* it. Refuse to knuckle under to conventional inhibitions. Take risks.

One can, for instance, save Our Heroes by gagging the giant space creature that has swallowed their transport so they can ride a stupendous wave of space vomit to safety.

"Over the top," mutters NetEx, giving Ew a sidewise glance, a petulant dare of assessment.

Ew swallows. One gets the impression he rather liked the flaming piss scene, in which Rygel, poisoned by Tannot root, became a secret weapon and saved the day. Over the top? Or just outrageously bold? Ew casually reaches a hand to his laptop keyboard for a little highlight and delete. "Self-centered," he says, an obvious diversionary tactic which nonetheless suits NetEx. "They seem to work together decently to get out of trouble—"

NetEx has taken a sip of his fruit concoction, which was a mistake as he now nearly snorts it out his nose. "Contrived luck," he says. "They are ever willing to betray one another, to walk away from one another . . . take that flaming piss episode—"

"'Thank God It's Friday, Again,'" murmurs Ew, who has perhaps done more reading than he let on.

"Typical of these characters—how long did they give D'Argo before they agitated to abandon him?"

Ew clears his throat. "They thought it was his choice to stay."

NetEx raises an eyebrow to correct him. "They didn't *care* enough to know for sure."

Ew's mouth opens. He might say "But . . ." He might point out that in fact, though D'Argo's crewmates were originally willing to go their separate ways if that's what D'Argo wanted, they nonetheless stuck around long enough to figure out that D'Argo was under the insidious influence of a population-controlling drug. He might be thinking that Aeryn—who had been up on Moya saving Rygel's life in defiance of her lack of training and scientific inclinations—came back to the surface of a planet too warm for her ultimate survival in order to help stage a rescue.

Or Ew might still be thinking that this is his chance to impress a person of NetEx's importance, and that to judge by that superciliously raised eyebrow, he clearly hasn't yet done any such thing.

Then again, he might just be thinking that eyebrow looks like Rygel's eyebrow in its most imperious mode. He clears his throat and offers, "There doesn't seem to be much loyalty between any of them . . ." and, seeing approval, barges forward. "Right from the start, the others have a little sneer in their voices when they say 'human.' Aeryn even includes humans when she says 'I always thought that lesser life-forms were useless . . . just something to be squashed.' Right there in the same episode where—"

And of course he stops himself, because of course he's realizing the contradiction of his own words. He's realizing that Aeryn was, in her inexperienced and brutally honest way, telling Crichton that she was wrong. Because he'd just saved her life. He'd just helped to save all of them, during a time in which Aeryn had been at her most vunerable, suffering from heat delirium. During a crisis in which she chose to ask Crichton, of all of them, for a mercy killing should it become necessary. She'd thought him squashable . . . and she'd been wrong.

CRICHTON: Fine. Well, on behalf of lesser life-forms everywhere, I accept the . . . compliment.

In fact, it was this adventure which represented the first pivotal points of trust and vulnerability for all of them, all strong individuals, bluntly invested in their own self-interest but slowly being drawn into a cohesive group. A group where the individuals did what they must to save the whole of them and where in one outrageous adventure, Rygel risked himself by going not only into the Monarch's dangerous nursery to help Moya's erstwhile crew understand what was happening, but by crawling right into the thick of it to open negotiations. Zhaan willingly subsumed herself to the Monarch to provide her a voice, and Crichton stubbornly held back his fears to insist they see the situation from the Monarch's narrow point of view, finding a way to work with her to save them all from the Peacekeepers who had come upon them in the midst of it all. D'Argo made a significant concession by working with Crichton's puny human plan of attack—and Aeryn risked her life so they could try it.

Not that this cooperation was any kind of permanent condition for any of them. That was clear enough even as D'Argo and Crichton rushed off to follow through on their plan. Crichton, hating to leave Aeryn, steeled himself to depart with D'Argo. "It's just you and me."

D'Argo didn't waste any words on platitudes. "Actually," he said, "It is just me. . . ."

Refreshingly blunt, these beings. They said what they meant... they meant what they said. They didn't apologize for who they were or what they wanted. They'd been through too much, and this was how they had survived... and intended to continue surviving.

And yet at the end of that incident, there was Aeryn... learning to think in a new way. Learning to discard assumptions. Learning, in fact, to be wrong.

Ew tries to salvage his blundering point with a wild leap. "And just when you think they can be trusted, that they have an understanding, Rygel declares Crichton prematurely deceased and tries to steal the boots off his still-living body!"

Well, yes. Very true. That's the Rygel we knew, loved and could depend on to act just according to his nature. Why, just consider his eulogy for Crichton—"John Crichton, unwelcome shipmate." Downright touching, wasn't it?

"I haven't even mentioned the worst of it." NetEx looks disgruntled, or maybe as though there's a belch caught in his throat. He catches the server's eye and nods at his empty glass, indicating he'd like a refill.

Ew jumps at the opening like a good sycophant. "Let me get that. It's the least I can do."

NetEx seems to agree. He nods graciously before diving back into his latest peeve. "The worst of it," he says. "The love arc between Crichton and Aeryn."

"I, er... thought that was supposed to be the best of it." Ew closes his laptop lid slightly, so there's no chance NetEx will get so much as a glimpse. Oops. I guess we know what *Ew* thought, anyway.

"What do you *not* do with a love arc in a prime-time drama?" NetEx asks, and then answers himself. "You do not kill the lovers—multiples of times!—and then bring them back and expect the viewers to trust you again. Didn't anyone learn that lesson with *Dallas*? You do not get action-based characters pregnant and take the baby to term! By God, you never let them have conjugal bliss in the first place!"

"Conjugal bliss," Ew repeats, apparently impressed with this phrase. Or perhaps with NetEx's willingness to bellow it in a public place.

"*Repeatedly*," NetEx says, an edge of righteous outrage in his voice. "And that doesn't even count all those momentary deaths—we're talking at least two distinctly so-called permanent deaths for both Crichton and Aeryn Sun. Not only that, but Crichton's own betrayal led to Aeryn Sun's first death. How can any viewership possibly remain invested in a relationship like that?"

Ew clears his throat and rubs a finger over that scruffy, almost-hidden-in-stubble soul patch again. Don't you just want to grab a razor? He says, "You've been thinking about this."

And true, NetEx has not consulted Ew's notes nearly often enough. Nor has he had time to absorb what's there. He's relying on his memory.

NetEx says tightly, "I've been involved in some discussions."

Hmm. Interesting.

But NetEx is still upset. "They did all the *don'ts*. It's like they went looking for—" He cuts himself off, puts an elbow on the bar and leans a little closer to Ew. Conspiratorial. "Look at that episode near the end of the second season. The one where Aeryn dies."

"Die me, Dichotomy" (2-22). If *Farscape's* irreverence came out anywhere, it was in its episode titles.

"Crichton *kills* her! How could anyone think this would work? He *killed* her," NetEx repeats, as if he simply cannot fathom it. "Cruelly. Callously. And she came back to love him. Compared to that, what's a little Luke-and-Laura post-rape marriage?"

Ew pushes his laptop lid all the way closed; it beeps a warning as it goes to standby. He sounds more certain of his ground, but still careful. Respectful. "He wasn't himself."

Literally, that is. Not with a Scorpius clone crawling around in his brain, exerting control and pushing all the buttons—including the one that sent Crichton's landing gear into the canopy of Aeryn's prowler and resulted in her death. How could anyone hate Crichton for that, seeing the agony of it distort his features? Knowing he hadn't been strong enough to resist Scorpius, knowing there was nothing he could do to now save her? Knowing his words—"Aeryn, forgive me"—fell on ears not deaf, but dead?

The very manner in which Aeryn Sun died—the way Crichton and even the entire crew responded—cemented and proved their relationship instead of destroying it. The way in which she returned to life, the sacrifice it took, made it clear the development was far from gratuitous. Rather than destroying viewer trust, it sucked the viewers in. They grieved as Crichton grieved.

But NetEx has gotten stuck on the subject. "And how could they think it would work to make her suddenly 'not dead yet!' Did they think this was a *Monty Python* skit?"

Suddenly *not dead yet*? It was far from so simple. There were no magic potions, no cheerful miracles. The means by which Aeryn's body was preserved on the very edge of death had been well established before she was revived. And the means by which she was revived....

A life for a life.

Zhaan pulled Aeryn back from that very edge of death, and then she paid for it. Not swiftly and easily, but over the course of time. Enough episodes so we, too, could understand the sacrifice, experiencing the denial and sorrow of Moya's crew. There were no freebies. No random punching of the reset button. No "oops, just kidding!" Aeryn knew it before we did—protested it and challenged Zhaan's insistence that Aeryn take her gift of life for Crichton's sake.

> AERYN: I can't. I know your thoughts. And I know what this will cost you.

And soon enough, so did we.

"And that's just for starters," NetEx says, close to babbling. "Next thing you know—within half a season!—Crichton's dead. But not before extensive—"

"Conjugal bliss?" suggests Ew.

NetEx stabs the counter with his finger, hard enough so it probably hurt. "Excessive! What were they thinking? Were they *trying* to bore the audience? To turn a pivotal moment into the mundane? There was no effort at discretion, at moderation, at—"

> STARK: What's the matter? Didn't sleep well?
> RYGEL: How could I? With them on the other side of this (raises his voice slightly)...very thin bulkhead!
> STARK: Bit noisy, were they?

"—good taste!" NetEx splutters. "Over the top! Did no one think of what happened on *Moonlighting*? Dave and Maddie hit the sack and the series was never the same!"

Change. Growth. Evolution. Consider it sometime.

Ew opens his mouth, but never gets a chance. "And then!" NetEx says. "Then they killed Crichton! Except, of course, he wasn't really dead."

Well, he *was* really dead. "Don't worry about me," he told Aeryn, trying to make it easier for her. "I've never felt better." And then he died. And he stayed dead.

Leaving Aeryn to manage a reunion with the *other* Crichton.

Leaving the viewers to grieve for them all. For Aeryn, who had lost the man she loved—had seen him beat Scorpius out of his head once and for all, had seen him discover the wormhole technology he had hidden in his own mind, had developed the intimate relationship they both craved—it didn't matter that there was a second "twinned" version of Crichton waiting aboard Moya. And the surviving Crichton lost Aeryn in a way he never expected—to himself.

But only *Farscape* would do it in such a way as to leave room for the whole thing to happen again...for the first time.

"And *then*!" sputters NetEx, really wound up by this point, "*Then* they both die! Together, this time. They turn to a crystalline substance in the beam of some weapon we've never heard of, and they're dead. Aeryn and Crichton and baby makes three. Dead. Just after Aeryn agrees to marry Crichton, of course. So who believes they're really dead? Who *would*, after what's happened before?"

"People worriebeing uncertd," says Ew, finally growing bolder. "When you know a show will do anything...then nothing's off-limits. It raised the stakes."

"Nothing's off-limits is right. Having that stumpy little Hynerian go diving for the leftover crystals, collecting them as he would gather food, which means there's going to be more—"

"Vomit," Ew says apologetically.

No point in wasting a good opportunity for more body fluids, after all. Rygel deposited the crystalline remains on the deck of the boat from which he was diving, offering them up with his own inimitable flair. And Ew seems to have caught on, finally. To the flair. To the value of going too far.

NetEx hasn't. NetEx isn't likely to. He's still carrying on. "*And* Aeryn Sun is pregnant. Some convenient fluke of Peacekeeper physiology keeps her from being certain of the father, since Sebacean women can tuck their little embryos away for development at a convenient time. Just like kangaroos. You think it's coincidence that show was filmed in Australia?"

"But it let them have the pregnancy and have their action, too," Ew observes.

"Ridiculous!" But NetEx's protests are beginning to carry a futile undertone. "Just as ridiculous as the way they had that baby born!"

"Which part, where Rygel incorporated the pregnancy, or the part where they transferred the baby to Aeryn at the last moment, or the part where she gave birth in the middle of a battle?"

"All of it!" NetEx sputters. "It's all over the top! It shouldn't have worked—none of it! How they possibly kept their viewers—"

"You've been studying," Ew realizes, bemused. "You know everything about this show. But why? It's not your show. It's not even one you seem to like."

NetEx settles back on his barstool, disgruntled. "I hate it. It's an expensive show that broke every character rule in the books—we've barely scratched the surface in this conversation! And yet. . . ." Definitely disgruntled. He takes a long swallow of his fruity drink. "I've been trying to figure out why the viewers are so damn loyal." And it remains unspoken but obvious—because NetEx would love to have a show like that. A show of his own.

But it's not likely. Because the *Farscape* folks learned what NetEx apparently cannot—that by throwing all of themselves into the show, by showing their heart and their soul and by going over the top, the viewers could trust them to be true to the characters and to the viewers. They wouldn't pull punches; they wouldn't take the easy way. They took the familiar . . . and made it entirely new again. And brought the viewers along for the ride, knowing only one thing for sure—they were never going to guess what would happen next.

A man walks into a bar, and the joke's on him.

> *Doranna was born writing (instead of kicking she scribbled on the wall of the womb) and never stopped, even though it took some time for the world to understand what she was up to. She grew up attached to college-rule notebooks and resisted all attempts at separation. Eventually she got a college degree (wildlife illustration) and had grand adventures on horseback in the Appalachians before ending up in the Southwestern high country with her laptop, dogs, horse and uncontrollable imagination.*

FLATULENCE, FOOD AND FORNICATION

RICK KLAW

Helium farts do seem a bit improbable unless Rygel runs on nuclear fusion (unlikely, given how much he eats). But the helium is not the point; the farts are. The farts, the eating, the sex, the greed.... Farscape's muppets were more real than most Federation captains, and far more interesting.

MY GRANDMOTHER INTRODUCED ME to *Star Trek*. I don't remember exactly when it was—it must have been 1974 or so—that I found her watching the show. Aware of my geek tendencies, she invited me to watch with her.

I was mesmerized. There was a smart, severe-looking dude with pointed ears. A buff, no-nonsense captain. A rock creature with glowing coals. I mostly remembered the creature. The Horta[1] burrowed its way through rock, oozing lava and threatening members of the crew. After Spock successfully mind-melded with the creature, the crew discovered that the Horta was the last of its race and actually a benevolent entity. Quite probably, this was my first exposure to humanist science fiction. In retrospect, "The Devil in the Dark" is one of the worst *Star Trek* episodes, but to this five-year-old, it was mind-blowing.

Watching *Star Trek* with my grandmother became a regular activity. At first glance, this seemed an odd show for my sixty-something-year-old grandmother to enjoy.[2] After all, she was a big fan of westerns and

---

[1] Legend has it that one day designer Janos Prohaska wore the costume in *Star Trek* producer Gene Coon's office. Coon was so taken with the creature that he wrote an entire episode around it.

[2] I never got a chance to ask her about it. By the time I began to wonder about this idiosyncrasy, my grandmother had passed away.

this was a show filled with spaceships and ray-guns. It wasn't until many years later that I put it all together. *Star Trek*, like most science fiction television, was nothing more than a western set in space.[3]

She soon introduced me to the the 1950s George Reeves *Superman* television show. At five, I was already a comic book reader and knew all about the Big Guy, but this was different. There he was on TV!

I began to wonder what else was out there, sending me on a never-ending quest for the elusive perfect science fiction show. Like *Star Trek* and *Superman*, I discovered in syndication *The Twilight Zone* and *The Outer Limits*. *Planet of the Apes*, *Quark*, *The Six Million Dollar Man*, *Battlestar Galactica*, *The Amazing Spider-Man* and others would come and go in an orgy of failed dreams and broken promises.

I also explored fantastic literature. I devoured the works of Bradbury, Burroughs, Matheson, Brown, Le Guin, Boucher, Dick, Sturgeon, Moorcock and others. My comic book reading continued unabated and reached a fever pitch in the mid-eighties, when creators like Alan Moore and Frank Miller burst upon the scene. By my early twenties, I had become a scholar of sorts, of both science fiction/fantasy and comics. My bookselling career was in full swing, and I had begun to dabble with editing and writing comic books.

Science fiction television offered nothing but a series of disappointments. Until 1987.

I refer to myself as a passive Trekkie. I know a lot about the *Star Trek* universe. I can name major characters, discuss individual episodes. I've seen every *Trek* movie in the theaters (including, to my dismay, *The Final Frontier* and *Nemesis*). But I won't rearrange my life to see an episode, don't write fan fiction, haven't read the novels[4] and you'll never catch me dressed up as a Klingon.[5] I did, however, watch the premiere of *Star Trek: The Next Generation* with both excitement and trepidation.

My roommate, several friends and I gathered to watch that first episode.[6] The premiere, "Encounter at Farpoint," was fair, but it showed a

---

[3] To be fair, so is most sf literature.

[4] Except one. I read the novelization of *Star Trek: The Motion Picture* back when the movie first came out. Ah, the folly of youth.

[5] Yes, I did see *Trekkies* and enjoyed the hell out of it.

[6] This communal experience seems unique to geeks and sport fans. You don't catch many groups watching *Jeopardy!*, *CSI* or *Survivor*, but science fiction and horror shows are different. I've known groups of people who got together for *Buffy the Vampire Slayer*, *The X-Files* and even (gasp!) *Highlander*. (The exception is *Melrose Place* and its ilk. I don't know if kids are getting together to watch *The OC* but it wouldn't surprise me.) Over the next seven seasons, I probably watched less than a dozen *Next Generation* episodes by myself.

lot of promise. Sure, we were introduced to perhaps the most annoying character in the *Star Trek* mythos ("Q"), and while the idea of a separating saucer section was interesting, how much could you really do with that?[7] But there was Captain Jean-Luc Picard.[8] He was the show's fulcrum right from the beginning, and over the ensuing years Picard developed into one of the most interesting characters on science fiction television. By the middle of the second season, I was hooked.

When the show ended its run in 1994, I was, once again, left with no science fiction television. The *Next Gen* spin-offs left me cold, and I never embraced *The X-Files*. My science fiction television viewing would remain intermittent until AggieCon 2000.

AggieCon bills itself as the oldest and largest student-run convention in the U.S.[9] Based on the Texas A&M University campus in College Station, Texas, AggieCon is completely managed by students.

I first started attending in the mid-nineties. At that show, I met Michael Moorcock and talked Joe R. Lansdale into contributing a story to my monster comic anthology *Creature Features*. With the exception of the 2001 AggieCon, which I skipped to get married, I have attended every one since.

While at the 2000 AggieCon, my future wife and I were relaxing in our hotel room after a hectic day at the convention. We sat flipping through the channels. Nothing. <click> Boring. <click> Stupid. <click> WHOA! We stopped on a show featuring a blue woman and a dude with tattooed tentacles on his face. It looked interesting, so we stayed tuned. Over the next hour we learned the blue woman was the priestess Zhaan and the tentacled warrior D'Argo. We met the human John Crichton, the aggressive Peacekeeper Aeryn, Rygel (a regal puppet[!] with some questionable manners) and a very large alien (another puppet) who was symbiotically linked to the living ship Moya. Quite by accident, I stumbled upon the most exciting science fiction show I had ever seen.

We watched the episode[10] in astonishment. On the Sci-Fi Channel, which up to that point had been mostly good for *Twilight Zone* reruns and being the brunt of the occasional joke, we saw aliens portrayed with

---

[7] Apparently, far less than most of us thought. In later seasons, the saucer bit was all but forgotten.

[8] When he portrayed Professor Charles Xavier in the *X-Men* films, Patrick Stewart joined the small fraternity of actors (including Harrison Ford, Arnold Schwarzenegger, Peter Weller and very few others) to become identified with two very popular genre characters.

[9] Aggiecon started in 1969. Guests have included Harlan Ellison, Michael Moorcock, Joe R. Lansdale, Wendy Pini, Roger Zelazny, Marion Zimmer Bradley and others.

[10] Which we later learned was "Back and Back and Back to the Future" (1-5).

real emotion, as well as beautiful imagery and mature sexual situations between different species.

We had caught our first episode after the opening credits. Luckily, we saw the credits on our next episode:

> My name is John Crichton, an astronaut. A radiation wave hit and I got shot through a wormhole. Now I'm lost in some distant part of the universe on a ship, a living ship, full of strange alien life-forms. Help me. Listen, please. Is there anybody out there who can hear me? Being hunted...by an insane military commander. Doing everything I can. I'm just looking for a way home.[11]

Luckily for us, this was just after the completion of the first season, so within six months we were caught up. We never missed another episode.

Farscape became our Sunday afternoon ritual. We routinely taped the episode on Friday night and watched it after lunch on Sunday. We would often discuss it for most of the afternoon.[12]

Over the next four seasons every major character was killed at least once (and, in the cases of Zhaan and presumably D'Argo, permanently), Crichton was cloned, and Moya gave birth. A variety of interesting alien cultures and worlds were introduced. The aliens were...well, really alien. Most science fiction shows tend to devise alien creatures from humans in fancy makeup and prosthetics. *Farscape* used traditional methods, but it also had some of the finest puppets ever.

Biological creatures were used in unusual ways to perform necessary and sometimes mundane tasks. Small leech-like creatures, Dentics, fed on food remnants from large creatures, thus they were used to clean teeth.[13] Most species in the *Farscape* universe were injected with translator microbes at birth in order to allow interspecies communication.

From the start there were many differences between *Farscape* and other science fiction shows. Beyond the superior writing, quality acting and gorgeous set design, the three tenets of life—eating, shitting and fucking—were an integral aspect.

---

[11] Opening credits voice-over from the first season.

[12] What a couple of geeks!

[13] And their urine gave off a minty fresh smell.

ZHAAN: Rygel, what a surprise. I see you're having something to eat. Is this your third helping or your fourth? ("DNA Mad Scientist," 1-9)

The deposed Dominar Rygel XVI not only organized the original escape with Zhaan and D'Argo; he was also one of the most disgusting creatures in the history of science fiction television. Nary an episode went by that Rygel did not fart, puke or piss. His race farted helium.[14] His urine could be explosive.[15] Hynerians had three stomachs. Watching Rygel eat was one gross spectacle.[16]

Rygel's vile bodily functions were an asset on more than one occasion to the crew of Moya and their allies. In "Thank God It's Friday, Again" (1-6), the crew was able to escape due in part to Rygel's explosive piss. After the crystallization of Crichton and Aeryn and the destruction of their bodies ("Bad Timing," 4-22), amphibious Rygel rescued the star-crossed lovers' pieces from the bottom of a lake. He swam down, ate the pieces and regurgitated them on land. The collected pieces were then reconstituted and the crystallization process reversed. And these were but two of the numerous times that Rygel's unique biology figured prominently.

Never has a show consistently displayed the fetid aspects of life with the honesty and frankness of *Farscape*. Rarely, *Star Trek* (in all its myriad forms) dabbled with the subject, and there was the infamous *Xena: Warrior Princess* lice episode, but that's about it.

D'ARGO: The bad news is that you are married and you must endure as a statue for eighty cycles in a strange world.
CRICHTON: What's the good news?
D'ARGO: Chiana and I are having fantastic sex. ("Look at the Princess, Part Two: I Do, I Think," 2-12)

Sex and sexual relations were another major element of *Farscape*. Like most mature Delvians, Zhaan had no self-consciousness about her body or her sexuality. In "Throne for a Loss" (1-4), the crew captured a young adult Tavlek, and Zhaan took his clothes for use in a plan to rescue Rygel from the Tavleks. The young man removed his blanket covering in hopes of intimidating Zhaan with his nakedness. She wondered

---

[14] Soon after it was revealed that Rygel farted helium, geeks all over the net were debating the realism of this. The consensus was that biological beings cannot fart helium. Whatever.

[15] When a Hynerian ingests Tannot root.

[16] Reportedly, after seeing how Rygel ate in "Premiere" (1-1), Brian Henson, the show's executive producer, suggested that there be as many Rygel eating scenes as possible.

aloud if his race had taboos about nudity, and the Tavlek told her that if they were all as ugly as she, they would. Zhaan gave him a coy smile and then showed him her elegant blue body. The boy shut up.

A wild and rebellious child, the runaway Chiana was a young woman who used her wits and wiles to get what she wanted. She often flirted and teased, using her seduction skills to get attention and put people at ease. Chiana's "abilities" often made her a vital part of Crichton's schemes.

During Chiana and D'Argo's romantic relationship, before and after the two-cycle break precipitated by Chiana's affair with D'Argo's son Jothee, their sexual activities were at times graphically displayed, far more so than in most science fiction television.

Star Trek (especially *Next Generation* and *Enterprise*), *Xena* and other shows toyed with sex, but it was not an essential part of the fabric of every episode of the series. With *Farscape*, sex was part of the culture. It was never excessive nor did it seem out of place.

There were two pregnancies during the course of the series. Early in season one it was revealed that Moya was with child. At the end of the first season, with Chiana and Aeryn's assistance, Moya's son Talyn was born.

In *The Peacekeeper Wars*, Aeryn gave birth to her and Crichton's son. As with everything on this show, there was a series of mishaps, including a brief period during which the child was carried by Rygel, Aeryn going into labor in the midst of a battle and Chiana playing midwife (sorta) once again. And D'Argo died, buying time for the crew (including the child) to escape.

Pregnancy is rarely present in science fiction television. Even when it is, such as with Deanna Troi in *Star Trek: The Next Generation* and Cordelia's pregnancy in *Angel*, the child is often the result of a malevolent force and not the union between two consenting sentient beings.

The basic biological aspects—flatulence, food and fornication—bring realism and the possibility of viewer identification to a science fiction show with several leading characters portrayed by puppets. At times Rygel was more real than James T. Kirk or Steve Austin. The motivations of Pilot were clearer than those of just about any of the characters on *Enterprise* or *The X-Files*. Through design or by accident, the use of these natural, essential commonplace elements enhanced *Farscape*, making it one of the finest science fiction shows ever.

I doubt my grandmother would have cared for *Farscape*, even though it is the best and most original science fiction show since the original *Star Trek*. It was too crude, too sexual, too weird.

Now that I think about it, she may have been amused with *Farscape*. Nana was legendary for her farts.

CRICHTON: And, there's life out here, Dad. Weird, amazing...psychotic life. And, uh...in Technicolor. ("Premiere," 1-1)

One of the more opinionated people in an industry of opinionated people, Rick Klaw is perhaps best known for the popular column "Geeks With Books" for SF Site. *A selection of his critical essays, reviews and other observations were collected in* Geek Confidential: Echoes From the 21st Century. *His writings have appeared in the* Austin Chronicle, Conversations with Texas Writers, Weird Business, The Big Book of the Weird Wild West, Gangland, Michael Moorcock's Multiverse, Science Fiction Weekly, Nova Express, Electric Velocipede, *KongisKing.net*, Fantastic Metropolis *and other venues. Klaw lives in Austin, Texas, with his wife, a cat and an enormous collection of books.*

LOOKING OUT FOR NUMBER ONE

PATRICIA BRAY

Remember Han Solo? Aggressive, self-interested, greedy and not particularly inclined to do the right thing. Except, like Humphrey Bogart in Casablanca *(and countless others), when the chips were down Han Solo came through, just as we knew he would. I assumed it would be the same in* Farscape; *that in the end they would always do the right thing. Then they cut off Pilot's arm.*

I MUST CONFESS THAT I WASN'T an immediate fan of *Farscape*. I watched the pilot episode, but I wasn't particularly impressed and didn't bother tuning in the following week. After all, I could see where this was going: human astronaut launched into distant part of space rallies crew of latex-covered aliens and fights for truth, justice and the American way. I've watched numerous sci-fi shows and movies, and I knew exactly where this series was headed.

I was wrong.

Fortunately fate intervened in the form of a twenty-four-hour flu. Confined to the couch, I channel surfed until I stumbled across the Sci-Fi Channel, which was airing a chain reaction of season one *Farscape* episodes. I tuned in and the first episode I caught was "A Bug's Life" (1-18), in which the crew of Moya was united—in their belief that Crichton couldn't possibly carry out his part of the plan. He was acting as captain not because the others recognized his heroic leadership, but merely because he fit the uniform.

I was hooked.

I pestered friends until I found someone who had taped the first-season episodes and then set about discovering this wonderful show.

Watching the pilot for the second time, I saw the clues that I had originally missed. The show started with a prison break, and from the very beginning it was clear that each person on Moya had his or her own agenda. Crichton wasn't saved as an act of mercy, but because the prisoners on board hoped to use his technology to make their escape. Realizing he couldn't help them, they locked him in a cell—but not before Rygel tried to make a separate deal with Crichton, just in case Crichton turned out to be on the winning side.

If the crew of Moya had had a motto, it would have been "Looking Out for Number One." Rygel was the most obvious example of this creed, with his constant schemes to sell the others out for his own advantage. When one of the crew was in trouble, Rygel was the first to vote to abandon them. Wisely, he knew better than to expect their help in return. Rygel made no apologies for his selfishness, and in this he was the most honest of them all. "What friends?" he told Crichton in "Self-Inflicted Wounds, Part One: Could'a, Would'a, Should'a" (3-3). "We were thrown together against our will and we're all just trying to make the best of it until we get the chance to screw the others and get what we want."

Rygel was not alone in his quest to get what he wanted regardless of the cost to others. Gentle, spiritual Zhaan held Pilot down while D'Argo chopped off one of his arms, the price Namtar had demanded in return for information on how to return to their homeworlds. Despite Pilot's screams, she refused to relent. After all, she reassured him, his arm would grow back. Eventually.

D'Argo's search for information to lead him to his son made him ignore Crichton and Aeryn's peril when they were trapped in the Flax. Only at the last moment did he return to rescue them, but even then his motives were self-centered: he did so not out of concern, but because he could not face his son with the knowledge that he had let his comrades die.

Unlike the rest of Moya's crew, Aeryn Sun had no home to return to. Her goal was simple survival, and her xenophobic upbringing ensured that she felt little sympathy for the alien species that they encountered. Even former comrades did not elicit her compassion. Upon discovering the stranded Peacekeeper Tech Gilina, Aeryn's instincts were to first interrogate and then execute.

Stark first appeared in the guise of a hero, sacrificing himself for the crew, accepting almost certain death. Yet when he returned to Moya, his need for revenge against Scorpius led him to withhold information, knowing none of the crew members would agree to rob the shadow depository if they knew of Scorpius' involvement.

Time after time Crichton endangered Moya and his friends with his search for wormholes. His side trip to examine a wormhole as Moya raced toward a planet that represented the only hope for the dying Zhaan had devastating results. Though he was chastened by this experience, he was unable to change this part of his nature. Crichton was an addict, and wormholes were his drug of choice.

Even Moya had her own agenda, putting the needs of her child ahead of the needs of her passengers. The demands of her pregnancy nearly killed the crew, and later she repeatedly ignored their peril in order to search for her missing son.

Whenever one of the crew was in trouble, the others would debate whether to abandon him to his fate or attempt to save him. When faced with a ship in distress, they did not leap to the rescue. Instead they paused to weigh the risks to themselves against any potential gain. A world in conflict did not bring forward an immediate urge to help, nor did they feel responsible for correcting the injustices that they encountered. Chiana was brought on board as a prisoner, and though some sympathized with her plight, no one was willing to endanger his or her own freedom to help a stranger.

The crew was briefly able to unite in pursuit of a common goal, but as soon as the immediate danger had passed, internal divisions would fracture the tentative accord. They weren't heroes. They weren't trying to save the galaxy or right wrongs. They were simply trying to survive, and to make their way home—one of the things that made *Farscape* different from almost every other sci-fi show on television.

The original *Star Trek* has been characterized as a crew of intergalactic Boy Scouts. Even the Prime Directive, which forbade interfering with other cultures, was not enough to stop their do-gooding ways. Like classic action heroes, Kirk and his crew took it upon themselves to right every wrong, a tradition upheld by their successors.

Stargate SG-1 started with a clear mission statement. Travel through the stargate, seeking out potential allies and technology that could be used to fight the Goa'uld threat. But this directive didn't stop them from intervening in civil wars, freeing slaves and endangering Earth by making new enemies. In *Stargate Atlantis*, soon after arriving on the water world the crew risked themselves to save others, imperiling both their own lives and their vital mission. But this was how we expected them to behave, because they are heroes.

In *Highlander*, even the other immortals mocked Duncan MacLeod for his tendency to rescue stray kittens and beautiful women. It was difficult to imagine how he had survived for four hundred years, and it seemed unlikely that he would survive for many more.

Quantum Leap was the ultimate example of a show driven by self-sacrificing heroics. Every week Sam Beckett leapt into someone else's life and was forced to stay there until he solved that person's problems. Sam's own wants and needs were always secondary. At the beginning there was a faint hope that each leap would be his last, but as those leaps piled up, week after week, one after another, it was difficult to pretend that there was any chance that he would in fact be able to return home. And yet, because he was a hero, we expected Sam to cheerfully keep to his assigned role and once more save the day.

Can you imagine what *Star Trek* would have been like had the *Enterprise* refused to put itself in danger? Or if the crew had paused to vote each time a life-or-death decision arose? We are shocked whenever Teal'c expresses an agenda of his own, disagreeing with the wisdom of Earth and Stargate Command. Heroes aren't allowed to take a day off, or to suggest that it is someone else's turn to save the universe. Week after week we tune in to our favorite sci-fi television shows and watch as our heroes set off to save the day. Again.

There isn't anything wrong with the shows I've mentioned, but to some extent they have traded character development for action. Jack O'Neill and SG-1 are willing to saddle up and save the universe each time in large part because they are not carrying the burdens of past failures. We watch these shows because we enjoy seeing how they are going to pull the rabbit out of the hat this time rather than because we are attached to the characters.

Farscape took a different approach, and because of that was able to offer incredible depths of characterization. The characters on *Farscape* could be hurt. They quarreled, they bled, they made mistakes, and they carried the scars of their failures with them. The characters were changed by their experiences. It is impossible to watch an episode of *Farscape* without taking into account where it falls in the overall story line. Faced with a similar challenge, the characters from early season one responded far differently from the people they had become by season four.

Consider John Crichton. In the opening episode he risked his life to save Aeryn Sun, a member of the military that was pledged to destroy him. As the series went on, John's idealism was tempered by experience. He had been hurt, and he had seen friends die. He was no longer quick to leap into the fray; indeed, he spent much of the latter seasons simply trying to keep himself and his friends alive. The man who had once tried to reason with his deadly enemies had become a man capable of killing thousands to get what he wanted.

"Every time we get involved, people die," Crichton reminded Aeryn in *The Peacekeeper Wars*. Even with the best intentions, they often made the situation worse rather than better. Nowhere was this more evident than in "Different Destinations" (3-5), in which their attempts to change the past resulted in the deaths of the very people they were trying to save. *Farscape* showed us that our heroes could be fallible, and that sometimes the very worst thing they could do was to try to help. When Crichton tried to save someone, we knew that he was fully conscious of all that he could lose and everything that could have gone wrong. We didn't have that same sense with Kirk or Picard, and don't with O'Neill.

While Crichton became more self-centered, Aeryn Sun underwent a reverse transformation. In her earliest days on Moya she was a reluctant passenger. She expected nothing from the crew other than to be left alone. Faced with certain death after her paraphoral nerve was destroyed, she was stunned by Crichton's decision to risk his life to try and find a cure. But as time went on, Aeryn showed her heroic side. At first she protected only her newfound comrades on Moya, but later it would be Aeryn who risked her life to save innocents, particularly the children that they encountered.

Even at the best of times they were, as Crichton once observed, a Jerry Springer kind of family. Yet a threat to that family was capable of uniting them. Whether it was rallying together to rescue Crichton from Scorpius' clutches, saving D'Argo from his own folly on the shadow depository or pursuing the kidnapped Aeryn Sun deep inside the Scarran Empire, the crew repeatedly risked their lives in order to save their friends and shipmates.

They were less likely to stick their necks out for strangers. Informed that he alone could ensure the survival of the Royal Planet and its millions of subjects, Crichton had no interest in playing the hero...until he learned that his alternative was to be handed over to Scorpius. Faced with the looming prospect of war between the Peacekeepers and the Scarrans, the crew of Moya was determined to stick to their neutrality.

The brilliance of *Farscape* lay in its complexity. The producers didn't take the easy way out, labeling one side as good and the other as evil. War itself was viewed as the horror, and rather than pit themselves against the might of two empires, Crichton and his friends chose to flee deeper into the Uncharted Territories.

It took the return of the Ancient Jack to make Crichton realize that he could not escape responsibility for the wormhole knowledge that he had unwittingly shared. Preventing the Scarrans from acquiring that knowledge cost Talyn's Crichton-clone his life, and gave us all the first glimpse of how horrific such a weapon could be.

When the Crichton on Moya learned of his twinned self's death, he knew that the job was only half-done: Scorpius had his own wormhole research program, thanks to the memories he had stolen. Crichton declared that he would stop Scorpius, and in this he was joined by Aeryn and Crais. The others refused to help at first, at least until Rygel rose to the occasion, showing that even he had a heroic side. Having witnessed the horrific power of the wormhole weapon that Talyn-Crichton had unleashed at Dam-Ba-Da, Rygel realized that the weapon was too powerful to fall into anyone's hands. When Crichton decided that the only way to stop Scorpius was to destroy the Command Carrier, Rygel agreed to risk his life, and helped convince the others to do the same.

And once again, having united to achieve a common goal, the crew then went their separate ways. They were not heroes by choice, but rather by necessity.

The Peacekeeper Wars miniseries picked up right where the regular series had ended, both literally, as John Crichton and Aeryn Sun were reassembled out of their component particles, and figuratively, as once again danger threatened, and the crew of Moya was forced to frantically seek a way out of their predicament.

The Scarrans and Peacekeepers were now at war, and the crew of Moya requested sanctuary from the Eidolons on Qujaga. Aeryn and John wanted nothing more than to be married and to raise their child in peace. But sanctuary was refused, and when Scorpius landed on Qujaga, it was clear that the Scarrans would not be far behind.

Scorpius tried to convince Crichton that wormhole weapons were the only hope of stopping the complete destruction of the Peacekeeper realm, and of saving the billions of lives within its borders. His arguments gained weight when we learned that the Scarrans had already attacked the Hynerian Empire; millions of Rygel's former subjects had perished. Even the Luxans had joined forces with the Peacekeepers, united against a common foe.

Crichton and the rest of the crew desperately sought to find a path to peace that did not require unleashing a weapon of mass destruction. But as the death toll rose, Crichton ran out of choices.

"I have to protect the people I love," Crichton told Einstein, attempting to convince him to unlock the wormhole knowledge buried within Crichton's mind. Doing so meant stopping the war raging around him—whatever the cost. Crichton would achieve peace, or he would destroy himself, his family and the rest of the galaxy trying.

At first the wormhole was small, barely noticeable. But as it grew geometrically, devouring everything in its path, the true horror of the weapon became clear. Finally everyone realized why Crichton had fought for so long and hard to avoid this moment.

Scorpius' reaction was to declare Crichton insane. The Scarran Emperor and Commandant Grayza were convinced that he was bluffing. That he would not destroy himself and his friends. But as the wormhole continued to grow, they were forced to realize that he was serious in his determination to achieve peace or else. And in this he was supported by his friends. Even Rygel faced the prospect of his imminent death with equanimity, declaring it a death worthy of a Dominar.

At the very last moment both sides agreed to Crichton's demands. Peace was achieved, but all involved had paid a high price.

Sometimes looking out for number one means saving the galaxy. Crichton and his friends hadn't set out to be heroes. They wanted nothing more than to be left alone to live in peace. But in order to achieve their goals, they had to reshape the very galaxy in which they lived. And this made their heroism far more real, far more believable than the rote perfection we see on so many other sci-fi shows.

Like Crichton and his friends, I do not see myself as a hero. I can't identify with those starship captains and quantum-leapers who save the day again and again without any thought for themselves. But there are people for whom I would give my life.

Each person gets the chance to be his or her own kind of hero, and I can think of no better inspiration than the gang from *Farscape*. When even Rygel can find his heroic side, there's hope for us all.

Patricia Bray is the author of the award-winning fantasy Devlin's Luck, which is the first novel in her bestselling Sword of Change trilogy. Patricia balances her writing with a full-time career as an IT project manager and claims credit for turning her coworkers into fellow Farscape fans. In 2006 she'll launch a new fantasy series with the publication of The First Betrayal. For more information about her books and upcoming convention appearances visit her Web site at www.patriciabray.com.

CRACKERS DON'T MATTER

JIM BUTCHER

Acclaimed novelist Jim Butcher analyzes "Crackers Don't Matter," the episode in which we discovered there was hope for humanity after all.

As a science fiction series, *Farscape* has what I consider a singular, enormous advantage over most other programs in the genre: it's perfectly willing to admit that Earth is a tiny and insignificant little place.

That's not such a shocking concept—after all, the *Animaniacs* sages Yakko, Wakko and Dot have been saying it for years. Yet from the content of the majority of science fiction programs extant, one would think it a radical idea. In Gene Roddenberry's *Star Trek* universe, of course, Earth is the center of an idealized civilization. J. Michael Straczynski's *Babylon 5* universe, while not nearly so Terra-centric as *Trek*, still placed our homeworld as the birthplace of a dynamic and formidable civilization. In the original inception of *Battlestar Galactica*, Earth was the Holy Grail of the remnants of a mortally wounded civilization.

Relatively few such television venues have depicted Earth as a place so unimportant that no one had ever even heard of it, much less bothered to have an opinion about it. Douglas Adams' Hitchhiker's Guide series, of course, did precisely that, depicting Earth as a place so uselessly unremarkable that it was paved over to help form a galactic highway. Ming the Merciless, archvillain of various *Flash Gordon* productions, regarded the Earth as a bauble to be toyed with and idly destroyed. The universe of *Stargate SG-1* depicts Earth as a scrappy underdog, surviving on its wits and luck more than any other single factor.

And then there is the universe of *Farscape*, where Earth is utterly insignificant, and where Earthlings, by the standards of a harsh and difficult universe, are slow, weak, fragile, half-blind and not very bright.

Which naturally brings us to John Crichton.

Poor Crichton. As our planet's representative Everyman in the *Farscape* universe, he had a lot of weight on his shoulders. Though one of the foremost minds of our world in the field of extra-atmospheric craft and phenomena, once he moved out of the kiddie pool and into the universe at large, all of his knowledge meant, in the words of a certain Man in Black, "precisely dick." His familiarity with the most advanced technology on Earth meant as much as a thorough knowledge of the use of medieval siege engines might to a modern military commander. Sure, there might come a time when the use of a catapult might just be critical, but honestly, what are the odds?

Which meant that Crichton's technological and mental assets were marginal, at best. And while he was in excellent physical condition (as is any astronaut IASA sends up), his best was barely enough to enable him to survive. Crichton probably represented the top percentile of what this whirling ball of mud had to offer, when both mental and physical skills are taken into account—yet if anyone Out There was playing kickball, Crichton would certainly have been the last one picked for the team.

After all, the *Farscape* universe was a tough place, and one that selected for a brutally Darwinian set of skills. A relatively small number of traits garnered respect from its denizens—first and foremost of which was strength, defined as the ability to kick someone's tail when the situation demanded it. Both Aeryn and D'Argo came from martial cultures, and both possessed training and talents in a broad spectrum of combat. Both could fly military craft, both were skilled in conventional engagements with small arms, and both were a threat in hand-to-hand combat. Both were far stronger and more fit than the average human being, both could sustain more physical harm than the average human, and, if that weren't enough, D'Argo also came custom-equipped with a paralytic poison stinger in the tip of a prehensile tongue.

A prehensile TONGUE, people.

The second trait the *Farscape* universe respected was intelligence—the possession of knowledge and the ability to apply it. Whether that knowledge was medical, political, scientific or practical, those who had it were valued. Zhaan's abilities as a botonist and pharmacist proved useful time and again. Rygel's political knowledge and his business savvy ensured that he always had a contribution to make to the survival of the group. Aeryn's knowledge of Peacekeeper procedures and tactical doctrine saved the crew of Moya more than a couple of times, and even Chiana gained some respect for her cleverness and abilities as a sneak, spy and seductress. Pilot, of course, probably had more sheer intellect than anyone else on board, and his ability to pilot and commune with Moya made him invaluable.

Finally, and perhaps a bit surprisingly, there was a widespread respect for spirituality among most of the denizens of the *Farscape* universe. Zhaan's position as priestess almost defined her status, both because of her wisdom and because of the potential access to extra-normal mental abilities many such mystics acquired. Stark, unlike Zhaan, could not really be said to have a great deal of respect, but his own extraordinary abilities were never taken lightly.

And then there was Crichton. Smaller, slower and weaker than virtually every threatening being out there, he could lay no serious claim to strength. He entered the *Farscape* universe as an utter neophyte, and almost none of the knowledge he possessed could be applied to the situations faced by Moya's crew. His spirituality was limited to seeing visions of Scorpius and the occasional hallucination about a wormhole alien who happened to look exactly like his father—and while that became more important as the series progressed, it took a while to kick in. When Crichton arrived in the *Farscape* universe, he was utterly unprepared for the kind of hardball game being played. In the view of Moya's crew, Crichton was little more than a liability.

Several things happened to convince his fellow crew members otherwise, none of which were clearer than the events of "Crackers Don't Matter" (2-4).

As a quick review: While negotiating with an alien for the purchase of a stealth device that would conceal Moya from the Peacekeepers, Crichton and company sailed into an area of particularly intense brilliance. The alien employed their own egos as weapons against them, confiding to them that only "lesser beings" would feel any effect from the light.

Naturally, the light began to have an incapacitating effect upon the crew, sending them into fits of utter irrationality while sustaining a steady level of paranoia. T'raltixx's lie about the rays' effect meant that no one on board was willing to admit that he or she was beginning to be affected. A bit more manipulation on the part of the alien put the crew at each other's throats while the alien reengineered Moya into some kind of giant light-generating device which he claimed would give him ultimate power of some kind.

(It looked to me like the alien, T'raltixx, had been soaking up the loopy rays at least as readily as anyone on the crew, but that's neither here nor there.)

The effect of this induced madness was a total inversion of the survival qualities of the crew: D'Argo and Aeryn's warrior skills were useless against a threat their minds could not rationally recognize. Their tendency to aggressively seize the initiative, usually of immense importance in a conflict, was turned against them, driving them to act upon utterly inaccurate judgments about their crewmates.

The advantages Rygel and Chiana enjoyed, their superior savvy and knowledge, were also utterly undermined by the disruptive effects of the light. Chiana and Rygel, both of whom had a somewhat fuzzy notion of personal property rights, were immediately crippled by the fear of their possessions being taken by others—their possessions being, in this case, about a million crackers: square nutrient wafers. Sure that they had to do all that they could to protect their precious property from the others, they immediately began plotting intrigues, each working on several different plots, alliances and betrayals.

Perhaps most dramatically, Zhaan's cool intellectualism and sense of remote spirituality were entirely subverted when the light sent her into a state of physical ecstasy. Zhaan was perhaps the most world-wise and experienced of the crew, and her intuition and intelligence often made her the first to be aware of danger. In this episode, however, her wisdom and intellect were of little avail, since she, as a sentient plant, spent the majority of the episode wracked with photogasms, and enjoying it.

Even Pilot, normally the gentlest, most rational and most stable of the crew, was easily led astray by T'raltixx when the alien was able to play Pilot's mixed feelings for the rest of the crew against him. Pilot's dedication to his principles of serving and protecting Moya's crew became a kind of understated hate for those who had not always acted with his best interests in mind—though admittedly, they did rip one of his arms off in order to trade it for a road map only a few weeks before. Though Pilot would normally not have countenanced such an intense reworking of Moya's internal systems such as the one T'raltixx undertook, his fear and long-repressed desire for a balancing of the scales between himself and several of the crew laid the stage for T'raltixx's plot and put everyone on board in mortal danger.

Heck, even the crackers had their value inverted. First considered a bland and horribly boring food supply, they were transformed by the insanity of the crew to a precious treasure worth fighting and killing for.

Here's where it gets interesting.

Just as the others had their strengths turned against them, Crichton experienced the same sort of reversal with his deficiencies. Because his senses were not as acute as everyone else's, he was less affected by the light. Because his mental processes were already fairly slow and unremarkable, the cognitive disruption caused by the light had the least effect upon him. Even the hallucinatory Scorpius managed to provide Crichton with a spot check against reality, helping him to hang on to his intellectual balance while the others had already plummeted into near madness.

Crichton alone managed to draw the crew together again, to mend the rifts that stretched between them and get them to recognize the true threat—the spidery alien T'raltixx. Because the others could not risk entering the light-filled chamber where T'raltixx had holed up, deficiency-riddled Crichton had to go inside and battle the alien alone.

Equipped with D'Argo's blade and a shield made from an armored plate from Aeryn's fighter, wrapped in a heat-resistant cloak from Chiana, slathered with a heat-resistant paste Zhaan made to protect his skin from burns and with the cloaking device hung around his neck like a particularly large and gaudy magic talisman, Crichton the deficient went out to fight the battle no one else on the crew could attempt.

Though still intoxicated from the light, Crichton managed to sneak in and assault T'raltixx. He defeated the alien, destroyed the light-generating equipment and saved the day, thus earning considerable respect in the eyes of Moya's crew. Crichton came through when none of the others could have.

While on the surface this was simply a somewhat silly and entertaining episode, the implied questions the story asked were surprisingly serious: What consists of value in a human being? Why are some traits more valued than others? What happens when the assumptions of value are suddenly trumped by a radically altered environment?

In the end, the episode posited a fundamental statement—that the overt skills, traits and talents so often valued by society are not always sufficient to meet the challenges of life. Like so much of the rest of *Farscape*, that statement supported the notion of humanity's very, very tiny role in all the vast reaches of the universe—it emphasized that our opinions of what traits embody an ideal human being are ultimately limited and shortsighted.

It stated that even those whom our society deems as valueless may have a more significant role to play in our future, and that one should not be too swift to judge what an individual may be able to contribute in the changing environment of our existence. It stated that the variety provided by those outside the mainstream of society may at some point prove useful, even necessary, and that a policy of tolerance is the wisest course.

It also implied that there are facets of the mind and the soul which may be far more important than more obvious survival skills—that things like courage, friendship and dedication may ultimately be as powerful and meaningful as military and political skills or a hyperactive intellect. Courage and loyalty managed to carry Crichton to a victory no one else could have achieved, despite his flaws. He established himself as a formidable (or at least competent) being in the eyes of his crewmates, who gradually began to realize that Crichton's iron nerve and occasional cleverness made him a worthwhile companion and friend.

Humanity is quite young. Our future is an enormous, unknown quantity with wonders we cannot yet even imagine, much less anticipate. We should not so blithely assume that what has always served us in good stead will universally continue to do so—and we must realize that if it should fail, we may be forced to turn to alternative skills, manners of thought and talents.

After all, you never can tell when someone like T'raltixx might drop by and undermine all our expectations, just as he did with Crichton and company. If so, we've got to make sure that we still have someone around to point out to us that crackers don't matter—people do.

Jim Butcher is a martial arts enthusiast with fifteen years of experience in various styles, including Ryukyu Kempo, Tae Kwon Do, Gojo Shorei Ryu and a sprinkling of kung fu. He enjoys fencing, singing, bad science fiction movies and live-action gaming. He is the author of the Dresden Files series, which includes Storm Front, Fool Moon, Grave Peril, Summer Knight, Death Masks *and* Blood Rites, *as well as the Codex Alera series. He lives in Missouri with his wife, son and a vicious guard dog.*

DON'T MAKE ME TONGUE YOU

JOHN CRICHTON AND D'ARGO
AND THE DYSFUNCTIONAL BUDDY RELATIONSHIP

MARTHA WELLS

*Can a grouchy, tongue-flicking, hyper-rageaholic strike up
a true friendship with a smart-alecky, half-insane, psuedo-
Sebacean? Not easily.*

IF THERE WAS ONE THING you could count on with *Farscape*, it was that it
would take you to some crazy-ass places and show you some crazy-ass
things.

I've always felt that one reason the show was able to take its viewers
to all those strange places is that the audience knew the core characters
so well, both human and nonhuman. Much of the first season was really
about the audience getting to know the characters, and the characters
getting to know each other. I actually had trouble getting into *Farscape*
at first because of that.

In fact, I didn't really become addicted until the latter half of the first
season, or even the beginning of the second. I saw the pilot episode, but
D'Argo, Zhaan and Rygel were all just yelling, scary aliens. Aeryn and
the Peacekeepers were yelling, scary human-looking Sebaceans. It was
the yelling that put me off. I figured, hey, if I wanted to see people yelling at each other, I could just turn off the TV.

My personal theory on why people get addicted to ensemble cast or buddy TV shows is that we get vicarious enjoyment out of the close friendships and family relationships those shows depict. It's just a theory. I haven't tested it on a control group or anything. But I know I tend to gravitate toward this kind of show, and that I have a particular kink for shows where two or more disparate characters find themselves coming together as partners or as a family.

So I should have loved *Farscape* from the beginning, right? Right. But I didn't watch the first part of the series with any attention to detail—at least not until after I got sucked into it by catching glimpses of the beauty and terror of the later episodes.

Being the kind of gutsy show that took chances, *Farscape* made the questionable choice to place us with an immediately likable viewpoint character, John Crichton, and dump him in with some irascible characters who were not immediately likable. We had to get to know them, to understand them, before we could like them; understanding between characters from different cultures and species was a common theme of the early episodes. The crew of Moya, alien, human and humanlike, did eventually become a family. A dysfunctional family, what with the yelling and the death threats and the ripping-off-of-arms, but still, a family.

Through the first season we got to know the characters as John got to know them, gradually discovering more about their past lives, their fears, their secrets and the events that brought them to be imprisoned on Moya. The one thing John had in common with his new companions from the beginning was that they were all lost and they all wanted to go home. D'Argo, Zhaan and Rygel had no more idea of where their home planets were than John knew where Earth was. Aeryn and later Chiana were the exceptions. They knew where home was; they just couldn't go back there without getting their brains sucked out. Even Pilot and Moya shared home-related fears: space was their home, they were accustomed to having a crew and found it comforting, and they didn't want to be left alone in the Uncharted Territories either. But it took all the characters time to realize how much they had in common. The emotional landscape of the series was always fraught, and in the first season the antagonism and conflict were more likely to come from John's friends and allies than his enemies.

Nothing on *Farscape* was easy, nothing was the way it first seemed. And John and D'Argo's relationship was the epitome of not easy.

Buddy relationships have long been a standard in movies and TV, with varied examples from Starsky and Hutch to Hercules and Iolaus in *Hercules: The Legendary Journeys*. Unlike many TV buddies, however, John and D'Argo didn't start off as friends. D'Argo, in fact, greeted John with the patented Darth Vader throat-grab-and-lift-off-the-ground move, and threatened to kill him.

John didn't realize at that point that D'Argo, Zhaan and Rygel were all kept in separate cells and didn't really meet until after their escape, not long before he arrived. At the end of the first episode it just seemed like everybody was yelling and threatening each other. Hell, it practically took five minutes of intense negotiation just to figure out who was going to let who out of the handcuffs in what order during their second escape from the Peacekeepers. Aeryn was scary, D'Argo was hitting and yelling, Rygel was just creepy, and John's only friend before the fade to black was a DRD with a limp antenna. Again, I can see why some viewers may have found the arguments, tension and distrust off-putting, especially if they, like me, turn on the TV for comfort and a little refuge from the arguments, tension and distrust of daily life. But *Farscape* was all about taking chances, and the yelling and tension was an important part of the emotional integrity of the overall story. These people were not only alien to the audience, they were alien to each other, forced to live together in a hostile environment; the show took us through the difficulties of that, step by noisy, fascinating step.

One of the biggest chances the show took was starting off its core buddy relationship with emotional and physical abuse and death threats. John's feelings on that were clear: early on he told Zhaan that with D'Argo and Aeryn everything was a test; he felt like he was trapped in a never-ending frat hazing at Alien U. The fact that John looked like a Sebacean Peacekeeper, the race that imprisoned D'Argo and was currently trying to run the crew down and kill them, didn't help the situation. It also didn't help that John was utterly new to the cultures and technology of the others on Moya.

Even though they were all from different alien races, the others did have certain elements of an interplanetary culture in common. Kind of like how we humans might not speak all of each other's languages, but we can mostly get around airports in foreign countries. We know what identification we need, and we can find the ticket counters and the restrooms, the snack shop and the taxis and other essentials, because those things are all fairly universal. When John was thrown into the mix on Moya, he knew nothing about the culture that these aliens shared in common. He didn't even know what Moya was, and had never before encountered the concept of a living sentient starship. He didn't know who was shooting at them and why they wouldn't stop. He didn't even know how to clean his teeth, and in the second season we learned that his eyes couldn't see the colors that some of the instruction signs were written in. The injection of the translator microbes that allowed him to speak the language didn't supply any of that common knowledge.

And D'Argo was not The Patient Guy, he was The Angry Guy.

John tried to connect with D'Argo long before D'Argo was willing to see John as anything but an annoyance. It made sense; we saw enough of John's past to know that he was used to close family, friend and working relationships. While John's relationships with Aeryn and Zhaan and Pilot, and even eventually Rygel, became close, D'Argo was the only other humanoid guy on the ship, and despite their physical and cultural differences, he and John had the potential to have a lot in common. John missed his dad and his best friend D. K., and he wanted a guy friend.

And then there were Zhaan and Aeryn.

Zhaan's line to Chiana, "My dear, I've kicked more ass than you've sat on," said it all. Zhaan and Aeryn were both strong, emotionally and physically powerful and occasionally scary women who also happened to be really hot. Considering that, John might have wanted a male ally. Somebody who understood where he was coming from. Somebody to talk to about how hot Zhaan and Aeryn were.

At the beginning of the series, D'Argo was separated from his people by his capture and imprisonment by the Peacekeepers. He told the others that he was arrested for killing his commanding officer but, as we found out later, that was a lie. And Zhaan, after finding out how old D'Argo was, told us that he was "but a boy." Though he had fought in two campaigns, D'Argo was not very old and not as experienced as he would have liked everybody else to believe. He came from a warrior culture and in many ways still felt that he needed to prove himself. His wife was dead, his son was gone, and he was a hunted fugitive stuck on Moya: when the series started, his life sucked beyond the telling of it.

In "They've Got a Secret" (1-10), we found out D'Argo was actually charged with the murder of his Peacekeeper wife, who was really killed by her own brother. After this experience, he didn't trust anybody. He didn't want to connect with anybody, let alone the weird little do-gooder alien with the off-the-wall sense of humor and absolutely no clue how to clean his teeth.

Finding out more about D'Argo's past didn't make him any less scary. In "DNA Mad Scientist" (1-9), D'Argo didn't make any apology for cutting off Pilot's arm in exchange for data and star charts that could have led him home. Even though the attempt failed miserably, D'Argo told Pilot that he would do it again if given the opportunity. That was a damn harsh thing to say to someone sitting there missing an arm. But D'Argo also brought a musical instrument that he had made up to Pilot's chamber and played it for him, and so we knew D'Argo felt more on the subject than he had been willing to say.

D'Argo was very clear that he didn't want a friend, and it took him a while even to admit that John could be a worthwhile ally. Even in "Exodus from Genesis" (1-3), when John said, "It's just you and me," D'Argo replied, "Actually it's just me . . . and you."

But over those first few episodes, John proved himself in spades. While John didn't know anything about the technology on Moya, he learned quickly, and he was a trained scientist.

Even though he started out as The Helpless New Guy, John quickly proved himself in battle. He could be a ruthless fighter when his own life or anyone else's was at risk, and he had no intention of letting himself, or his new friends, be captured. He also rapidly became The Guy With the Ideas; John's problem-solving abilities were even better under stress, and the crew quickly came to value that. He was a brilliant guy for a human, which made perfect sense—he wouldn't have been flying the experimental space module for IASA in the first place if he wasn't.

But while these qualities helped D'Argo see John as an ally, what really set the stage for their close friendship were John's essential qualities of loyalty and trustworthiness.

In "Back and Back and Back to the Future" (1-5), John had a vision where he heard D'Argo reveal that he had lied about the true nature of the crime he had been imprisoned for. Revealing this to D'Argo was the only way to convince him of the danger, but John sent Zhaan and Aeryn out of the room first so he could tell D'Argo privately. John's bone-deep understanding that the existence of the secret wasn't his to reveal, that it was a terribly private thing for D'Argo and that it was up to him to choose whether or not to reveal it to the others, was an important insight into John's character. In the middle of a desperate situation, he was still willing to take the extra minute to safeguard D'Argo's privacy about an issue that didn't mean much to John but was intensely important to D'Argo. It was a clear sign to both D'Argo and the audience that John could be trusted on a very basic level. D'Argo understood that kind of trust was rare in the Uncharted Territories, and that it could mean the difference between capture and freedom, death and life.

Of course, John still had to take the opportunity to rub in the fact that D'Argo had been fooled by the alien woman. D'Argo asked, "Do you mock me?" and John answered, "D'Argo, I mock all of us. . . . You're not the first guy to have his head snapped off by a chick."

This all helped establish the bond between John and D'Argo. And since the audience was going to view the trip through this wonderfully strange, often frightening and sometimes disturbing landscape through John's eyes, it was nice to know he was a guy we and the other characters could trust. Even if it took the other characters a while to understand him. "What is wrong with him?" Aeryn asked in frustration at one point. "He is Crichton," Zhaan answered philosophically.

In "Thank God It's Friday, Again" (1-6), we got John hiding for three days from D'Argo's Luxan hyper-rage. D'Argo's temper was played for laughs in this episode, with Aeryn teasing John about hiding so well that they couldn't find him to tell him that D'Argo had left the ship. It was also implied that hyper-rage was sex-related, and that all D'Argo really needed to calm down was to get laid. But *Farscape* never let the character relationships become stagnant. Big betrayals and small betrayals occurred as the characters learned more about each other and the pain of the past was exposed. Sometimes people were what they seemed; sometimes they were better, or much, much worse.

The constant conflicts and what they revealed about each character eventually brought the crew closer together, and the audience closer to the crew. Another key moment between John and D'Argo was in the episode "Till the Blood Runs Clear" (1-11), where John had to pretend to be Butch Crichton, a bounty hunter, in order to save the group from a vicious pair of Blood Trackers. D'Argo (surprise, surprise) leapt to the wrong conclusion, deciding John had betrayed him. After resolving this confusion and hurling insults at each other until they both calmed down, John said wearily, "This isn't going to work. We're never going to be friends." D'Argo replied, "Friendship is a lot to ask." But they did agree to be allies. Then D'Argo refused to "abandon" John in battle, though it would have made tactical sense. "Great," John said. "We can be buried together." Well, they nearly were.

But in a lot of ways, the bounty hunter episode gave John the key to dealing with D'Argo: as John pointed out, D'Argo did like to be The Alpha Male, The Guy in Charge, and he was having a problem assigning John a role in his personal scheme of things. John and D'Argo quickly developed a pattern to deal with this: D'Argo bit John's head off, John bit back, and they got on with business. John quickly learned that the best way to deal with Luxans was to be as irascible with them as they were with everyone else. In "Bone to Be Wild" (1-21), D'Argo blamed John for chasing after M'Lee and leaving Zhaan alone. John replied that it was instinct, and that everything D'Argo did was instinctive, with the unspoken corollary that D'Argo should shut the hell up. D'Argo growled and did. They had come a long way from the Darth Vader throat-grab-and-lift-off-the-ground move. They were still dysfunctional, but in a functional way.

The fledgling bonds between John and D'Argo were tested over and over again in the first season. In "The Flax" (1-13), D'Argo had the chance to salvage a Luxan ship containing star charts that could have led him back home to his son. But John and Aeryn were trapped in a damaged shuttle, and if D'Argo stopped to salvage the Luxan ship, he knew they might die. After some hesitation, D'Argo chose John and Aeryn, and he was fully aware of what that choice meant. D'Argo wouldn't betray his allies; especially allies who were becoming friends. The audience knew that now, too, and we cautiously felt a little more comfortable that our new TV friends wouldn't kill each other at the first opportunity.

Conflicts between John and D'Argo and all the characters continued to reoccur throughout the series. John had always known that D'Argo's temper could snap out of control; it happened often enough. In "Revenging Angel," in the second half of the third season, D'Argo mistakenly thought that John had done something to sabotage D'Argo's ship and accidentally knocked John into a coma. John spent much of the episode in a dream in which he imagined D'Argo was trying to kill him. But as the series progressed, D'Argo became wiser and more mature, more aware of his own failings and more in control of his temper. John, on the other hand, got crazier—partly as a result of the Scorpius clone in his head and partly because of his traumatic experiences. So you eventually got episodes where John was the nutjob and D'Argo was the one talking sense.

The last really important first-season milestone in John and D'Argo's relationship, and in fact in John's relationship with all the characters, was in the episode "Jeremiah Crichton" (1-14). John was feeling like an outsider and tired of the others blaming the human for everything that went wrong. He had a hissy fit and took a ride outside Moya in his module. But Moya starbursted prematurely and John was left believing that his new friends had abandoned him to his death. Fortunately, he was able to land on a planet that bore a close resemblance to a primitive Earth-type desert island paradise. Unfortunately, there was something on the planet that was draining power, and John was now stranded there.

John then became The Angsty Guy for three months, thinking his new friends had seen an opportunity to dump the weird annoying human and leapt at it. But the starburst was an accident, and the others had actually been searching for John the entire time. And it was D'Argo who refused to abandon the search when Zhaan wanted to face the fact that they might never find John. Luxans might have had a corporate policy against apologies, but D'Argo did admit to guilt, saying that John was only in this situation because they drove him away. That was one of the cool things I grew to love about D'Argo: once he let you in, he didn't let you down. Though he had told John that friendship was a lot to ask, he took the concept of "allies" seriously. More seriously than John had realized.

"Jeremiah Crichton" was where we got our first real look at the D'Argo of later seasons. He was beginning to deal with his personal demons, and instead of just being The Guy Who Yells, we started to see him as The Guy We Like. He was no longer the one-dimensional angry warrior figure of the first couple of episodes. He was more thoughtful, more aware of his faults and able to admit to his mistakes. Of course, he still yelled, but we liked that, too. He was becoming the character that the others would come to trust so much they actually made him The Guy in Charge.

When Rygel and D'Argo arrived to rescue John in "Jeremiah Crichton," they found him still majorly piqued. "You smell like dren," D'Argo greeted him. "You look like dren." D'Argo actually unbent enough to explain what happened, and made John understand that it was an accident. Their reunion was very understated, and nobody said what had happened in so many words. But the audience had known for a while now that D'Argo wouldn't betray John; now John knew it too, and that changed the tone of their relationship.

The dysfunctional part kind of fell by the wayside after that, but John and D'Argo continued to bicker and snap their way through most of their adventures. That's part of the classic buddy relationship, but these two guys had a lot more reason to yell at each other than most. D'Argo's life had made him The Angry Guy for a lot of valid reasons, and he was never hesitant to say what he thought. Or yell what he thought.

John and D'Argo never had a comfortable relationship, but none of the relationships on *Farscape* were comfortable, and they were never meant to be. *Farscape* was never meant to be a comfortable show: it was scary and poked you in unpleasant places; it ripped arms off and stuck needles in people's eyes. Understanding other people and accepting their differences in real life isn't comfortable either. I tend to think that was what that first season of *Farscape* was all about.

Frankly, it took me a few episodes to get used to *Farscape*. But I was glad I did.

Martha Wells is the author of seven fantasy novels, including Wheel of the Infinite *(HarperCollins Eos, 2000) and Nebula Award nominee* The Death of the Necromancer *(Avon Eos, 1998). The* Wizard Hunters *(HarperCollins Eos, May 2003) was the first book in her fantasy trilogy taking place in the world of Ile-Rien from* The Element of Fire *and* The Death of the Necromancer, *and her newest novel is the second book in that trilogy,* The Ships of Air *(HarperCollins Eos, July 2004). The third book of the trilogy,* The Gate of Gods, *will be released in 2005. Her books have been translated into eight languages, including French, Spanish, German, Russian and Dutch.*

DEAR JOHN

A LETTER OF REPRIMAND FROM THE NEW BOSS

TEE MORRIS

Ever wonder how our space agency would behave if Farscape had been a real mission? Here we are, a planet not even united in the best way to drink beer—either chilled, warmed or at current room temperature—and suddenly we find ourselves part of a network of wormholes that stretch into the deepest parts of our galaxy . . . and beyond. Our intrepid intergalactic explorer, John Crichton, would be considered a hero by NASA, right? Now, the administration would be given the kind of funding not seen since the Space Race of the sixties, right? And as far as public opinion and image, it would be considered "cool" again to be an astronaut, right?

Maybe. In a perfect world. But remember, it isn't the dreamers or adventurers calling the shots. It's the suits. Their spin on Farscape would be far different. . . .

FROM: National Aeronautics and Space Administration
DEPARTMENT: Project Administrator
1969 Kennedy Way
Cape Canaveral, Florida

TO: Cmdr. John Crichton
RE: Cancellation of Farscape Project

Dear John:

As I am newly appointed to this upper-management position here at NASA, I have just recently become aware of your top-secret research project code-named "Farscape." Having reviewed the footage (cleverly pawned off to the general public as science fiction) that had been leaked to news resources such as the *Washington Post, Sixty Minutes* and *Access Hollywood*, I note your passion and zeal for this, NASA's most ambitious project to date. You have more than upheld the name of your father, Captain Jack Crichton, in your heroics and bravery when facing dangers of the great unknown, and there is nothing that NASA could do, or would do, to take away from your accomplishments in not only surviving such hostile conditions, but settling down and starting a family. Your ingenuity, fast thinking and ability to troubleshoot truly is a credit to your name, and we at NASA applaud you for such talents. However, after reviewing your debriefing sessions and the numerous field reports still coming in from outside resources, I must step in and make an executive decision to pull present and future funding from this project.

At this point, I'm sure you will expect me to say something along the lines of "This is not an easy decision, Cmdr. Crichton, and it pains me to do so . . ." but I do not intend to do anything of the sort. On the contrary, the more I type, the better I feel. A weight is being lifted off my shoulders with each word of this correspondence, a correspondence that I can only hope will reach you through the experimental channels now established since your last visit to Earth and thanks in part to the data you left behind on the Moon for our retrieval. (More on this particular matter later.)

As you read this, your mind is probably racing through your past five years in the area of the universe you described in your debriefings as the "Uncharted Territories," the question of "Why?" asked again and again as you review your achievements. Well, Cmdr. Crichton, just because you lived to tell of your experiences does not necessarily define them as "successful." In fact, the reason NASA is pulling all funding from the

Farscape Project is because of its greatest liability: you, Commander John Robert Crichton, Jr.

The following reasons behind our decision to cancel the Farscape Project are listed in detail, as follows:

Misrepresentation of Earth on Foreign Worlds. I am fully aware that you were not prepared for the wormhole phenomenon the Farscape Project created, but be that as it may, you were thrown into a part of the universe unknown to us. Regardless of whether you volunteered for the position or not, you became, in a sense, Earth's ambassador to these strange new worlds. The members of the Overhead and Planning committee were unanimous in agreeing that additional training would have helped you fulfill this role more competently, but I myself am unanimous in concluding that if you had just taken a moment—just a moment—to think before opening your mouth, there would not have been so many botched First Contacts (or, as we at NASA are now referring to them, **BFCs**). For example, you were involved in a First Contact scenario with a farmer and her son, during which you initially told them they had been *chosen* to serve as the emissaries between their world and ours. Later on you were compelled to inform her that Moya was, in fact, part of a prison breakout. On account of this, her world's government has deduced that Earth is some sort of penal colony, and has been trying to contact the United Nations in order to discuss possible prisoner exchanges. As NASA headquarters is based in the United States, this is a public relations disaster for the country as well as this agency.

We are also deeply disturbed by what we at NASA are calling "The Katratzi Incident," which involved you holding Scarrans and Sebaceans under your influence by means of nuclear terrorism. I have no doubt that your time on your own in the Uncharted Territories was stressful and that improvisation was a necessity, but did you really think you were representing Earth and its world governments properly? While the United States is working very hard to improve its overall image globally, you did nothing more than perpetuate the "obnoxious American tourist" stereotype, only this time wearing a WMD for your belt buckle. This incident did not go over well with my peers here at NASA. You were, and still are, a representative of this agency and this planet, and should have considered the first impression you were giving during your consistent First Contacts in the outer reaches of the known universe.

Poor Orientation of Alien Races to Earth Culture. Building on the complications and problems of your numerous **BFCs**, we at NASA were under the impression that after five years of exploring new and uncharted areas of our universe you would have made more of an effort to familiarize your shipmates with Terran culture. Before being injected with translator microbes, NASA administration thought that the Luxan of your crew was bestowing upon the President of the United States and his Chiefs of Staff a greeting of his native world. On closer inspection, we discovered that the first words Ka D'Argo delivered to the leader of our country were "Yes. No. Bite me." We have yet to divulge this information to the White House, but they are starting to grow anxious, and I am running out of convenient excuses as to why we do not yet know precisely what words were exchanged that day. I cannot simply tell him it was a traditional Luxan felicitation. (See later note: **Farscape Project Overhead and Operations Exceeding Original Projections.**) Otherwise, we will have the President of the United States addressing the UN and its world leaders with "Yes. No. Bite me" (see earlier note on trying to improve country's image), although I do not doubt he has come close on certain occasions. Building on this theme, how can we overlook that D'Argo's final words in battle were not the traditional pledges and oaths of the Luxan Battle Cry he told us of, but a repeating chant of "I'm Your Daddy"?

Further evidence of this cultural contamination came to our attention when we received images taken from Moya's databanks of a visit you paid to a Peacekeeper memorial. During the Venek siege on the defenseless monastery, bystanders recalled the battle cry of covert Peacekeeper forces to be the words "Tony Montana!" On cross-checking these references, we discovered that for several centuries Peacekeepers went charging into battle invoking the name of Tony Montana. We also found out that the Mother Superior of this monastery was repeating the phrase "the one called Crichton" right up to her death. What we at NASA have dubbed "The Peacekeeper Memorial Incident" will be addressed again later in this reprimand.

Is this how you have represented our planet over the past five years in the outer reaches of our galaxy? By dropping pop culture references that manage to become heroic icons of their worlds?

Misuse of NASA Property. Let me make clear that I fully understand that *Farscape 1* is an experimental research craft, and that there were intentions for its design and technology to be developed over time. I also understand that, as you were stranded in the outer reaches of the known universe, you would have to improvise and adapt your module for its new environment. The reports of where you took *Farscape 1*, however, have my boxers in a knot, and I have to wonder if you have forgotten who footed the bill for this experimental craft—a craft that you have essentially turned into a Ford Mustang sitting in a driveway on a set of cinder blocks. NASA received reports of your initial arrival to Peacekeeper-patrolled space, and were a bit alarmed at how *Farscape 1* was clipped by a fighter-class vessel (what Officer Sun referred to as a Prowler). From there, the module went on to become your own personal houseboat on the planet Acquara, a second car for Officer Sun on several occasions and your own personal wormhole hot rod for you and your guests. We at NASA are not sponsoring a taxi service; we had qualified you *and only you* to fly this *multimillion-dollar* experimental module. We also did not intend for you to make *Farscape 1* your own beachfront cottage.

This blatant misuse of NASA's physical property really steams me, but not as much as your flagrant abuse of NASA's intellectual property.

The data you have collected over the five years you spent in the Uncharted Territories (including the area designated as Tormented Space) is, whether you believe so or not, the property of NASA, not—I repeat, *not*—your own personal bargaining chip for ship repairs, hostage exchanges or forcing peace treaties on two warring races. I couldn't give a rat's ass if the Farscape Project's original intent involved theories of gravitational acceleration. It still led to the creation and navigation of wormholes and therefore the associated knowledge is still considered part of the Farscape Project. Who makes that call? You, the supposed scientist? No, you don't. I make that call. Why? Even when you are cavorting with a myriad of extras from George Lucas' latest project, I'm still the boss. I decide what the law is around here. In the end, your mission and its resulting data is NASA property. Your findings belong to us! End of story.

Now if you want to publish your memoirs, go on *Oprah* and talk about the complications of interpersonal relationships with aliens (seeing as you had so many—please see later note **Improper Conduct Befitting an Officer**), or if you want to endorse Dentic Toothpaste and make guest appearances at science fiction and fantasy conventions as the star panelist of their science tracks, be my guest. However, you cannot negotiate to be the center star on *Hollywood Squares* with the wormhole data you obtained while on NASA's bankroll. You just can't! Albeit, in light of what you did with the data in question, I would have rather seen you in the center square than playing fifty-yard-line referee in a war between the Sebaceans and Scarrans. (See earlier notes **Misrepresenta-**

tion of Earth on Foreign Worlds and Poor Orientation of Alien Races to Earth Culture.)

Farscape Project Overhead and Operations Exceeding Original Projections. No, no, wait—let me rephrase this bullet point: the Farscape Project has not only thrown NASA's budget completely out of whack for the next century, Earth is trying to put several millennia of differences behind them and do something that would make John Lennon proud—we are all trying to get along. Not because we want to, but because we are *forced* to! Why? you may ask. As you and the network of wormholes you have opened have introduced our world to well-armed, highly eccentric, outwardly aggressive and downright spooky sentient life-forms, movies like *Independence Day* and *The War of the Worlds* are starting to look like Michael Moore documentaries. The loss of *Farscape 1* hurt NASA financially, but not as much as bereavement pay and lawsuits that immediately followed on account of two NASA ground personnel (you know—the kind of personnel who have *safe* jobs in space exploration!) connected to this project. Then there was the stunt you pulled, leaving your wormhole notes and calculations at the site of your father's last moonwalk. Very nice, John. Might I ask what in God's name you were thinking? Maybe your intentions were good. Maybe you were high off of Moya's coolant fumes. I don't know what you thought or intended, and come to think of it, I don't very much care.

Perhaps you are thinking about calling us to the legal mat on this particular point, weighing the scientific benefits and cultural exchanges your adventures brought to our world. Before you call the law firm of Pip & Guido, I direct your attention to the expenses that the Farscape Project accrued upon and since the arrival of Moya in Earth orbit. The ladies in your company enjoyed several lavish shopping sprees, Chiana and Sikozu in particular discovering the joys of establishments such as Saks Fifth Avenue, Macy's, Movado, Helzberg Diamonds and Godiva Chocolatiers. (And I won't even begin to discuss the tab your future wife, Aeryn Sun, left for us at Victoria's Secret.) Their bills paled in comparison, though, to that of His Royal Eminence Rygel XVI. His Royal Eminence racked up figures matching the Cassini probe's budget thanks to the numerous 1-900-number phone calls he enjoyed during his visit. All these expenses fell under the Farscape Project.

Still, these extravagances were minor compared to blowing off the cobwebs from a mothballed Saturn V rocket (something not accounted for in this decade's NASA budget, or the next decade's for that matter), as we wanted to be certain that NASA—and not some other government agency, be it from this world or somewhere else—obtained the worm-hole information that you left behind on the Moon.

Should I bore you with the numbers for training just one astronaut for a moon launch? No? How about the cost to fire a Saturn V rocket? All these costs we were compelled to put under the category of the Farscape Project as we are now scrambling to face Scarrans, Peacekeep-ers, Zenetan pirates, Nebari, Budongs, Tribbles, Orion Slave Girls and God-knows-what-else that will want to take advantage of Earth, a plan-et that has now become Metro Center in some sort of cosmic subway network.

While you may think this is mere administrative paranoia I am spew-ing, you might also want to consider exactly how and from where we are getting these detailed reports of your exploits in the farthest reaches of the universe. The answer has a lot to do with your **BFCs** and those wormholes you oh-so-conveniently created within Earth's proximity. We've been receiving frequent missives from a variety of races, all of whom are looking for you, and they have been entertaining us with many a yarn of your exploits. Only a few have managed to survive the trip through the wormhole. The Acquarans were the first. Fortunately when they landed their spacecraft on *terra firma*, they managed to do so during this year's Hula Bowl halftime show when the guest marching band was performing a salute to science fiction themes. The incident not only went unnoticed, but was hailed as one of the best performanc-es ever put on by the Marching Royal Dukes of James Madison Univer-sity. The two other **BFCs** of yours we've had to contend with involved a Luxan delegation that we greeted with what we *thought* was their tra-ditional salutation (please see earlier note concerning **Poor Orientation of Alien Races to Earth Culture**) and a portly mechanic who tried to sell us some weak knockoff of *our* wormhole data (please see earlier note concerning **Misuse of NASA Property**). Fortunately, when I finally came to after getting "tongued" by the Luxan High Minister, I was able to patch up the diplomatic issues that had arisen from the insults ex-changed, thereby making their perilous journey through the wormhole worthwhile. As far as the mechanic goes, Furlow has made an excellent addition to the NASA family as Director of Development and Research. (It's a good thing she remains unaware of how cheap we are getting her. Due to the financial turmoil that your antics have put us in, there is *no way* we could afford someone with her talents and abilities otherwise!)

Speaking of the NASA family, we have also needed to hire more em-ployees for the Farscape Project whose sole purpose has been to come up with names for the many incidents attributable to your interaction and interference. Thanks for helping our family grow, John.

Even though physical traffic through your wormhole network has been sparse, we are fielding many complaints, queries and comments concerning you via radio and video signals. Once a week we have to assure representatives of Lyneea's government that we are not planning any invasion of her homeworld, nor are we interested in trans-wormhole prisoner exchanges. One particularly tense communiqué included heated exchanges with a Peacekeeper-Venek survivalist cult that insisted on visiting the shrine of the famed warrior John Crichton and his brother-in-arms, Tony Montana. We remedied this potentially dangerous situation by broadcasting through the wormhole Brian De Palma's remake of *Scarface* (again, billing it under expenses for the Farscape Project). Apparently the film was well received, and the Veneks are now hungry for more Al Pacino. Shall I give you the cost for intergalactic rights to the films *Heat* and *Scent of a Woman*? Hoo-ah!

Out of all the stories that have come back to us through our numerous wormhole correspondences, the one with which I was particularly impressed was how you went sailing off into the sunset after threatening to destroy your corner of the universe with a wormhole-driven chain reaction of biblical proportions. From what we were told, you really were not certain if you could stop it, and I for one have to question whether you even considered how long this science experiment of yours would have taken to reach Earth.

This act alone would validate this reprimand, but, John, I have saved the best for last. Knowing you flyboys and how very Tom Cruise you all think you are, it is the following infraction that literally pushed me beyond this side of sanity and which I now, with a strange maniacal glee, type out as a black mark on your permanent record. It is high time that skilled pilots, after millions of dollars invested in time, training and hardware, are held accountable for their sophomoric behaviors and raging hormones.

Improper Conduct Befitting an Officer. Before I begin to explain how you, Commander John Crichton, stand accused of such a violation, I feel compelled to define in layman's terms "First Contact." First Contact is an initial meeting between two races, at least one of which is of extraterrestrial origins. Simply put, that is how we regard the term here at NASA.

That being said, and disregarding the **BFCs** accrued during your time in the Uncharted Territories, I must ask: why have you deemed this simple, clear and *unobtrusive* definition of First Contact inefficient? It is a safe assumption that when this term was first coined, it did not take into account the extravagant amounts of bodily fluids you swapped between alien races in your time off-planet. Long before you settled down with the Sebacean woman, Aeryn Sun, there was what NASA refers to as "The Johnny Apple-Crichton Incident." According to our reports, a royal dynasty will be bearing your offspring several decades from now on account of a DNA match obtained during a coronation ceremony. Our investigation team decided to dig a bit deeper and try to ascertain exactly *how* this DNA was exchanged. Needless to say, this investigation made us all here at NASA very uncomfortable, so much so that we considered hiring Rygel XVI's 1-900-numbers for possible freelance consultant work. Fortunately, there was very little embarrassment around the DNA match process. This independent investigation uncovered, though, one of the more appealing aspects of the Breakaway Colonies, as well as the reason for your enthusiasm for staying on the Royal Planet. Perhaps you looked at this culture's casual wrestling of tongues as "speed dating," but your lack of inhibitions has now led to the interference and irreversible alteration of millennia-old bloodlines. Would I call this a **BFC**? Absolutely! While you may have enjoyed the party, a First Contact should never constitute knocking up representatives of a Royal Family, even if you were absent during the marriage consummation. And still, this was not enough for you. As we discovered in our frequent communications with Peacekeeper High Command, you managed to place yourself in the company of one Jenavian Charto, a Peacekeeper covert operative with whom you enjoyed a few moonlight skinny-dips.

There is also the matter of Peacekeeper Commandant Mele-On Grayza that, reports lead us to understand, is carrying *someone's* baby. NASA investigators are still trying to discover the party responsible for this pregnancy, but many of the signs I see point to you. We do realize that Commandant Grayza has a certain "thing" about her, and we empathize, but for God's sake, you've got a doctorate from MIT in theoretical sciences. You are supposed to have an analytical mind and be able to deduce how things work. As her "happy gland" (along with everything else from the waist up) was in plain view, couldn't you have come up with a theory that led you to figure it out and keep *it* in your pants? Now we face a possible intergalactic paternity suit which does not thrill our legal offices, especially following the recent wrongful death suits (please see earlier reference, **Farscape Project Overhead and Operations Exceeding Original Projections**). To her credit, Commandant

Grayza is remaining tight-lipped about who the father is, but it stands to reason it has to be you. Why? Maybe because of the accounts from the Acquarans' heir-to-the-throne Rokon who shared strong words about you locking lips with his fiancée, Lishala, in between the times you were searching for your lost shaker of salt on your houseboat *Farscape 1* (please see earlier reference, **Misuse of NASA Property**). We also have the records (and the subsequent obituary) of a Peacekeeper technician named Gilina who was so enamored with you she got her skinny butt fragged on account of it.

And finally there is your visit to the planet LoMo, referred to by NASA as the "Uncharted-Territories-Gone-Wild Incident." I don't think I need to go any further concerning that evening, an evening best forgotten by everyone.

There are others—*many* others—who are sending messages via the wormhole wireless, all trying to ascertain your whereabouts. As it stands, you are sporting a track record with women that would make James Tiberius himself look at you and say in reverence, "Stud." This is not behavior that best befits an officer of the United States military. And yes, while the rank you carry could very well be looked at as an honorary title on account of your duties as an NASA Science Officer on specific shuttle missions, it is still a title of the United States Armed Forces and should be honored as such. There are just certain things— *and people*—you don't do when you are an officer and a gentleman. Hell, there are things you just don't do when you're a gentleman, but for some reason you just had to "give it a go" and find out what it would be like, didn't you? When all signs read "Do Not Enter" you put the pedal to the metal and went ahead into undiscovered country. Oh, don't give me that look, John Robert Crichton—you know *exactly* what incident I am referring to right now! I am referring to the "Every-Man's-Dream Incident," where an anomaly involving the Leviathan's shield harmonics and Halosian weaponry caused your consciousness to switch bodies with Peacekeeper Officer Aeryn Sun. Now, being male myself, I can understand the curiosity; but there is just something highly disturbing about the "stress test" you subjected on Officer Sun's endowments. We won't even question the scientific validity of "I'm a guy. They were right there." I sincerely doubt, with a conclusion such as that, the Nobel Prize is in your future.

I now review this reprimand, and as high as my blood pressure rises, I must admit that you were not a complete failure in your project. No, complete failure would have involved Earth being pulled into an intergalactic war that we are, at present, hardly prepared to face. Instead, we are merely preparing for inevitable close encounters with more of the many cranky aliens you encountered—made cranky, perhaps, by one of your numerous **BFCs**. Be that as it may, your antics (at least, the ones made public knowledge on your last visit to Earth) have gained popularity, especially on the Internet and through panel discussions held at "cons" across the country. Yes, Cmdr. Crichton, you have fans. Apparently, they *relate* to you, finding the mistakes and the responsibility you acknowledge and accept refreshing. You are a hero who is far from perfect, knows he is far from perfect and, if blessed with a bit of luck, can end his day on a perfect note.

Perhaps your charm, good looks, black leather pants and "Good Ol' Blue-Eyed Southern Boy" routine has worked on the general public, but it's not flying with me, Sparky. And it is for the reasons I give above that I am compelled, for the sake of NASA's public relations image, the good of the country and the safety of the planet, to pull the plug on this disaster and present to you your intergalactic pink slip. To quote America's richest pop icon, *"You're fired."*

On a closing note, I do think that you should be proud of one accomplishment coming from the Farscape Project. Now, with this out-of-control network of wormholes making us another rest stop in the galactic spaceways, providing technology that we as a planet may not be able to control and uniting us as a world out of sheer terror at what might in the future be coming to dinner, NASA has been asked to spearhead an in-depth program for deep space exploration. With your five-year mission in front of this program's oversight committee, a proposal is on the board to draft and implement a golden rule for humans to, going forward, follow to the letter, insuring that no alien culture is manipulated, interfered with or influenced once we set foot on their soil. I have even come up with a name for this rule: *The Prime Directive*. (Catchy, don't you think?) Thanks to you, I believe that space travelers from Earth will in the future think before they boldly go into the great unknown.

Enclosed you will find a copy of your pay stub itemizing backpay accumulated during the five years you spent in the Uncharted Territories; but in light of the infractions depicted in this reprimand, I gave the authorization to use said backpay to begin covering expenses for the adjusted price tag of the Farscape Project (please refer to...oh screw it, just start from the part of the letter that begins with "Dear John" and work your way down!). As stated earlier, I do not wish to trivialize your survival instincts or the resourcefulness you have shown in the Uncharted Territories or Tormented Space, but as the detailed issues in this reprimand will show, there are certain contraventions that cannot and will not go ignored or unaddressed. Therefore, consider this reprimand, the accompanying transcripts of depositions, the DVD of recorded audio and video communiqués and the enclosed release documentation as the end of the Farscape Project, your termination from NASA's employment and the release of any liability NASA may face in the future as a direct result of others' past, present or future contacts with you or your offspring.

Should you wish to appeal this executive decision, tough noogies!

Sincerely,

Alan Armstrong, Project Administrator
National Aeronautics and Space Administration

Tee Morris' writing career began with his portrayal of Rafe Rafton at the Maryland Renaissance Festival, which led to his coauthoring of MOREVI: The Chronicles of Rafe and Askana. *He then appeared in* The Complete Guide to Writing Fantasy, *a finalist for* ForeWord Magazine's *2003 Book of the Year. Both of his 2004 releases,* Billibub Baddings and the Case of the Singing Sword *and* The Fantasy Writer's Companion, *also earned the distinction of being* ForeWord Magazine's Book of the Year *finalists.*

2005 saw the podcast of MOREVI *(a first for* The Dragon Page Radio Show*), the release of* MOREVI's *sequel,* Legacy of MOREVI, *as well as the coauthoring of* Podcasting for Dummies *and paying homage to his favorite television show,* Farscape. *Find out more about Tee Morris at www.teemorris.com.*

THE BIG BROTHER

AMY BERNER

Will the real Bialar Crais please stand up? Was Crais the hyper-disciplined Peacekeeper officer who rose to command a major warship? Or the out-of-control maniac who disobeyed orders to pursue an unimportant human to the edges of known space? Or the wise father figure who befriended the wounded Talyn? Or the hero who sacrificed himself for his friends? Crais can seem like an irresolvable contradiction until you remember one key fact. Amy Berner remembers, and explains.

WHEN BIALAR CRAIS AND TALYN sacrificed themselves to save Moya and the rest of the crew in "Into the Lion's Den, Part Two: Wolf in Sheep's Clothing" (3-21), my jaw dropped with a very loud clatter. I know I wasn't the only one. How could this be? *The* Bialar Crais, who held the title of "crazed military commander" in the opening credits until being superseded by Scorpius? Was this the very same Sebacean who had chased John Crichton far into the Uncharted Territories, hell-bent on revenge? When did he become the martyr type?

But now that I've had a chance to look back at the series, I realize that all of our jaws should have stayed exactly where they were. That "hell-bent on revenge" issue was the big clue. After all, Crais never was your average Peacekeeper captain, and the roots of that revenge were also far from average for any Peacekeeper.

We witnessed several facets of Crais during his seasons on *Farscape*:

Captain Crais the Peacekeeper, Vengeful and Insane Crais and Talyn-Bonded Crais (well, also Red-Heel-Wearing Policeman Crais and Fairy Tale Ogre Crais, but as those were only products of Crichton's imagination, we'll let those slide). But these all had one factor in common: through it all, Crais' identity always hinged, in one form or another, on being the big brother.

THE BROTHERS: TAUVO AND TALYN

Crais demonstrated his abnormality from the very beginning, although we didn't have enough knowledge of Peacekeeper society at first to realize it. During those initial episodes, we saw Crais as a bad guy, and bad guys don't need to have reasons for their irrationality.

For example, in the series premiere, Crais was unconcerned with the report of casualties until he learned that his brother was one of those killed. Freshly emerged from that wormhole and an easy target, John Crichton was labeled a murderer, even though a recording of the actual events showed it to be an accident. If he were human, this huge overreaction by Crais could be blamed on the emotions resulting from his brother's death, but this was a very un-Peacekeeper-like reaction. Such an intense response had to come from somewhere, or rather, somewhen: childhood.

Crais wasn't raised as a Peacekeeper. He and his brother Tauvo were recruited together from a farming colony and given the "honor" of military service. Looking back, Crais described his parents as "compassionate, moral, emotional" ("Dream a Little Dream," 2-8), all descriptions of individuals completely unlike Peacekeepers. In the flashback of their last moments at home generated by the evil sorcerer Maldis in "That Old Black Magic" (1-8), we learned that his father's final, sad request of young Bialar was that he look after his brother.

His request contradicted normal Peacekeeper instructions. Those born inside the organization were taught to forgo all family ties in favor of those to their superiors and to their units. The identities of a Peacekeeper's parents were normally unknown. Therefore, siblings should not be a factor in their lives. But while Crais rose high in the organization, he never completely bought into all of their philosophies.

As the oldest boy in his family, Crais had to be responsible. He fit the firstborn "overachiever" mold, as well as possessing the competitor personality that oldest children tend to have. From what we know of their hierarchy, his ascendance to Peacekeeper captaincy must have been hard-won. He was driven to succeed and appeared to be devoted to serving the Peacekeeper precepts—but at that point, those precepts were working out just fine for him.

During his tenure with the Peacekeepers, one of his major pet projects was the genetic engineering of Leviathans, blending their DNA with Peacekeeper technology to produce hybrid gunships. Until Talyn, these attempts were unsuccessful, and Talyn himself was flawed. Still, Crais had no problem going to extreme measures to achieve his ends in this project; when capturing Moya, Crais had the uncooperative existing Pilot killed, replacing her with the younger, more eager Pilot we know and love. Crais the Peacekeeper also had a penchant for permanently removing anyone who might get in his way, including Leviathan expert Velorek, who planned to sabotage his cruel Leviathan experimentation, and Lieutenant Teeg, the only subordinate aware of the orders to recall him from the Uncharted Territories.

He caused more than his share of Peacekeeper deaths, so his obsession with avenging the death of one Peacekeeper would seem irrational to his superiors. Now, Crichton-chasing may have seemed to be a major Peacekeeper hobby, but the goal of most of that chasing—primarily by Grayza and Scorpius—was the wormhole knowledge locked up in Crichton's head, not Crichton himself. Crais did not have this valid excuse. Tauvo Crais should have been just one more lieutenant under his command, with no further emotional bond involved. Revenge for killing a fellow Peacekeeper had its place, absolutely, but Crais crossed several lines by disobeying the orders of Peacekeeper Command to continue his pursuit.

Crais had promised his father that he would look after his brother, and he had failed. The promise he made as a child became more binding than his years of Peacekeeper training. He risked court martial, incarceration and execution in the name of vengeance, all for Tauvo and for his own wounded pride.

As Crichton repeatedly escaped his grasp, Crais' discipline finally began to take control over his rage. However, Scorpius' arrival had greater impact, as the half-Scarran stole Crais' command out from under him. For someone who was always first in any situation, this could not be tolerated. As a child and as a Peacekeeper, he had always been top dog. Crais needed a new option.

To Crais' way of thinking, taking the newborn Talyn from his mother was a perfectly natural thing to do under the circumstances. After all, he had been taken from *his* family as a child. Plus, as the architect of the Peacekeeper/Leviathan gunship project, he felt a responsibility for Talyn. The bond was established in his mind before the gunship was ever born. He understood what this new hybrid Leviathan was capable of better than anyone else. Talyn satisfied Crais' need for a ship and base of power after Scorpius supplanted Crais' place in the fleet. And in Talyn, Crais would again have a brother: someone to protect, but also someone with the instincts of a warrior, just like Tauvo.

Why choose, even subconsciously, a half-Leviathan as a new brother and not someone more, well, bipedal? It wasn't simply because his options were limited. Crais' Peacekeeper-bred racism and belief in class structure was firmly ingrained, and he was unable to see any of the other males on Moya as equals. There were no other male Sebaceans in Crais' life after leaving the Peacekeepers. Crichton might have looked the part, but Crais never could have formed a friendship with him: he could never fully let go of the fact that the human's sudden appearance was the cause of Tauvo's death. Aeryn's strong feelings for Crichton only soured his opinion of the human more, though Crais did build up a grudging respect for Crichton, especially after the Crichton twin on Talyn died of radiation. In Crais' defense, Crichton never fully trusted Crais either, so there was nothing upon which to base a friendship on either side. If it weren't for Aeryn, neither of them would ever have helped the other. The only other males nearby were both former prisoners and of other species: D'Argo, Stark and Rygel. Talyn was, in his own way, an equal, as he was a power all his own. Plus, due to his breeding, Talyn was the most Peacekeeper-like of all of them, save Crais himself.

BUILDING A NEW FAMILY UNIT

Peacekeepers shaped Talyn into a tool, just as they had shaped both of the Crais boys. With their inherent kinship as the major motivating factor, Crais saw another path for them both. After an exchange with Scorpius in "Mind the Baby" (2-1), Crais explained the meaning of it to the young Leviathan gunship: "You are not his concern, merely a tool he can use or barter away. This is how the Peacekeepers treat their own—you, me, Officer Sun. But we are alike now, orphaned from all we ever knew. We have only one another to rely upon. You must believe me. Trust me." Crais drew on their similar situations in order to emotionally bind Talyn to him, becoming the central figure in the young gunship's life.

Crais mentioned Aeryn Sun in his list of the members of this new family unit, and, in his opinion, her presence would have made his and Talyn's life ideal. There were many similarities between the two former Peacekeepers (more than Aeryn liked to admit). But while Aeryn had a large support group as she made the transition from Peacekeeper to free-thinker, Crais did not. With a stronger support system, he might have had a better ultimate fate. Instead, he had only his past experiences and memories to draw from. Unlike Aeryn's experience on Moya, there was no tenth-level Delvian priest to calmly support him, nor a Pilot to reassure him, nor a human to daily challenge his long-held beliefs.

Without outside support, Crais reverted to form—his original form, the one that did not have a chance to mature into being. His last experience as a family member was as a child; as an adult, he had to feel his way through. He did not always make the best choices, but it is a credit to him that he tried.

Crais' childhood with loving parents may have been a distant memory, but it still stayed with him throughout his life. He built on the foundation of his early years, and this foundation became the basis of his love for Talyn and Aeryn. Without his happy-family background, it would never have been possible for these feelings to develop. If he had succeeded in setting up a situation in which only he, Talyn and Aeryn explored the Uncharted Territories together, he would have rebuilt a perfect family unit for himself.

As much as other characters (and the audience) didn't want to believe it, Crais made a true effort to both please and protect Aeryn, especially when it came to the situation with her mother. For example, he showed Aeryn the holo of her mother visiting her as a child. Yes, he tried to please her in part so she would come away with him and Talyn, but his motivation was primarily to bring her joy. This was not something he was practiced at, and it was an extraordinary development for him that he even made the effort.

Of course, Crais did have an ulterior motive for obtaining a ship and later gathering a crew around him. There was no chance to rejoin the ranks of the Peacekeepers, even if he had wanted to, and he knew far too many Peacekeeper secrets to be allowed to run about freely. Having "bodyguards" handy was a good thing for him. However, he likely could have found protection from another source; this arrangement with Talyn was vastly preferable to him.

But Talyn chose Crais as his captain just as much as Crais chose Talyn as his ship. Some of this was due to Crais' influence, as he undermined Aeryn's original bond with Talyn by brainwashing the confused child into believing that he was the hybrid's only real friend. According to Crais, they were kindred, and Talyn agreed. Crais communicated with Talyn more effectively than did Aeryn, Moya or anyone else. When Talyn received more confusing input than he could handle soon after birth, Crais became the only person that he trusted. Talyn offered Crais the direct neural interface to his systems—the "hand of friendship"—willingly and without it being asked of him, but they understood each other on a basic level even before that offer.

Aeryn, Stark, Rygel and one of the Crichton doubles originally joined Talyn to draw the retrieval squad away from Moya—a squad led by Aeryn's mother, Xhalax Sun. This situation, and Xhalax's apparent lack of maternal feelings toward Aeryn, was more typical of the traditional relationship between family members in the Peacekeeper organization than Crais'. However, Aeryn did have a dim memory of her mother visiting her one night and revealing that she was conceived in love. Both the visit and that type of procreation were completely against regulations. Aeryn had the institutional upbringing that Crais did not, but that moment was enough to lay the foundation for Aeryn's future development away from the Peacekeeper mold. If one nighttime visit had that much impact on Aeryn, imagine how much impact Crais' entire childhood with a loving family must have had.

With Talyn's suddenly expanded crew, Crais tried to remain the primary decision maker, his well-practiced role as a Peacekeeper captain but also a version of his "big brother" role from childhood. Understandably, the other denizens of Talyn didn't trust him. Based on past history, you can't blame them. He repeatedly made decisions that he believed were in the best interests of everyone without consulting the people affected, such as when he spared Xhalax rather than killing her, letting Aeryn believe that her mother was dead. Crais thought that this was the way to keep them safe from a woman he believed to be irredeemable. He had plenty of good reasons for this belief, from her single-minded persistence in carrying out her orders to her laughter at Talyn being named for Aeryn's father. When Xhalax and Aeryn met again, it was Crais who finally killed her, despite Aeryn's belief that, like her, her mother could be rehabilitated.

FULL CIRCLE

Talyn and Crais spent months together far from Moya's influence. They returned occasionally, each time with mixed results. In this new persona of Hybrid Gunship Captain, Crais often chose to eschew violence instead of actively pulling Talyn into that course of action. Talyn possessed enough violent tendencies of his own already without exposure to additional violent situations. They did return to the group when Moya's insides were flambéed in order to stand guard during her rehabilitation (although Aeryn's death was enough of a distraction that their enemy was able to sneak in anyway).

Paralleling Crais' instability in the first season, Talyn became unstable out in the world. The deep bond between Talyn and Crais even caused neural feedback and painful blistering in the Sebacean, but despite it all, Crais wouldn't abandon the gunship. Instead, he did what he had to for his Leviathan "brother." Crais struggled to keep Talyn's behavior in check. He wasn't always successful at it, but no one could have done a better job.

When Talyn became too unstable to function, too often a danger to himself and others, Crais chose the only plan that could keep the gunship alive: shutting down almost all of his systems until the volatile personality could be replaced. He faced the difficult choice of returning Talyn to the mental state of a newborn child to save him. However, another option presented itself before that became necessary: a warrior's death while fighting an enemy. A death like Tauvo had.

And the enemy needed to be fought. Scorpius' wormhole project was bad news; Crais knew it as much as anyone. He and Talyn participated in Crichton's ruse to board Scorpius' Command Carrier and destroy the project from within. Not a bad plan, but Crais discovered before the others did that it would fail. Making both the audience and the other characters believe that he had betrayed them, since duplicity was perfectly normal for him if it helped him achieve his own ends, he notified Scorpius of Crichton's plans.

Crais lulled Scorpius into a sense of safety while he and Talyn prepared to go to starburst from within the Command Carrier. This plan would free Moya, allow the others to escape, give the crew of the Command Carrier enough time to abandon ship and would destroy the existing wormhole technology. The only casualties would be Crais and Talyn, but Crais learned as a Peacekeeper about acceptable casualty numbers. And, as with so many of his other decisions, Crais set up his sacrifice without bringing it to the group first. He knew that it was their best and only plan, and so he made the call. True to form, he felt that it was his call to make.

He convinced Talyn by calling on his bond with the hybrid. As warriors and as brothers, they chose to die together, helping their extended family and dealing a mighty blow to their enemy. What better way to go out could there be for either of them, who really had little to lose except each other? With the cannon removed from Talyn, their ability to starburst became their weapon. Crais explained the situation simply: "The rest have been captured. And Moya...Moya will soon be enslaved....Unless we do something. Something radical. You and I...together" ("Into the Lion's Den, Part Two: Wolf in Sheep's Clothing").

Together. Neither of them would have been able to make this sacrifice alone. Like any family, together they became more than the sum of their parts.

Crais would again have been left alone once Talyn's memory had wiped. The gunship would no longer have had the personality that Crais had come to know, nor would Talyn have still trusted him. Their bond would have been destroyed, leaving Crais with no one. There was no place for him with the Peacekeepers, and he never had a place on Moya. There was only one place Crais mattered, and that was with Talyn, as Talyn's captain.

Tauvo. Talyn. For both, he was the big brother. This shaped his actions, his emotions and, finally, his death, taking him from crazed pursuer to savior. He might not have been able to save his blood brother, but in saving Aeryn and Moya (as well as the lives of many innocents), he found redemption for that failure. And he had his brother by his side when he did it.

Amy Berner has a not-so-slight obsession with the science fiction and fantasy genres. Using what spare time her "day job" and her cats let her have, Amy pops up all over the place with reviews, essays and short stories. Amy is also a contributing author to the anthologies Five Seasons of Angel, The Anthology at the End of the Universe *and* Alias Assumed: Sex, Lies and SD-6. *She is a regular columnist for DarkWorlds (www.darkworlds.com) and lives in San Diego, California.*

A HITCHHIKING PILOT

THE INTELLECTUAL PARASITE GOING EVERYWHERE AND NOWHERE VERY FAST

JEAN RABE

Pilot's decision to bond with Moya, even putting aside the blatant illegality and immorality of it, is difficult to justify. Bonding with Moya dramatically reduced his life span and severed his connection with his race. No mate, no children, no company of his own kind. In return for all of these sacrifices he earned the dubious honor of space travel—although he can never leave his chair. What is Pilot, really? Jean Rabe has a theory.

F OR A LONG STRETCH OF MEMORY Pilots and Leviathans have lived harmoniously, each race sharing intimate knowledge of the other and enjoying varied experiences as they starburst together across the galaxy. Outsiders have continually sought to intrude on this relationship, wanting to learn about the multifaceted pairing between Pilot and ship. Since first learning of the unique relationship between the two by way of Cmdr. John Crichton's return to Earth, our universities have devoted sciences and no doubt scientists' lifetimes to it, filling library shelves and lecture halls and coming away with enough multilayered postulations to keep a legion of anthropologists occupied.

If only they could look away from the biological and psychological complexities of the pairing and seek a simple justification for the bond between the two races, then their curiosity would be sated.

The explanation is an easy one: they would see that a Pilot is little more than a rider glued to the saddle of a wide-ranging mare. Before the Peacekeepers, the Leviathans were much like Earth's horses—of some intelligence and curiosity, benevolent and frequently on the move. The addition of a Pilot is akin to that of a rider on a horse, with the Pilot steering his or her Leviathan toward specific locations, helping take care of it and providing companionship.

In this particular horse-and-rider relationship, no stirrups or reins are needed. Let us take in our discussion the example of one of the most infamous Pilot/Leviathan pairs: Moya, and her Pilot. The two can communicate with a neural link. Pilot is able to sense Moya's moods, anticipate her starburst jumps and tell when she is not feeling well. His moods often reflect hers, in much the way the husband and wife of a long-married couple mirror each other's feelings. And while the psychological complexities of the pair might suggest a more sophisticated pairing, the basic facts show it is a simple symbiosis, less complex than the one between a termite and its protozoa.

While Pilot helps keep Moya running efficiently, there is little to suggest that Leviathans can't manage on their own—they certainly did before the Pilots came along. And it was clearly not necessity that forced Pilots to team with Leviathans, as the former race existed for centuries without the ships. It was desire and curiosity, factors which—as hallmarks of sentient beings—do not typically play a part in symbiotic relationships on Earth. And it was possibly the influence of the Peacekeepers, forcefully nudging the two races together, that sealed the proverbial symbiotic deal.

A GLANCE AT SYMBIOTIC LIFE

Throughout the galaxy, the majority of life-forms have one primary thing in common: they must eat. Often this involves competing for food and preying on other species. This in turn also involves avoiding being preyed upon.

One exception is a symbiotic life, where two different creatures coexist and share food and other necessities—the term "symbiosis" itself comes from an ancient Greek word that roughly translates as "living together." In all symbiotic relationships, at least one of the two life-forms benefits. Pilot could not leave his planet without Moya, let alone starburst across the galaxy to see other worlds and races. Yet for all this increased mobility, he is still like a child who can "look but cannot touch." He cannot venture onto any of these worlds or interact with any of these races... unless a member of one of those races comes to him in his "den." It is a wonderful and sad life Pilot embraces, and a worse one than faced by most symbiotic creatures we see on Earth.

Therefore, his symbiotic existence is not an evolutionarily beneficial one—nor would we expect such a manufactured partnership to be so. Pilot cannot have a family and produce offspring, and his life span has been shortened: rather than the thousand-year span he would have enjoyed, he lives only as long as the ship with which he is bonded, a mere three hundred cycles. So there are serious negative implications to the joining. His relationship with Moya, then, must be classified as an intellectual symbiosis—he gains information and experiences by being with her.

That said, there is no question that the creature called Pilot shares a symbiotic existence with Moya, the Leviathan, and one that, at first glance, appears to be a sophisticated form worthy of scientists' and anthropologists' time and libraries' space. Certainly Moya's other crew members view it as an impressive shared existence, as no doubt do a plethora of sociologists. Perhaps that is because they are too close to the two species, or because they feel a need to consider the coexistence something elaborate because it is set in the exotic locale of space.

However, looking deeper into the lives of these two connected beings suggests that Pilot is little more than an intellectual parasite, a knowledge-seeking hitchhiker stealing a ride only to see the galaxy. Pilot was forced upon the Leviathan; Moya had no choice but to let him come along. Symbiotic relationships are not always mutually agreed on; mushrooms, after all, do not get the preapproval of the compost heap they intend to grow on.

But while we have established that a Leviathan can function without a Pilot, it is also clear that Leviathans prefer not to go it alone—hence the relationship can still be classed as symbiotic. It is just a matter of determining what type of symbiotic relationship is involved. Understand that there are overlaps in the various types of symbiosis; scientists admit that the lines are blurred as far as many pairings are concerned, and the lines with Pilot and Moya are blurred as well.

A CLEAN RELATIONSHIP

A "cleaning symbiosis" can be found between many species on Earth. For example, the little plover bird cleans the teeth of crocodiles along the Nile River. The crocodiles open their mouths to accommodate the plovers, allowing them to feast. The birds act as natural dentists at the same time.

The cleaner wrasse is a small fish that tidies up after sharks, eating the scraps the sharks leave behind without ever becoming a meal itself. Another fish, the remora, attaches itself to a shark or rides close in its bow wake. These fish usually eat parasites, keeping their shark buddies healthy.

While Pilot does not clean Moya himself, as he can't move about well enough under his own power to tend to any such task beyond dusting off his control panel, he does direct the DRDs to scurry about the Leviathan, cleaning and effecting repairs in his stead. So in this instance, the relationship could be considered a cleaning symbiosis. But that's not enough of a classification—the crew could just as easily pick up mops and pails and do the work themselves.

MUTUALISM IN SPACE?

When a symbiosis results in benefits to both organisms, the term used is "mutualism." For example, consider the algal growths and fungus of lichens on Earth. One can discover clumps of fungus on the root systems of many plants, including a wide variety of trees. These fungal growths dig into the roots and let the plants absorb nitrogen from the soil through them. In return, the growths get the carbohydrates they need to live. Some types of fungus also protect their host from harmful bacteria. Similarly, Pilot has dug his "tendrils" into Moya, pulling nutrients from her. In turn he helps protect Moya from the occasionally destructive urges of her crew, at the very least acting as a buffer between the ship and offending individuals. Further, he acts as companion, navigator and stationary bodyguard. So, while Pilot and Moya benefit each other in a similar fashion to mutualistic Earth relationships, Pilot is far more dependent upon Moya than she is upon him. When Pilot was temporarily ripped from Moya, he was given few arns to live. Only reattaching him to the ship saved his life. So while the Leviathan was able to live without Pilot, he clearly could not survive without her. It is established that there is some benefit in the relationship for the ship, a hint of mutualism, but not enough to satisfy the term scientifically.

COMMENSALISM PERHAPS . . .

There are creatures on Earth that fall into a particular symbiotic classification, called "commensalisms." In a commensalistic relationship one species tends to benefit, while the other is largely unaffected. This seems to be the case with Pilot and Moya.

The term "commensalism" roughly means "joining together at the table," and refers mainly to food-sharing associates: one creature lives off the uneaten food of another. On Earth, the shark and the previously mentioned remora is a perfect example. The small remora clings to the shark for sustenance via a sucker. The shark leaves the remora alone as it feasts off scraps the shark isn't interested in. Apparently the remora is beneath the shark's notice; it doesn't harm the shark in any way. Another example is a type of barnacle that can be found on whales' mouths eating to its heart's content. And some barnacles have a commensalistic relationship with other species of barnacles. Pilot fish (an interesting name, eh?) are another example of such a relationship, though biologists don't yet have all the details. The fish swim along with the sharks, perhaps because of an instinct to school or perhaps because they can go farther and faster while caught up in the "draft" of the sharks' movement. In any case, it is clear they, like the remora, eat tidbits the sharks overlook.

Not all such commensalistic relationships are aquatic. Consider the tiny termite. There is a one-cell creature living in the termite, a microscopic protozoan, that turns wood cellulose into sugar, which is then digested by the termite. Harmless bacteria live in human intestines, as well as the intestines of other Earth creatures. They exist on food that passes through our bodies, perhaps even helping us by gobbling up unsafe particles. There are similar relationships in the plant world. Consider epiphytes, plants that grow on other plants. These hitchhikers do not steal food from their host; rather, they simply soak in the sunlight from a better position. Epiphytes include orchids, some members of the pineapple family and Spanish moss. And a case could be made that many species of birds share a commensalistic existence with the trees they build their nests in—the birds depending on the trees for shelter, and the trees not suffering for it.

Though you could say that Pilot has, in effect, nested in Moya, he is clearly more dependent on her than an orchid is on a tree. His circulation system is tied to the Leviathan; therefore his health is a mirror of hers. Further, once bonded, a Pilot receives his nutrients from his ship and would starve without her, though being bonded means the Pilot no longer has to worry about obtaining food on his own. His regeneration is also keyed to the nutrients he receives from his Leviathan: Moya's Pilot was able to regrow limbs, and while it is possible that Pilots can regenerate on their homeworld, it is also likely that the shared nutrients from the Leviathan facilitate regeneration—or at least speed it considerably.

PILOT THE PARASITE

Perhaps a better case can be made for calling Pilot little more than a simple parasite, living off Moya and growing rich with knowledge. In the scientific sense, a parasite is a life-form that lives in or on another creature, referred to as the host. The parasite gains sustenance through its host, and in the process does some amount of damage. For example, ticks and fleas live off the blood of deer, dogs and even people. At times, the host loses only the tiniest amount of blood and is basically unaffected. Occasionally, however, the host might get an infection from a tick's wound, or catch some malady from a flea.

Scientists likely would argue that Pilot is far from a tick. They would claim he is beneficial rather than harmful, or at worst is benign. However, the harm comes when Pilot asserts himself to get Moya to do this or that, go here or there, starburst at the crew's request. The harm is in exerting, at times, undue influence. He shaves away her free will and bends her to his own goals.

There are several other examples of parasites on Earth. Viruses are parasites, thriving on the host body while making the host feel miserable. Tapeworms are parasites, growing fat off their hosts' meals. Fungi and bacteria are parasites, as are the lice that trouble parents and school-age children. The plant world, too, is full of them.

Pilot may not make Moya ill or keep her from flying from system to system. He may not promote infection, as hurting her would likely kill him as well.

But no matter how noble his speeches or clearly stated his intent to look after her, he still steals her energy. Pilot is a space-faring parasite.

PILOT THE PARASITIC POLYP

Pilot might, in fact, be likened to a deep-water polyp. This polyp, found off the coast of Newfoundland on Earth, is known to adhere to the shells of hermit crabs. The polyps are able to bud—to reproduce—and the resultant growths carpet the crab's shell. The polyps then dissolve the shell, in effect eating it as a parasite would, and become the new "shell," growing at the same rate as the host crab. The polyps protect the crab, and the crab does not need to shed its shell to find a larger one as it normally would as it grows. The colony of polyps are able to travel with the crab, seeing the wonders of the ocean floor, whereas, left to their own devices, they could not have moved much of anywhere.

Pilot has—literally—attached himself to Moya and sees the galaxy as a result. He's seen a wormhole or two, met races he'd never dreamed of, watched planets explode and played a part in a few heroic endeavors. Pilot would never have had such opportunities without the Leviathan. He would have remained on his watery homeworld...one more polyp without a crab...one more parasite going nowhere.

Instead, Pilot goes a great many places, while at the same time—fused in his den—he is going nowhere at starburst speed.

Jean Rabe is the author of fifteen fantasy novels and more than three dozen fantasy, science fiction and military short stories. Her latest work is the Finest series from Tor Books, and the upcoming Return to Quag Keep with Andre Norton. Her hobbies include visiting museums (particularly ones filled with old planes and military gear), playing an assortment of games, pretending to garden and participating in fantasy football leagues. She shares her Wisconsin home with her husband, two dogs that wrap themselves around her feet while she works at the computer and a parrot named Trouble, who chatters incessantly.

THE FALL AND RISE OF RYGEL XVI

BILL SPANGLER

Rygel, short of stature and long of arrogance, came off as a tin-pot Napoleon—although, considering Rygel's 600 billion subjects, perhaps it was Napoleon that was the tin-pot Rygel. If Rygel is Napoleon, he's Napoleon in Elba, exiled and powerless, but no less greedy, no less vain and no less real. The reality of Rygel—his humanity, if we can put it such—is one of the great triumphs of Farscape.

I WAS SITTING IN A LOCAL THEATER, watching *Star Wars, Episode II: Attack of the Clones* for the first time. On the screen, Obi-Wan Kenobi, Mace Windu and Yoda were discussing the safety of Senator Amidala as they were walking through a corridor of the Jedi Temple.

Actually, Obi-Wan and Mace were walking. Yoda was sitting in a hovering platform that enabled him to keep up with his companions.

So how did Yoda get Rygel's ThroneSled? I wondered. Yoda himself predates the Hynerian by quite a few years, but in this scene he was definitely showing Rygel's influence.

The creators of *Farscape* may not have been thinking in these terms, but I like to think of Rygel XVI as the Anti-Yoda. The deposed Dominar of the Hynerian Empire is everything that the diminutive Jedi Master isn't. He's greedy, self-centered and gluttonous and passes helium when nervous. In lesser hands, a character like this would have been used solely for comic relief, and certainly Rygel often filled that role. At the same time, though, he was given clear motivations for his actions and the ability to rise above his instincts, to become a hero.

111

Creating such a complex character required a unique synthesis of contributions from several sources. Jonathan Hardy provided the Dominar's voice, while a team of puppeteers brought Rygel to life on the soundstage. John Eccleston was the lead puppeteer during the first season, followed by Matt McCoy.

These performers were supported by outstanding scripts. David Kemper, one of the creative forces behind the series, described Rygel this way in the last issue of the *Farscape* magazine: "For sheer joy of writing, nothing can beat Rygel. I have stated many times before that I believe he is the smartest, cleverest, most complex character on the show. Let's not forget he was the ruler of hundreds of billions of subjects. He's got to know more about things than he lets on. That means that there are many places to look within him where a writer can find surprising moments."

Rygel definitely surprised *Farscape* fans over the course of the series.

Many times, Rygel appeared to be ruled by his... well, let's call it his heightened sense of self-interest. However, even a quick look at his background shows that it would have been very difficult for him to turn out any other way.

As he liked to point out, Rygel XVI was the Dominar of the Hynerian Empire, ruler of 600 billion subjects. Since Rygel was known to embellish the facts when it suited his purpose, it's difficult to say how accurate this number was. However, it is possible to say that the Hynerian wielded some real power.

According to the episode "Exodus from Genesis" (1-3), the empire was established by Rygel I, otherwise known as Rygel the Great. In the novel *Dark Side of the Sun,* author Andrew Dymond says that the Dominar's summer palace was built by Rygel IX, more than a thousand cycles before the events of the story. So the Hynerian Empire can be called well-established, regardless of much time separated Rygel the Great and Rygel IX.

The empire's population appeared to be sizable, even if it didn't reach the 600 billion mark. In "Infinite Possibilities, Part Two: Icarus Abides" (3-15), it was established that a billion Hynerian subjects died at the hands of the Charrids, who invaded the empire during the reign of Rygel XI. In *The Peacekeeper Wars*, Rygel's cousin Bishan told him that millions had died as a result of the fighting between the Scarrans and the Peacekeepers. In the first episode, Rygel mentioned in passing that he received his translator microbes "at birth," which suggests that he was being prepared for life in a cosmopolitan, racially diverse culture.

It's probably safe to assume that young Rygel didn't have 70,000 servants waiting on him, as he claimed in the episode "The Flax" (1-13). On the other hand, it's probably also safe to assume that the Dominar-to-be didn't lack for any comforts. As Dymond notes: "All Rygel had known from the moment his eyes opened and cool gray-green Hynerian daylight had first bathed his face had been the diligent attention that maids, butlers, dressers, chefs and myriad other servants had paid his every whim. He was their destiny. The royal blood of generations flowed through his veins, pulsed in his heart. He was Hyneria of Hyneria. The Dominar-To-Be. And woe betide anyone who did not make their life's business to know it."

This extravagant but insular life was taken away from Rygel shortly after he ascended to the throne. His cousin Bishan took over the government and turned his rival over to the Peacekeepers. Specifically, Rygel was turned over to the notorious Selto Durka, who tortured him. He was moved from Durka's Command Carrier, the *Zelbinion*, before that ship was destroyed by the Nebari. However, Rygel spent roughly 130 cycles as a prisoner before he escaped with the others inhabiting the Leviathan Moya.

At first glance, life on Hyneria and life in a Peacekeeper prison couldn't be more dissimilar. To Rygel, though, they must have had one important point in common: in both cases, his self-interest, his very survival, had to come first.

How did Rygel survive his incarceration? Over the course of *Farscape*, Rygel proved he could be physically vicious under the right circumstances, such as when he bit Aeryn Sun in "I, E.T." (1-2), and when he finally killed Durka during the "Liars, Guns and Money" arc (2-19, 2-20, 2-21). He decapitated the former Peacekeeper and carried his head around on a pole.

This viciousness might be a trait that Rygel developed while in prison. However, it might also be a characteristic common to Hynerians. It would help to explain how they built an empire.

Rygel also demonstrated several times that he was a masterful trader and negotiator, combining his best royal swagger with an ability to identify his opponent's weaknesses. These skills proved to be useful for everything from acquiring supplies to tricking Zenetan pirates into leaving Moya in "The Flax." In that same episode Rygel told Zhaan, "Bluffing is what the game is all about." He may have been referring to Tadek, the strategy game he used to hoodwink the Zenetan leader, but he may also have been referring to the game of diplomacy.

Rygel's negotiating skills may have earned him other advantages while in prison, such as continued use of his ThroneSled, his relocation to Moya and, ultimately, the acquisition of the key codes which allowed Rygel, D'Argo, Zhaan, Moya and Pilot to escape.

The Hynerian apparently spent some time on Moya before the escape. In the first season, Zhaan said that Rygel had been on board Moya longer than anyone except for Pilot, and D'Argo said he had been on board the living starship for eight cycles.

In any case, Rygel's negotiating skills switched on the instant he met John Crichton in the first episode of *Farscape*. He tried to form an alliance with the bewildered human, saying, "I'll look after you now, and you'll look after me later." This attempt to strike a deal did not succeed, but many others did.

The former Dominar's insistence that the universe recognize his obvious superiority caused some strain in his relationships with his fellow escapees. Not long after they gained their freedom, D'Argo admitted, "I've been searching for a reason not to jettison him at the next refuse dump." After being bitten by Rygel, Aeryn swore that, "Someday you will die at the hands of a Peacekeeper."

At first Zhaan was the member of the group most willing to treat Rygel with respect. She called him "Your Eminence"—apparently the proper way to address a Dominar—when trying to get him to work with the others. She also told Rygel—in "Exodus from Genesis"—that part of the spirit of Rygel the Great resided within him. Even the Delvian priestess, however, would eventually lose patience with him.

At times, it seemed as though Rygel was interested in nothing but his own comfort, even when Moya was being pursued by the Peacekeepers. In "Exodus from Genesis," he decided he had time to assemble art supplies and take up painting (self-portraits, of course). Other times, though, he could be remarkably progressive. In "Jeremiah Crichton" (1-14), Rygel learned that one of his ancestors, Rygel X, exiled a race called the Acquarans from the empire and marooned them on a planet with a device that prevented them from ever having modern technology. Not only did he say that the Acquarans had been "terribly wronged," Rygel denounced the priesthood that had kept this information away from the rest of the population. "The highest sacrilege is purposefully keeping your own people ignorant and subjugated for your own glorification," he proclaimed.

On a more personal level, Rygel dealt with the mental wounds left by his torture in the episodes "PK Tech Girl" (1-7) and "Durka Returns"

(1-15). In the latter, Rygel was recaptured by Durka, whose real personality had become dominant again after cycles of Nebari conditioning. When he threatened Rygel with more torture, however, the Hynerian called him "pathetic" and "a failure."

"You never broke me, you only made me stronger," he said. "Even if you kill me, I'll be laughing at you, because the last thing I'll be thinking of is you on Nebari Prime for another hundred cycles, being ground back down into nothing."

Even Aeryn admitted that Rygel handled himself well.

Rygel came to another important realization in "Family Ties" (1-22). Ironically, this episode began with Rygel at his most devious and selfish, trying to negotiate a deal. He told the Peacekeepers that he was willing to help them capture John Crichton—and the wormhole data locked in his memory—if they gave him the resources he needed to return to Hyneria and overthrow his cousin.

When he realized that he wasn't going to get what he wanted, Rygel returned to Moya. He bluntly admitted that he did try to betray them, but said that the others should still accept him because, ultimately, nothing happened. (It's possible that he actually believed this, but it may also have been another demonstration of Rygel's belief that "bluffing is what the game is all about.")

Later, though, in an emotional confrontation with Crichton, the Dominar commented on his usual self-interest:

RYGEL: Look, I know—I know I can be selfish, but, given a change, I
    can usually—
JOHN: Do what, do the right thing?
RYGEL: Yes.

Acknowledging that self-interest is not automatically the right thing was, in itself, a remarkable admission.

Gradually, Rygel showed more loyalty and respect to Moya's other passengers, behavior that sometimes puzzled him. In the text story "Faces," by *Farscape* writer and executive producer Richard Manning, the Dominar reflects on placing the Royal Pendant in Aeryn Sun's coffin.

He hadn't meant to give her his Royal Pendant. He had worn it to her funeral to honor her, but as he'd approached to pay his last respects, he suddenly found himself placing his most treasured possession into Aeryn's casket. 'You are more worthy of this,' he whispered, also to his surprise.... He'd acted on impulse, which he knew was foolhardy behavior from a Dominar. Yet he'd meant what he said. . . .

"Faces," which appeared in the *Farscape* magazine, illustrates the extremes of Rygel's behavior. In it, even as he recovers Aeryn's body from an ice-cold lake and makes an awkward attempt to console Zhaan, Rygel is trying to make a separate deal for a ship to take him back to Hyneria.

The question of returning to Hyneria also came up during *The Peacekeeper Wars* miniseries. Bishan sent a message to Moya asking Rygel to return home and lead the forces protecting the Hynerians against the Peacekeepers and the Scarrans. It was probably a sign of how badly things were going that Bishan felt it necessary to locate Rygel (remember, it's been at least 130 cycles since he turned Rygel over to the Peacekeepers) and to make such an offer.

Rygel's response to the message was, "If he thinks I'll return to a shared throne, he is beyond deluded." (What Bishan was offering—if anything—was never made clear.) That appeared to be the end of the matter...only it wasn't.

Later, D'Argo told Chiana that Rygel had asked the Luxan to return to Hyneria with him. D'Argo asked Chiana to come too, visualizing a rustic, peaceful existence for them both. It may have been that D'Argo and Rygel were talking about general postwar plans. However, it may also have been that Rygel wanted to bring the biggest, fiercest-looking member of Moya's crew back with him when he challenged Bishan for the throne.

D'Argo, of course, never realized his dream of a peaceful life. Near the end of *The Peacekeeper Wars*, though, Chiana said that she was still going to Hyneria. Whether dealing with Chiana alone was part of Rygel's plans is a story that may never be told.

Gigi Edgley, the actress portraying Chiana, said in an interview that she felt Chiana and Rygel didn't trust each other because their personalities were so similar. However, they each respected the other person's skills. (If Chiana found Nebari Prime stifling, it's hard to say what she would have thought of Hyneria without D'Argo at her side.)

In addition to making plans for his future, Rygel played a major role in saving Aeryn, Crichton and their unborn child in *The Peacekeeper Wars*. He enabled John and Aeryn to be brought back to life (again), only to discover that he had become a surrogate womb for their baby. The embryo was eventually returned to Aeryn, but not before Rygel formed an emotional bond with him. Rygel may have decided that, in some sense, the child was his. However, when he offered to hold the baby while the others made a perilous leap off the roof of a building into Moya's docking net, Rygel seemed to be showing genuine concern.

Rygel even managed to recover the ring that John gave Aeryn when he proposed, holding it in one of his three stomachs until the appropriate time in their wedding ceremony. (Crichton rinsed it off before putting it on her finger.)

Maybe Rygel sold his ThroneSled to Yoda in order to finance his return to Hyneria. That's a trading session I'd like to see. Yoda wouldn't know what hit him.

> *Bill Spangler has written both fiction and nonfiction based on TV science fiction series. In addition to articles in* Xposé *and* Wizard's Sci-Fi Invasion, *he has written original comic book stories based on* Alien Nation, Quantum Leap *and other shows. Bill and his wife Joyce live in Bucks County, Pennsylvania, with two ferrets and a dog.*

ZHAAN: PLANT, PRIEST, ARCHETYPE

JOSEPHA SHERMAN

Orgasmic plant, fierce peace-lover and smart-assed wise woman, Zhaan was a contradiction and a delight. She was the glue that held the crew together in the early seasons, and her character was subtle, complex and unique. Unique, but not without precedent, as Josepha Sherman explains.

ZHAAN, OR MORE PROPERLY Pa'u Zotoh Zhaan, the blue-skinned, bald, mystical and lovely Delvian priest and sentient plant, is certainly one of the most unusual and intriguing characters ever to have appeared on *Farscape*. Even though her character left the series, killed at the beginning of season three, her popularity remained strong throughout the remaining year that the series ran, and still remains strong even now, after the series was canceled, with many Internet sites dedicated to her, different types of images created of her, from digitized alterations of actual photographs to artwork—including Peacekeeper "wanted" posters—and games and music designed around her. The Pa'u Zotoh Zhaan fan sites cross international borders, appearing in the languages of almost all the countries that received the show, including France, Spain, Germany, Italy and Russia. There are even people who claim to be following the Delvian Seek, Zhaan's religion.

But why should the character of Pa'u Zotoh Zhaan have remained so continually and internationally popular regardless of the viewers' cultural or national backgrounds? Part of it is, of course, simply the appeal of the mysterious. And there is no denying that Zhaan's alien beauty attracted many viewers as well. But those aspects of mystery and beauty are hardly exclusive to Zhaan, and whether taken alone or together they still would not have been strong enough to account for the continuing cross-cultural interest in her character.

The real reason for her appeal lies beneath those more obvious aspects. What makes Pa'u Zotoh Zhaan a genuinely memorable creation, even if most viewers aren't consciously aware of it, is something far older and far more fundamental—it is the irresistible impact of the archetype. Archetypes are those basic images that are "hardwired" into every human psyche regardless of race, religion or culture, which we respond to whether or not we realize what's happening. For example, no version of the archetype tale of "Beauty and the Beast" has ever failed to be successful, and another archetype tale, "Cinderella," has been collected in over nine hundred versions and still turns up as the plot of many "chick-lit" novels. And as a sentient plant and dual-natured kind nurturer and fierce-eyed destroyer, Pa'u Zotoh Zhaan is undeniably an archetypical figure on several different levels.[1]

ZHAAN AS PLANT DEITY

The first and most obvious of Zhaan's archetype images is sacred and sentient plant. The concept of the sacred plant alone, though, is too broad a topic to truly fit her. Sacred plants occur throughout the world's botany, after all, in countless forms and with countless uses, from the holy lotus of Buddhism and Hinduism to the equally holy hallucinogenic peyote of the Huichol of Mexico. Zhaan's role as Pa'u may make her sacred, but her plant species is not sacred in itself. The image of Zhaan as a sentient plant is a little more accurate. The fact that there have been scientific (and nonscientific) debates as recently as the turn of the twenty-first century about whether or not plants can be considered sentient and that books like *The Secret Life of Plants*[2] have been so successful shows the power of the concept of the intelligent plant. A quick look at the world's religions, mythology and folklore reveals numerous sentient plant-beings, including those who, like

---

[1] Early psychoanalyst Carl Jung (1875-1961) first defined the term "archetype" as an inherited pattern of thought or symbolic imagery that is present in all humans. Examples of the most common of these archetypes include the Shadow, the Wise Old Man/Woman and the Trickster.

[2] Tompkins, Peter and Christopher Bird, *The Secret Life of Plants* (New York: HarperCollins, 1989).

Zhaan herself, have warm wisdom or dark aspects. In the Jain faith, for instance, every living thing, including plants, is believed to hold a jiva, or soul. In Greek mythology, hamadryads were, in a way, sentient plants, since they were inextricably linked to their trees. As tree spirits, minor deities, each of the hamadryads was born with a specific tree, lived within that tree, and died when it died. They acted as guardians of the forest, so by modern conservationist standards they could be considered beneficial beings. There are similar tree beings in India, such as the voluptuous Vrikshaka. In ancient Armenian beliefs, plane trees had spiritual powers, able to link the living with their dead ancestors by conveying messages to the living from the afterworld in the rustling of their leaves. In ancient Persian lore a talking, spiritual tree in India prophesied the truth to Alexander the Great: that he would die young. And in medieval lore, the mandrake plant represented the darker side of sentient plants. Said to be roughly human-shaped, it was supposed to scream loudly enough to kill or madden people when it was uprooted.

In addition, the transformation of a human into a tree occurs with surprising frequency in Greek mythology: Daphne, for example, when pursued by the god Apollo, begs the gods for help and becomes a sacred laurel.[3]

However, the plant deity is not Zhaan's strongest archetypal link. Far stronger is her embodiment of the concept of duality.

ZHAAN AS DUAL-NATURED

In mythological and religious terms, duality refers to the existence of two whole but opposing attributes within one being. A fairly common concept within the world's past and present belief systems, duality is generally seen as an aspect of a deity or other spiritual being. In Christianity, for example, Jesus is usually spoken of as having the dual natures of mankind and divinity. In Roman mythology, the god Janus was literally portrayed as a two-faced deity, looking to the past and the

---

[3] While sentient plants, let alone sentient plants that are as highly evolved as the Delvians, aren't found anywhere on Earth, scientists have been debating about whether there might be some form of plant intelligence. And indeed there are some oddities on our planet that do seem to hint at a vegetable form of wisdom, such as the Stilt or Walking Palm (*socratea exorrhiza*) of the Amazonian forest. Thanks to the combination of poor soil and scant sunlight, this tree is able to "walk" on its aerial roots. The tree can move toward more light by growing more roots in that direction and letting the roots that are in the wrong direction die off. A Stilt Palm can "walk" about seven feet a year.

future simultaneously. Shaman masks of the Pacific Northwest often can be opened and closed to reveal two different faces representing two different natures, human and spirit. In what is now Turkey, the Iron Age Hittite civilization of the first millennium B.C. employed the emblem of the double-headed eagle—probably the distant ancestor of the Russian and Polish double-headed eagle—which symbolized, it is believed, secular power and religious power.

Pa'u Zotoh Zhaan falls into the duality concept three times over.

ZHAAN AS HEALER AND DESTROYER

Zhaan, seen in her gentler aspect of priestly purity-seeker and healer, is definitely an image of the archetypal Mother Goddess, the warm-hearted divine nurturer who cares about and for all living things. Every culture within human knowledge has had some form of this archetype, whether it is the Greek Demeter (with her guardianship of all growing things), the ancient Egyptian Isis (the loving, powerful wife and mother) or the modern Western version of Mother Earth (Gaia, the living planet Earth). In the Hindu belief system, to which we will return shortly, the Mother Goddess is a many-faceted being known as Devi.

This warm and loving side of Zhaan's nature is clearly shown throughout the series. From the very first episode it was obvious to viewers that she had taken on a mothering role toward the others soon after coming aboard Moya. In fact, Zhaan was charmingly tender toward Moya herself, and to Moya's baby, the genetically altered Talyn, refusing to believe that Talyn couldn't be saved. It was Zhaan who had kind words toward Pilot and D'Argo (with hints that she might feel something far warmer toward the latter, sensuality also being an aspect of a Mother Goddess). She was gentle with John Crichton, who was warily feeling his way in his new surroundings, and even was relatively tolerant of the sharp-tongued, selfish Rygel, seeing in him something worthy and working to bring out the best in him. She was particularly motherly toward him during "Durka Returns" (1-15), during which Rygel was forced to confront his former tormentor and face his fears.

This didn't mean that Zhaan let Rygel get away with anything, including self-pity or rudeness. That would be out of character for a helping being. When Rygel asked indignantly, "What am I? Chopped mellet?" Zhaan retorted calmly, "Of course not. I can stomach chopped mellet."

Zhaan, in her aspect of nurturing mother figure, was a major part of the episode "Throne for a Loss" (1-4). In it, she was confronted with a sullen alien boy addicted to a drug that turned his people into vicious warriors. Zhaan pitied him and did her best to bring the boy out of his drug addiction and change his determination to be as vicious as the rest of his race. She acted as a true counselor, doing whatever she needed to do to aid him, and remained absolutely unshockable despite the boy's surly attempts to discourage her. That she failed to turn him from his path of self-destruction added an element of genuine tragedy to the story, but that the boy made his own choice could hardly be seen as Zhaan's fault. She did all that was possible without taking away the boy's right to choose. It was her gentle determination to make a difference, her caring for others, that was the point. But she was not too good to be believable. As Zhaan herself commented in "PK Tech Girl" (1-7), "I'm a trusting soul at best, but not to a fault."

This brings us back to the subject of Devi, the Hindu Mother Goddess. Although Devi is a good, gentle being who, in her aspect as Durga, takes up arms only for just causes, such as demon slaying, Devi has her dark aspect as well. In this other form, she is also Kali the destroyer, the dark mother: literally, "the black one." Whereas Devi is always seen as a gentle, maternal figure and Durga as a righteous one, her other aspect, Kali, is frightening and deadly. While she is not evil, she does represent the ferocity of killing madness and the power of death. Kali is usually portrayed as being four-armed and bearing weapons—or weapons and enemy heads. She wears a long necklace of skulls and a girdle of dead men's arms. Her eyes burn red, she is smeared with blood, and, in a close parallel to the story of Zhaan's dark side, she stands with one foot on the dead body of her husband.

Indeed, Zhaan in her dark aspect, her fierce, flame-eyed madness, is a terrifying and perilous being who might well be inspired by Kali. In the days when Zhaan was still on her homeworld of Delvia, the planet was a peaceful one. Most of the people were members of the Delvian Seek, a spiritual discipline consisting of many levels, each with its own rewards, although there was the danger that a seeker who strove to achieve new levels too quickly might be driven insane. Those who successfully reached a certain level became Pa'us, Delvian priests.

Pa'u Bitaal was a powerful member of the ruling conservative faction of Delvia. He was Zhaan's spiritual counselor—but he soon also became her lover, joining his life force with hers by sharing Unity. But Pa'u Bitaal refused to step down when his term of office was over. Instead, Bitaal and the other conservative Pa'us hired the Peacekeepers for, as they put it, "external security." That, of course, proved to be a deadly mistake. Under the Peacekeepers, Delvia was quickly turned into a slave state, and any of its people who tried to rebel or simply protest were promptly arrested by the Peacekeeper forces. Zhaan's own father was captured and sent to an asteroid camp, leaving her ignorant of his fate. Heartsick and raging over what she saw as Bitaal's betrayal of their people—and of her—Zhaan the revolutionary became Zhaan the dark archetype and, like Kali, let her dark madness have free rein. She murdered Bitaal while they shared Unity.

That murder was the crime for which she was imprisoned by the Peacekeepers. It was during that imprisonment, of course, that Zhaan consciously turned from her dark aspect and, like Kali fading and the Devi aspect returning, found her nurturing aspect as she worked her slow way up toward enlightenment. But even so, even after having reached the Tenth Plateau in her search for perfect understanding and unity with all life, Zhaan was never quite able to keep her dark side repressed. The darkness still lurked just behind her tranquil blue façade, and it could appear suddenly and in startling and unexpected ways. One jarring example happened aboard Moya in "DNA Mad Scientist" (1-9). The devious Namtar offered the desperate Zhaan, Rygel and D'Argo a chance to get the star maps to their homeworlds in exchange for some of Pilot's DNA. (Namtar, fittingly enough, may have been named for a minor god of the underworld in Sumerian mythology, Namtar, who brings disease and pestilence.) But Pilot refused to give up any DNA samples—primarily because Namtar wasn't after a few bits of skin but rather a whole arm. Zhaan didn't hesitate. With Rygel's help, she coldly and efficiently participated in chopping off one of Pilot's arms, giving as excuse only the rather cold-blooded statement that it didn't really matter since Pilot, who regenerated limbs, would soon grow a new one.

But it was when Moya arrived at a mysterious Delvian colony (in the episode "Rhapsody in Blue," 1-12) that Zhaan's aspect as red-eyed destroyer appeared in its full fury. The Delvian sect that had been sheltering there had tricked the crew of Moya into coming to their planet with the goal of forcing a meeting between their leader, Pa'u Tahleen, and Zhaan. Her fellow Delvians insisted on learning how Zhaan had managed to suppress her inner darkness, the killing madness. The sect had difficulty in controlling the darkness in themselves and that darkness had too often destroyed those among them who were seeking to become Pa'us. But Zhaan refused to give them the information because she knew it would be used to kill, not to heal. And so Pa'u Tahleen tore the information from her mind in what came close to mental rape. That violence hurled Zhaan out of any hope of self-control into a dark, savage maelstrom of madness. She could not hold onto reality, and her eyes burned red with fury. Until John managed to save her through Unity, the ferocious Zhaan was truly a manifestation of the dark side of the Mother Goddess, Kali the destroyer.

ZHAAN AS SEXUAL AND ASEXUAL BEING

Pa'u Zotoh Zhaan not only fit the archetype of the healer and destroyer in one. She also was the personification of an even more unusual mythic duality: Zhaan was a sensual, even sexual being—but was also, at the same time, celibate or even asexual.

When we first saw Zhaan in the premiere episode, there seemed to be no doubt that she was a sexual—or at least a highly sensual—entity, especially where D'Argo was concerned. In fact, D'Argo said to her rather suggestively, "I have heard of your kinds of practices, your...appetites. I have heard of something known as the...Fourth Sensation." It was never explained, and the viewer could only wonder what sexual oddities were implied. However, from that point on, suggestive language was never used toward her again.

Still, in that first impression, Zhaan did appear to be the image of another archetype: the goddess of love (or, often more accurately, of lust). If both the "light" and "dark" sides of her nature are considered together as a whole, Zhaan could be said to resemble a figure such as the Sumerian Inanna—later to be known as Ishtar—goddess of both love and war. Inanna is often portrayed as a beautiful woman, usually naked or holding her robes open—but is just as often portrayed as a fully armed warrior. Zhaan's determined saving of Stark and their bonding resembles Inanna's equally determined rescue of her lover, Dumuzi (later Tammuz), from death by following him to the underworld and winning him back.[4]

But when Zhaan and D'Argo are considered together, that goddess archetype is slightly altered. The Hellenic Greeks reduced the power of the goddess of love and war, separating those two attributes and turning Ishtar into Aphrodite, the goddess only of love and lust, not war. But the

---

[4] For a more complete version of the myth of Inanna, see one of the many translations available in English.

memory of the earlier version of the goddess seemed to have inspired them to make Aphrodite into the lover of Ares, god of war, bringing the two attributes back together in the process. In similar fashion, Zhaan, when considered in conjunction with D'Argo in the earlier episodes, appeared to be an Aphrodite-like figure, with D'Argo, of course, in the role of Ares.

But first impressions can be deceptive, and sure enough, that first image of Zhaan and D'Argo, we soon learned, was not an accurate one after all. They were not lovers, and later (in the episode "Bone to be Wild," 1-21), we learned that Zhaan, regardless of her very womanly appearance, was not even a mammalian woman at all, but rather a plant. Instead of bones, her people had cartilaginous fibers, and their tissue structure was cellulose.[5]

It is Zhaan's plant nature, in fact, that brings up the topic of asexuality. We were shown that there were both male and female Delvians, and presumably both genders were necessary for Delvian reproduction. But we also saw Zhaan in the process of literally running to seed, producing toxic pollen in instinctive self-defense—and the implication was that if Zhaan had been left untreated, she might well have reproduced by budding before dying. Of course, it was made clear in the episode "Self Inflicted Wounds, Part One: Could'a, Would'a, Should'a" (3-3), that the pollen was merely a Delvian response to extreme stress, the way that an Earthly plant might produce blossoms or run to seed if it were in similarly stressful conditions—but the idea of asexual plant reproduction was clearly part of that concept. Does this mean that Delvians didn't have the mammalian version of sex at all? Since there were male and female Delvians who did look mammalian, the possibility of mammalian types of sex can't be ruled out—but it does seem more likely that sentient plants capable of producing pollen would also have had an asexual exchange in the manner of plants.

Asexuality was also implicit in her reaction to intense light. Those "photogasms," the extreme, clearly pleasurable response to bright light, might seem to mirror human sexual responses, but they actually had little to do with any mammalian concepts of sex: they were the exaggerated responses of a plant. Although Zhaan did—and indeed had to—eat solid food, including meat, she also did, or so she told John, have a form of photosynthesis that let her take energy from sunlight as do Earth's plants.

---

[5] Since Zhaan ate meat without qualms, and even seemed to need it at regular intervals, it appears likely that the Delvians evolved from carnivorous plants such as Earth's Venus flytrap or the various forms of sundew.

There are no precise parallels to this aspect of Zhaan in the Earth's mythology. There are several asexual gods, such as the hermaphroditic Egyptian Hapy, god of the Nile's fertile flooding, who has a fat man's body and a woman's breasts, and the Greek Chaos, who has no true gender.

However, there are two mythic comparisons that can be made that cover both of the aspects—sexuality and asexuality. In the first case, scholars believe that the Greek goddess Artemis, the cold, apparently utterly chaste goddess of the hunt, may actually have had a dual nature similar to that of Pa'u Zotoh Zhaan. Artemis, as said above, is generally portrayed as being a fiercely celibate goddess, at least in most of the surviving myths—yet, in apparent contradiction, some of the other myths about her also state that she needs to renew her virginity every year by bathing in the pure waters of the spring Canathos. It seems unlikely that a completely celibate goddess would need to renew what she had never lost. Instead, that very need for a renewal of virginity implies a sexual nature coming into conflict with an asexual one. Artemis may well have had two cults, one worshipping her chastity and the other her fertility.

In the second mythic comparison, in ancient Scandinavian belief Gefion was said to be a vegetation and fertility goddess—but the same myths state that she was also the patron of virgins. Fewer details are known about her than about Artemis, but in one account, Gefion is described as a virgin herself. In another, it is claimed that she had four sons. Once again, there is that unlikely dichotomy, that dual nature, of fertility and chastity.

Perhaps, then, Zhaan, Artemis and Gefion could be said to be dual beings, contradictions, at the same time both sexual and asexual.[6]

ZHAAN AS SACRIFICE AND REBORN BEING

Zhaan represented yet one more archetype of duality. This one, in fact, is one of the most powerful in and most strongly resonant with most of the world's cultures. It is the archetype of the dying and resurrected hero or deity. To that is linked the equally powerful mythic motif of the hero or deity's sacrifice—or self-sacrifice.

The slain and reborn hero or deity is often linked in the world's my-

---

[6] It's possible that Artemis, despite her standard image as a virginal goddess, was originally a fertility goddess, as the famous statue of the Ephesian Artemis implies. That statue is either many-breasted, or wears severed male genitalia as ornaments.

thology with vegetation, specifically with the endless cycle of the seasons. The archetype story may take the form of the ancient Egyptian myth of the god Osiris, ruler of the Egyptian pantheon, who was slain by his envious brother, Set, and resurrected by his wife, Isis, who reassembled Osiris' dismembered body and used her magic to return him to life. Or it may be the relatively recent—possibly postmedieval—British ballad of "John Barleycorn," the personified and "sacrificed" barley cut down and then "resurrected" as whiskey. But the basic shape of the story is always the same.[7]

In such sacrifice and resurrection myths, the deity's skin is often portrayed as green, such as is the skin of the resurrected Osiris, and is clearly a symbolic link with the returning vegetation. Of course, Zhaan's skin is blue, not green, but her link to vegetation is obvious.

Blue-skinned deities and heroes do appear in world mythology, although they rarely have a clear connection with vegetation. In Hinduism, for instance, divine avatars such as Vishnu and Krishna, those who are worthy and capable of fighting evil, are portrayed as having blue skin, symbolic of pure sky or water. In ancient Egyptian mythology, the sun god Amun (alternate spelling Amen) was sometimes shown with blue skin to indicate his sacredness and purity—giving us echoes of Zhaan once more.

But perhaps the most dramatic aspect of this archetype is the idea of the willing sacrifice, its close cousin the self-sacrifice and the willingness to give up one's own life to save another's. This concept in its three forms is a major point of several religions, including Christianity, Hinduism and Buddhism. It also appears in ancient mythology, for instance in the myth of Odin, where Odin willingly makes himself a sacrifice by hanging himself on a tree so that he may gain wisdom. And in the Tarot deck, the Hanged Man card is often read as an image of willing self-sacrifice.

In the case of Pa'u Zotoh Zhaan, she proved herself to be a willing sacrifice not once but twice. A Pa'u's life energy could be transmitted through Unity to another being, although it meant a great drain upon the giver. Zhaan freely shared Unity with Aeryn to save the dying wom-

---

[7] The myth of Osiris, his murder by his jealous brother, Set, and his recovery and resurrection by his loving wife, Isis, together with the vengeance of their son, Horus, on his uncle, can be found in any good book of Egyptian mythology.

The ballad "John Barleycorn" can be found in many collections of British balladry, and is, in its various versions, in the public domain. Barleycorn is barley, used in the brewing of malt liquor or whisky. The first two stanzas show why it is considered a vegetation death and rebirth ballad (see ballad reprinted at the end of this essay).

an, even over Aeryn's objection and even though Zhaan knew as well as Aeryn that saving Aeryn would fatally weaken Zhaan herself.

After she rescued Aeryn from the brink of death, Zhaan quickly began to run to seed. The only way for the others on Moya to save her, she told them, was to find a safe planet where she would be able to root to regenerate.

But so powerful an archetype as the willing sacrifice is not so easily denied. During the frantic search for a proper planet for Zhaan's regeneration, Moya collided with an alien vessel on the edge of a wormhole. The two ships became so thoroughly merged from the collision that it soon became painfully clear that the only way to separate them without them both going through the wormhole and being lost was to destroy one of them. The aliens were killed during their attempt to sabotage Moya, but Moya remained trapped, tangled with the other ship. If Moya was ever to be freed, someone had to pilot the alien ship free, with the understanding that the alien ship would then be pulled into the wormhole and destroyed. It was Zhaan who made the ultimate sacrifice. She made a farewell speech to her friends in the two-part episode "Self-Inflicted Wounds" (3-3, 3-4), that sounded like the essence of that willing sacrifice: "Now I know I shall meet my goddess and be accepted to her bosom. Sensitive D'Argo, exuberant Chiana, wise Rygel, selfless Aeryn, innocent Crichton. My children, my teachers, my loves, there is no guilt, there is no blame, only what is meant to be."

After that, she triggered the alien ship's generator and gave her life for the lives of her friends.

But rebirth is also part of this archetype. Indeed, in the Mayan myth of the Hero Twins, their rebirth is made possible only through their sacrificial deaths, once by fire, once by beheading.[8]

Could this aspect of rebirth through sacrificial death apply to Pa'u Zotoh Zhaan? Perhaps it could. Zhaan was, after all, a plant being. The act of budding in plants is actually a natural act of cloning, in which the "offspring" is genetically identical to the "parent." Perhaps the fact that Zhaan was in the process of budding at the time of her final sacrifice means that a new young Zhaan might have somehow survived—and that in a way that means that Pa'u Zotoh Zhaan herself will be reborn.

---

[8] The entire myth of the Hero Twins can be found in the Mayan sacred text, the *Popol Vuh*, available in many English translations.

THE BALLAD OF JOHN BARLEYCORN

There were three men come out of the West
Their fortunes for to try
And these three men made a solemn vow
John Barleycorn must die.
They ploughed, they sowed, they harrowed him in
Throwing clods all on his head
And these three men made a solemn vow
John Barleycorn was Dead.

They've left him in the ground for a very long time
Till the rains from heaven did fall
Then little Sir John's sprung up his head
And so amazed them all
They've left him in the ground till the Midsummer
Till he's grown both pale and wan
Then little Sir John's grown a long, long beard
And so become a man.

Josepha Sherman is a fantasy novelist, folklorist and editor, who has written everything from Star Trek *novels to biographies of Bill Gates and Jeff Bezos (founder of Amazon. com) to titles such as* Mythology for Storytellers *(M. E. Sharpe, Inc.) and* Trickster Tales *(August House). She is the winner of the prestigious Compton Crook Award for best fantasy novel and has had many titles on the New York Public Library Books for the Teen Age list. Most current titles include* Star Trek: Vulcan's Soul: Exodus *with Susan Shwartz, the reprint of the Unicorn Queen books from Del Rey and the forthcoming* Stoned Souls *with Mercedes Lackey, for Baen Books. She is also editing* The Encyclopedia of Storytelling *for M. E. Sharpe. For her other editorial projects, you can check out www.ShermanEditorialServices.com. When she isn't busy writing, editing or gathering folklore, Sherman loves to travel, knows how to do Horse Whispering and has had a newborn foal fall asleep on her foot. You can visit her at www.JosephaSherman.com.*

MY IMAGINARY FRIEND

JODY LYNN NYE

Insanity as a survival strategy? It's so crazy that it just might work!

Everyone has known someone who seems to be listening to an inner voice. Most of the time we call it intuition. Some call it their guardian angel or the voice of God. Very small children have imaginary friends, and recent studies have stated that having an invisible companion is a "healthy indication of cognitive and social awareness"[1]...at least if you outgrow these presences by the time you're six or seven years old.

A number of unhappy people claim they hear voices that tell them to commit grievous wrongs. They are mentally ill. There are also human beings who hear many characters speaking inside their heads, interacting in more or less lively ways and in improbable situations. They are writers. Passersby who hear them expostulating with the aforementioned characters sometimes think they fit into the category of the mentally ill. Most of the time, they do not.

But I digress.

Whether they come from the soul, the imagination or the creative muse, these "voices" are all generated from within. They have not been imposed from without.

In an increasingly crowded world, the confines of one's own brain is the last true bastion of privacy. A good deal of one's sanity is dependent

---

[1] Hulbert, Ann, "Are Imaginary Companions Good for Kids?" Slate.msn.com, 2/1/05.

upon being able to retreat to one's own personal thoughts, to process the events of the day without outward criticism or scrutiny. One's thoughts about other people remain private, as do one's insecurities, hopes, lusts and longings. The psychological implications of an outside personality insinuated into a sane mind are shocking.

So what would you do if someone went and stuck a coherent personality in your mind, one that could browse through your memories at will and was designed to rat on you to its creator? That Earth astronaut John Crichton was able to handle the introduction of a neurochip in his brain, let alone a neural clone with a very distinctive personality, is admirable. Yet couldn't the intrusion have turned out to be more beneficial to him than harmful?

Before his capture by the half-Scarran Scorpius, Crichton was already under considerable strain. As an IASA astronaut, Crichton had to be in robust physical and mental health to even be considered for the Farscape program, let alone chosen for it. He was brave, clear-minded and not easily deterred, with a firm belief in who and what he was, but even the most sane man, no matter how much fortitude and good humor he had, would find it difficult to cope with finding himself dozens if not hundreds of light years from home in the company of multiple intelligent alien life-forms, including a plant who looked like a statuesque six-foot-tall woman with blue skin and a multiarmed, shell-headed symbiote who flew a living ship. Especially since said ship was being pursued with intent to kill or capture by the only race in that part of the galaxy that looked at all like the human beings that he had left behind. Crichton's early trials also included an encounter with a seemingly all-powerful race of elder beings, the Ancients, who placed in his mind the knowledge of how to create a wormhole, the first substantial intrusion upon his mental privacy by an alien race. Compared with what happened next, his treatment was mild.

In Scorpius' hands, Crichton was subjected to the Aurora Chair, a scientific device that revealed his memories and thoughts to Scorpius as easily as if the half-Scarran were watching television. Crichton was mostly unable to protect himself from this invasion, though his tough mind allowed him to keep certain minor thoughts private. Additionally, "firewalls" had been added to his subconscious by the Ancients to protect the knowledge they had given him. That and his own native stubbornness prevented his mind becoming the proverbial open book. Still, Scorpius was able to access enough information to make Crichton vulnerable to blackmail and threats against his homeworld and his friends. When he escaped from the command center, he was unaware that a complex electronic gadget, the neurochip, had been placed in his brain, a second strategy to obtain the information that the Aurora Chair had failed to get.

The main program in the chip, a neural clone of Scorpius himself, did not manifest itself until Crichton himself was under further mental strain, when the crew's hard-won food supply was threatened by parasites and he learned that Scorpius had issued a message on the communication beacon system offering a reward for Crichton's capture. The beacon appeared to have triggered his subconscious to reveal the clone to him. Since the clone informed him that he was not supposed to be able to see it, it is possible that the differences between Sebacean and human anatomy and neurochemistry allowed him to perceive it, thus beginning the difficult relationship between Crichton and the unwelcome visitor in his head.

Harvey, as the neural clone came to be called (Crichton had a gift for handing out nicknames: "Harvey" was the name of the 6-foot 3½-inch invisible rabbit in the eponymous novel by Mary Chase about a happy-go-lucky millionaire who claimed Harvey as his best friend), appeared first at the edge of Crichton's field of vision but later appeared to step directly out of the message beacon and assume full "reality," at least to Crichton. From the beginning Crichton knew that this being was not real, but his reactions under stress caused him to attempt to speak to it, and even to shoot at it. Crichton did not appear to be frightened by the sudden appearance of the interactive hallucination, and immediately deduced that Scorpius had done something to him to generate the neural clone.[2]

It is the opinion of Dr. Jeffrey S. Nye, eminent neuroscientist and helpful brother of this author, that if a patient presented to a psychiatrist claimed that he was hearing and seeing an alien being that no one else could see, he would be diagnosed as showing the Schneiderian first-rank symptom of schizophrenia. Auditory hallucinations are a product of the auditory cortex in the temporal lobe of the brain; visual hallucinations originate in the visual cortex in the occipital lobe. Harvey was a complex creation, a triumph of Peacekeeper science. The neurochip, implanted in the brain close to Broca's area, which controls speech function, could easily have been made to stimulate both cortexes to achieve

---

[2] Curiously, except at the very beginning, his companions aboard Moya never questioned Crichton's claim that he was seeing an image of Scorpius. It's possible that their willingness to believe him helped him hold on to his sanity against the years-long onslaught from within.

a full illusion while the program searched Crichton's memory for the information it sought.

From the beginning, Harvey's chief goal appeared to be breaking down Crichton's mental resistance. He followed Crichton around Moya expanding on childish pranks Crichton pulled on friends in his youth, events that Harvey had discovered in Crichton's memories. Harvey kept insisting that revenge was a vital part of Crichton's mental makeup, a charge Crichton denied, and with reason. In fact, vengeance was much more a part of Scorpius' personality, but the lines between Crichton's personality and the clone's blurred somewhat as time passed.

As he had to work with the images and metaphors available to him from Crichton's subconscious, Harvey often appeared against a background of one of Crichton's memories, wearing outfits that looked ridiculous over Scorpius' habitual attire of black, crocodile-print vinyl, and using (or misusing) images that only a Terran of a particular period in history would know. Because memory is a complex thing, Harvey often got references wrong, such as when he enthused about pizza with margarita shooters. Crichton had to correct him: no one drinks margaritas with pizza.

Harvey would pop into Crichton's consciousness at the most inopportune times, distracting Crichton when he needed to concentrate on the disaster *du jour*. Harvey created annoying illusions and hammered away at Crichton's sanity, frequently telling him that he was out of his mind. Crichton often agreed with him, just to annoy him back. He resented Harvey dredging up personal remembrances and especially his insinuating himself into them, a violation of those precious memories. If anyone had ever wished to have a secret friend so he would never be alone again, seeing what an annoying pain in the posterior Harvey was would remind him that there are worse things in the universe than being lonely. Harvey also seemed to get more pleasure out of Crichton's stored recollections of enjoyable things than Crichton did: beer, movies, women, sunny beaches, his family. Less out of amusement park rides, however, which seemed to represent moments of crisis to the clone.

At the same time, Harvey's task involved preserving Crichton's life, not because he cared about him but because the clone needed him to survive long enough for it to uncover the information it required and be retrieved by Scorpius. At times Harvey popped up with information that Crichton could not possibly have found on his own to help save him from danger. At other times, he would offer observations that could have been provided either by the clone or by Crichton's own subconscious. The clone was the only element out of place in an Earthlike illusion designed by a Scarran captor to break him. Harvey gave Crichton just enough information to challenge him into coming up with a way out of the situation. He also nudged Crichton's system to metabolize the Nebari "wonderfulness" drug, allowing him to resist their control. A flash vision of the clone was often a harbinger of the real Scorpius' appearance, giving Crichton a chance to prepare to deal with the encounter.

Harvey had means to protect himself. A mental block prevented Crichton from speaking about the neurochip. The chip also contained a function that kept Crichton from hurting or killing Scorpius directly or indirectly. That function, which was likely to have been designed to affect the medial frontal cortex,[3] must have caused Crichton considerable mental distress as it robbed him of free will. As time went by and Crichton began to defy the strictures of the programming, the clone was forced to take a more active role, like misleading Crichton in order to keep the clone's presence a secret, or whispering orders.

Their relationship was an adversarial one. Crichton never warmed to the concept of having a permanent boarder in his subconscious. He may have played chess with him once in a while, but he was not happy. Though he must have been aware of the clone a good deal of the time, Crichton seldom brought it up to his companions on Moya, and did his best to ignore it whenever he dealt with a crisis.

Harvey did not enjoy being ignored; he was endowed with Scorpius' personality, after all. He taunted and annoyed Crichton whenever he appeared. He challenged Crichton to defend his own thought processes, forcing him to face what was real and important. Crichton was no willing victim, though. He held his own amazingly well, dealing with the intruder by denigrating him, calling him names and picturing him in humiliating outfits and situations. Crichton saw only one advantage to having Harvey haunting him: with Scorpius' clone interacting directly with his subconscious mind, he was gaining an innate understanding of how Scorpius thought and acted. However, that did not mean that he was able to counter every action the clone inside him took.

The fact that, unless Crichton was very tired or injured, he never broke down and lost control was impressive. That is, unless you count the little lapse during which he ended up drowning his girlfriend.

[3] Nachev, Parashkev et al., "Volition and Conflict in the Human Medial Frontal Cortex," *Current Biology* vol. 15, 122-128, Jan. 26, 2005, Imperial College of London and University College London. http://www.fil.ion.ucl.ac.uk/~grees/downloads/nachevreeshusain.pdf.

As long as Crichton was alive and the chip unretrieved, the neural clone would be present if not always apparent, mining through Crichton's eclectic memories to find the technical information about wormhole creation that Scorpius required. As he came closer to achieving that task, Harvey's urge for survival became more and more desperate. At last, he was able to take over Crichton's body. He proved that he would go to any lengths to break free to broadcast a call to Scorpius for retrieval, including knocking Zhaan unconscious with a devious plea for her to enter Unity with him and smacking Aeryn's Prowler out of the sky with his own flyer, an action which resulted in her death. Crichton's consciousness managed to reassert itself at that moment, but he was too late to save Aeryn. He allowed himself to be clapped in chains, uncertain whether Harvey would manifest himself again. The clone had to go. He allowed a Diagnosan to remove the chip from his brain.

It was a shock to both him and Harvey when, after the Diagnosan performed the operation, the clone was still there in John's head. It did not vanish even after Scorpius appeared to take possession of the chip and try to kill the Diagnosan. Crichton was left in a shocking condition, his brain exposed and speech center damaged. For a time the horrible possibility loomed that the only person with whom he would ever hold a coherent conversation again was Harvey, the clone in his mind. The fear might have broken a lesser man. Crichton had already proved his resilence, but his resistance to Harvey energized his struggle to remain sane.

Once he was restored, Crichton took firm control of the situation. He developed a means of internal mental control that allowed him to banish or summon Harvey at will, to the clone's obvious annoyance. He seemed to put more action and more detail into his mental life. In punishment for causing him to kill Aeryn, Crichton beat up the clone and threw him into a dumpster, to the wild cheers of a crowd as imaginary as Harvey himself. Winning seemed to give him the strength to fight for his sanity.

The balance of power between Crichton and his unwanted boarder shifted from that point on in Crichton's favor. Without the chip's power supply and hardware, Harvey was no longer as strong as he had been. Crichton summoned him whenever he felt like having someone to talk to. Dependent upon John's goodwill for his survival, Harvey became pathetic and whiny. Whereas before Crichton complained (to D'Argo, who had the opportunity to meet Harvey within the mind of the alien Kabaah on the leisure planet LoMo in "Scratch 'n' Sniff," 3-13) that Harvey just showed up to give him bad advice, the clone had now begun to mislead him deliberately. (Crichton was in further mental crisis after having been accidentally cloned himself, with a Scorpius present in each of the two Johns, hereafter referred to as John-green and John-black.)

In the same way that a child's imaginary friend helps him or her develop social perception, Harvey's knowledge actually provided Crichton with understanding of alien behavior, particularly that of beings that Scorpius had personally known well. Probably based upon Scorpius' previous observation of Crais' character, Harvey informed Crichton that Crais was holding information back from him. The insight aided Crichton in creating a diversion, using Crais' fear, that allowed both him and Harvey to survive a dangerous situation.

Harvey also insisted that Jack, the Ancient, would kill both Crichton and Harvey if he knew of Harvey's presence in Crichton's mind. As it turned out, Harvey was half right. Upon learning of the clone, Jack held back from unlocking the formulae in Crichton's mind that could have been used to build a much-needed weapon. Instead, he created a power surge that killed the clone in John-black's mind. But John-black was killed not long afterward, leaving John-green and his Harvey clone alive aboard Moya.

Crichton couldn't escape from Harvey's gibing even when in a coma. While Crichton lay unconscious from a critical blow to the head, Harvey insisted his only hope of recovery lay in revenge. Crichton refused to believe it; his sense of self continued to hold strong. Crichton strongly resisted the clone's interference, knowing that his reason for living was his love for Aeryn. His body might have been weak, but his mind was resilient enough to bring him back from near death. Harvey, as a fully realized adult personality, challenged Crichton to make his own choices and defend them firmly.

By that time the clone feared encountering the original Scorpius and was more inclined than ever to help Crichton, answering questions more or less honestly and assisting him in unlocking the remaining wormhole equations stored in Crichton's mind, as long as he was allowed to survive. Harvey had become more of a friend to Crichton than Scorpius had ever intended, turning on his creator and refusing to fulfill the original reason for his existence in favor of continuing his own life, limited though it was.

Harvey's agenda had become his own preservation, and he did whatever was necessary to keep himself out of Scorpius' reach. He feared being destroyed. The clone had evolved his own reality, and wished to maintain it ad infinitum. He saw many advantages to living in Crichton's mind, enjoying culture, flavors, sounds and women, all courtesy of the Earthman's memory. Harvey attacked what he saw as Crichton's Achilles heel: Aeryn. He reached into Crichton's subconscious to give him the information about Aeryn's condition that the man could not have otherwise heard when Noranti whispered it into his ear, but not until it was too late to stop Aeryn from leaving Moya in her Prowler. On her return, deathly ill and accompanied by Scorpius, Harvey seemed to take pleasure in telling Crichton he might have to kill Aeryn before the illness did. Once again the nagging voice forced Crichton to steel himself mentally and find another solution to the overwhelming problem at hand: saving Aeryn's life. While in this case it was doubtful that Crichton would have given up, there were other, smaller crises from which he might have chosen to walk away if not for Harvey's voice in his ear.

Despite Harvey's best efforts at keeping Crichton from getting too close to Scorpius, Crichton, desperate to be free of Harvey's intrusive presence, enlisted Scorpius and Sikozu to evict the clone. Harvey pleaded his usefulness, but Crichton wanted his privacy back. The process worked, and Harvey was gone. Crichton was relieved, ready to resume his new life.

But Scorpius had lied to Crichton. Some time later, when the astronaut was once again emotionally vulnerable, soothing the newly rescued Aeryn, he saw a vision of what could be Dracula's living room in scratchy, cinematic black and white. The coffin on the bier popped open to reveal a new and improved Harvey, one with long claws and a Transylvanian accent. This new Harvey was utterly loyal to Scorpius and dedicated to a new cause: the destruction of the Scarrans. In that cause the new Harvey could transmit Crichton's thoughts and feelings directly to Scorpius. Crichton must have felt overwhelmed by the betrayal. To believe for all those months that he had been freed of the interfering clone and to be enjoying private memories and inner thoughts only to discover that the seeds of a new and more powerful intruder had been planted at the very moment the first one was removed must have been devastating. To his credit, Crichton's mental strength rose to the challenge. As before, Crichton was compelled to protect the information Scorpius had gathered, and to his horror he realized that to prevent that eventuality he had to go rescue the hybrid from the Scarran flagship. The mental war he must have been waging within himself all the way there manifested in the seeming irrationality he displayed in the audience hall before the Scarran emperor. It could have been the beginning of a mental breakdown, but Crichton once again demonstrated his resilience.

Harvey stayed quiescent from then until near the conclusion of *The Peacekeeper Wars*, when Crichton was preparing to build the wormhole weapon. The clone produced another illusion of Earth, a construction site for Harvey & John's Construction and Engineering, Wormhole Weapons to the Stars. Crichton, needing a clear mind and fed up with Harvey's mining of his precious memories, managed to "fire" Harvey, pushing him out of the way to do the job by himself.

When he next saw Harvey, the clone was dying. His job was finished, since Crichton's brain no longer contained the wormhole knowledge he was supposed to garner, and the Scarran menace had been quelled. In one final dip into the rich cultural tapestry of Earth, he paid tribute to the motion picture *2001: A Space Odyssey*, as Harvey, gray-helmeted since he had no visible hair, appeared as "Old Dave," dying in a silk-covered bed in a stark white room with elegant gold furnishings, facing "Young Dave," Crichton, who wore a space suit. In a moment of pathos, Harvey informed Crichton that from then on he would have to make all of his decisions on his own. The clone died, pointing to the monolith that had appeared behind Crichton. The last traces of the program had been eradicated.

It would be surprising if Crichton felt anything but relief to finally be left alone in his head with his own thoughts. He was free at last, not only of Harvey but of the Ancients' interference, since their formulae were removed after the wormhole weapon was deactivated. Yet Crichton shouldn't have dismissed the thought of Harvey without some measure of gratitude. Making his own decisions put him at risk for making more mistakes than he had with Harvey present. Without that nagging voice, that irritating presence imposed upon him against his will, that keen knowledge of alien culture, weaponry, geography and above all, psychology, he might not have survived his experiences at all. "Imaginary" or not, Harvey may have been the best friend John Crichton ever had.

Jody Lynn Nye lists her main career activity as "spoiling cats." She lives northwest of Chicago with two of the above and her husband, author and packager Bill Fawcett. She has written over thirty books, including The Ship Who Won *with Anne McCaffrey, a humorous anthology about mothers,* Don't Forget Your Spacesuit, Dear, *and over seventy short stories. Her latest books are* Strong-Arm Tactics *(Meisha Merlin), and* Class Dis-Mythed, *cowritten with Robert Asprin (Meisha Merlin).*

UNIVERSE ON A BUDGET

A TOURIST'S GUIDE TO *FARSCAPE*

ROXANNE LONGSTREET CONRAD

Galactic travel is fun, of course, but your time is limited, and you don't want to waste it in last season's pleasure spot. And, let's face it, safety is a concern, what with rampaging Peacekeepers and power-hungry Scarrans, and those are just a few of the dangers lurking for the unsuspecting tourist. What you need is a good guide.

So, YOU WANT TO VISIT OTHER LANDS? Meet new and interesting beings? Experience culture and adventure?

Well, you *could* just trust to luck and go unprepared, like the infamous Hooman adventurer John Crichton. Just pop an orbiter through a handy wormhole and trust your luck to find food, shelter and beings who won't sell your skin as a coat. But is that wise?

With this guide to food, transportation, accommodations and sightseeing in Peacekeeper space, Scarran territory and Tormented Space (should you be crazy enough to go wandering around in there), you can tour the universe in comfort without getting frelled by the unscrupulous along the way.

Special features include:

- How to eat like a Hynerian on an exiled Peacekeeper's budget
- Are you a hostage or a guest? Five ways to tell the difference

141

- SPECIAL VENDOR INSERT: Visit the newly remodeled Gammak Base Day Spa!
- Insanity: making it work as an amusing party trick

PEACEKEEPER-CONTROLLED SPACE

PEACEKEEPER HOMEWORLDS

The Peacekeepers, bless them, are hard workers, and they do ensure safe travel through most of their controlled space. If you don't mind a succession of challenges, stops, rude questions, suspicious glares and constant demands for your credentials, you're safe as houses...as long as you don't make them suspicious.

If you're lucky, you'll never have to visit the interior of a Peacekeeper ship...but if you're not, grab your own fuzzy slippers and pillow, and bring your own Dentic. Traveling at state expense in PK space is efficient, but not comfortable.

And whatever you do, don't make them angry. You won't like Peacekeepers when they're angry.

SECURITY: It's unlikely you'll be allowed to visit a Peacekeeper homeworld. They are notoriously xenophobic, probably because of that ongoing trouble with the Scarrans, so if your outward appearance tends away from Sebacean norms, you might consider another tourist destination. Or at least subscribe to one of Intergalactic Insurance Consortium's ransom-and-rescue policies, always popular with adventurers. And surprisingly affordable, given the high cost of cloned body parts.

SAFETY: ★★★★★

HOSPITALITY: ★

ACCOMODATIONS: If you're intent on visiting a Peacekeeper planet— *any* Peacekeeper planet—it's a bit like visiting your stern old aunt's house for the summer: you'll have a safe, boring stay, in painfully nondescript surroundings and on lumpy mattresses. Don't bother wasting time looking for the best place to stay; given the Sebacean mania for standardization, all hostels are the same, except for necessary differences for those who breathe alternate atmosphere mixes, compulsively mate or have a tendency to cannibalize other guests.

COMFORT: ★

DINING: While the food won't be anything to vid home about, there will be plenty of it. Of course, as befits a military culture, it will be served at strict intervals, and woe to you if you don't have your feet under the table in time. And you'd better *like* it. There are no regional varieties to food cubes and protein paste, so don't bother asking. And don't bother to try to charm them. Presenting your compliments to the chef will only earn you contempt, as Peacekeepers don't believe in positive reinforcement.

CUISINE: ★

ENTERTAINMENT: Peacekeepers like to drink intoxicants, but only off duty, of course. This presents a bit of a problem for the owners of such establishments, as PKs are almost *never* off duty, and when they do drink, they turn belligerent and destructive to even the sturdiest bar furniture. Therefore, most PK leisure facilities are owned and operated by the Peacekeeper government, and cater exclusively to their own.

Sub-rosa establishments flourish near major ports, however, and a few credits slipped to a non-Sebacean at your hostel may net you the address. If you're going, however, pack body armor, a pulse pistol and (preferably) a bodyguard or two. There won't be any Peacekeepers on duty to keep things calm.

> TIP: Don't eat the gakh; it's imported and rarely still moving on its own. Some canny bar owners have taken to re-animating the gakh with temporary applications of high voltage. Don't be taken in.

LEISURE ACTIVITIES: ★★

If you're looking for a cultural event, such as theater, music, dance or art, look elsewhere. Peacekeepers don't waste their energy on what they consider "frivolous occupations," although they will import it from elsewhere. But why settle for a road show company from Delvia—obviously desperate for work, or it wouldn't travel to a PK homeworld—when you can stop off on that lovely world and see the grand mysteries?

CULTURAL VALUE: ★

SIGHTSEEING: Unless you like solid, four-square architecture that reminds you of wartime bunkers, and grim-looking martial statues, we'd advise you to save the sightseeing for later in the trip.

GRATUITIES: Tipping a Peacekeeper, no matter how friendly they might look, is a very bad idea. One tends to like one's skin attached to one's musculature, or one's exoskeleton left intact; Peacekeepers are somewhat hotheaded about their personal dignity. A simple "Thank you" will suffice and let you save your credits for areas of space where tips are called "bribes" and are much more gracefully accepted.

PEACEKEEPER COMMERCE PLANETS

If you're looking for adventure, you'll find it here. Peacekeepers don't allow alien species full access to their homeworlds except in rare cases, but they've established these Commerce Planets as outposts where a huge variety of life-forms can sell, buy, barter and steal. (Although we don't recommend stealing in Peacekeeper space. The penalties for theft are harsh, as are all PK penalties, and can range from imprisonment on a Penal Colony to "Community Service," the most dreaded of all sentences. There's nothing worse than serving as a bathroom attendant on a Commerce Planet.)

SECURITY: As with all planets in Peacekeeper-controlled space, Commerce Planets are, of necessity, secure on a broad scale. (Either secure, or lifeless balls of rock.) Infractions to the peace are dealt with harshly, promptly and permanently. We urge you not to be an example displayed gruesomely to others.

SECURITY: ★★★★★
HOSPITALITY: ★

ACCOMMODATIONS: Hostels are available a dozen to the block on PK Commerce Planets, and almost all of them cater to specific species. If you're a Luxan, you'll find a sturdily built room block with all the comforts of home, temperature-corrected for comfort, with plenty of room to swing a Qualta Blade if you're in the mood (and we know you always are). Delvians can find ample and ambient environments in which to meditate upon mysteries (some complexes even include sunrooms, which come equipped with strict privacy locks).

The same holds true for virtually any known species. Technology and equipment vary from simple bed-and-bath cabins without computer access to fully stocked suites possessing the capability to run an entire merchant empire from your exquisitely comfortable armchairs. The Hynerian block housing, in particular, is well-known to be astonishingly sumptuous, though the furnishings are smaller than most species find comfortable and the rates would stun even the most well-heeled casual traveler.

COMFORT: ★ TO ★★★★★ (*varies according to species and income level*)

DINING: If you're not required to visit for business, dining is one of the best reasons to schedule a landing on a Peacekeeper Commerce Planet. Home-cooked (or uncooked) meals from a thousand different species. Exotic spices. Meats, fish, worms and vegetables from literally unnumbered worlds, many not proven to be addictive or dangerously poisonous. If you're an aspiring gourmand, a visit to one of the Commerce Planet's Meal Blocks is for you. You can sample from a dozen different food bars in one stroll, ending at the Medicant's free clinic to be certain that the *tsychis* you nibbled doesn't find your stomach(s) an inviting growth medium.

> TIP: Be sure to pack anti-in-digestion products and pu-rified drinking fluids. And never accept anything from a being who offers it for free. The antidote will cost far too much.

CUISINE: ★★★★★ (*for variety*)

ENTERTAINMENT: Commerce Planets weren't established just to promote trade of goods, but to encourage trade of cultures and services as well. On any Commerce Planet you'll find a wide variety of leisure activities to thrill even the most demanding traveler, from Luxan war dances to Delvian ballet. Even the Peacekeepers have been known to put on a show, though this mostly involves unscheduled live-ammunition war games within the city block. Performance artists occupy most street corners, and entrancing music fills the air in sectors where species possess a sense of hearing.

> TIP: Avoid the oil wrestling emporiums, unless your ca-sual wear is wash-and-wear.

LEISURE ACTIVITIES: ★★★
CULTURAL VALUE: ★★

SIGHTSEEING: If you're of a fearless disposition, visit the Colarta sectors for a glimpse of these mysterious executioners of Peacekeeper law. When not out wreaking officially sanctioned carnage in hopes of winning their freedom from Peacekeeper rule, Colartas love to garden, and their public spaces are some of the most beautiful and exotic on any world. For architectural delights, look to the famous Delvian buildings found on Commerce planets: minimalist, strong and open, they welcome travelers to participate in meditations and physical delights alike. (If nudity is a cultural taboo for you, you might want to miss this stop.)

LANDMARKS AND POINTS OF INTEREST: ★★★

GRATUITIES: Generally, tip waitstaff, room attendants, bath attendants, drivers and menacing-looking beings who block your path. Some of these may demand all of your available credits, but can generally be haggled down to a reasonable price. If the negotiations go badly, however, try not to start any pitched battles, as the Peacekeepers might overreact. (See our section on *Security*, re: lifeless ball of rock.)

UNCHARTED TERRITORIES

"You don't want to go in there," said an unidentified Peacekeeper officer interviewed for this publication, "but if you have to go, take an armed escort. A warship, preferably. You have no idea what you're getting into."

There's a reason these territories are uncharted. Peacekeeper expeditions sent in often fail to return, or return with incomplete information at best. The Uncharted Territories are full of chaos, war and a hardy pioneering spirit…the universe at its most vital and dangerous. Beings from a million origins mix in varying states of war and peace, and it's rare indeed to come across someone of your own race. Inhabitants on these worlds are generally in the Uncharted Territories because they couldn't survive in their native space—because they were being hunted for crimes, or because they were generally of unpleasant, uncivil dispositions.

Go armed and dangerous, if you must go at all.

TRANSPORTATION: The first challenge is, of course, getting there. Most reputable cruise lines won't go anywhere near the Uncharted Territories, so you'll have to rely on third-rate cargo haulers or disreputable mercenaries barely a step above piracy (and sometimes a step below, as in the case of the Tavleks). In either case, you won't be on a leisure cruise. Expect to work for your passage.

Even if you have your own ship, you'll be prey for a variety of dangers, from rampaging Space Plants to intelligent microbes, so be wary, keep weapons at full and never, ever trust *anyone*, including your own ship's crew.

EASE OF TRANSPORTATION: ★

SPECIAL FEATURE

How to Eat Like a Hynerian
on an Exiled Peacekeeper's Budget

Could you go from being sole ruler of 600 billion beings to a disgraced, impoverished Peacekeeper prisoner? Anything is possible. Should you find yourself walking on the skinny side of the poverty line, here are a few tips from the famous Dominar Rygel XVI, former traveling companion to John Crichton, beamed directly from his Royal Palace on Hyneria.

(His Royal Highness would speak to you directly, but matters of state prevent. However, his plumber was kind enough to vid a few words for our records.)

If you're smaller than they are, good. Let them underestimate you. Fight dirty. Cheat. Lie. Steal. And if things turn against you, always look pitiful and small. (And if you're not smaller than they are, even better. Might makes right. It's worked on Hyneria for thousands of cycles.)

Accept charity. Some of those frelling idiots might actually give you food if they think you're hungry. But always remember, charity is only good if you're the one receiving the goodies.

Be ruthless. If someone refuses you a meal because of a silly thing like being able to cough up money, stick their heads on poles and display them until decomposition interferes with your appetite. Service will be more respectful in the future.

Watch your friends closely. Not just for treachery—ancestors know there's no friend you'll ever have who shouldn't be suspected of that—but for any sign of ill health. If they do turn up dead, there's profit to be made. But wait a memorial interval—maybe an arn—before rifling through the possessions of your dead companions, for decency's sake. After all, somebody's going to get what's there, and it might as well be you.

Look for bargains. If you're fortunate enough to have a stomach like a Hynerian, and are able to eat foul decomposing things that could sicken even a Scarran, so much the better. It's amazing what people throw out.

And last: don't be on a budget. Force everyone else to sacrifice. That's the way the Dominar does it.

Editor's note: The producers of this volume do not condone lying, cheating, sticking heads on pikes, betraying your friends or rifling through their possessions for the odd coin. However, it does seem to work for Hynerians.

ACCOMMODATIONS: Friendly—or even nonfatal—landfalls within the Uncharted Territories are few and far between. We suggest you prepare for a long on-board stay. If you must take the free air, however, we suggest the planet **Acquara**, which gave shelter to Hooman adventurer John Crichton during his sojourn in that area. The planet of **Litigara** has some pleasant aspects, but the overabundance of lawyers will signal all but the dimmest visitors to move along. Quickly.

Our primary recommendation is reserved for the **Breakaway Colonies**, which are Sebacean homeworlds without the unnecessarily difficult Peacekeeper rules of order. As an added benefit, you may be allowed to visit the **Royal Planet**, which is quite aesthetically pleasing.

We do *not* recommend extended visits to the rebuilt **Gammak Base Day Spa** (although we did accept their advertising money)—even with its recent makeover, this former torture-and-prison facility is simply not up to galactic standards. The hot stone massages would be a nice touch, if the stones were not *red* hot and a great deal heavier then most species would find comfortable. And the Aurora Chair, for all its improved plush upholstery, is still not comfortable in its reclining position.

COMFORT: ★ *(at best)*

DINING: Palatable—or even comestible—food is few and far between in the Uncharted Territories. You might have to trade often for local fare and should be quite careful about alien spices and unfamiliar vegetables. Inquire closely about the origins of some of the meat dishes if your species has strong taboos against cannibalism.

CUISINE: ★ *(even for the adventurous palate)*

ENTERTAINMENT: There is very little formalized entertainment to be had in the Uncharted Territories, so far as official reports have shown. One visitor reported, "There are a hell of a lot of half-dressed alien chicks and some damn fine booze, but I wouldn't try those little white things they serve at parties in there. Oh, but you should check out the Nebari lap dances. Real fine."

LEISURE ACTIVITIES: ★
CULTURAL VALUE: ★

SIGHTSEEING: A brief stop-off to the **Royal Cemetery Planet** might be the very thing to remind you of the gloomy, short nature of life. Travelers with a sporting interest might explore the mazelike caves, and in rare cases, be invited to "Take the Stone," which is a bit like the curious

Hooman sport of flinging one's carcass from a high object with only a stretchy belaying rope to keep one from achieving terminal velocity. Only without the inconvenient rope. *Not recommended for those with weak cardiovascular systems, nervous dispositions, spicules or exploding brain cavities.*

LANDMARKS AND POINTS OF INTEREST: ★★★

GRATUITIES: If you survive an encounter with anyone in the Uncharted Territories, there is no need to offer a bribe. Offering one beforehand, however, may ensure you are able to end your business peacefully.

THINGS TO AVOID: Sheyangs, for spitting fireballs and generally being inconvenient companions on a long journey. **Dam-Ba-Da Depot**, unless your vessel is in extreme distress, for overcharging and occasional murder. Zenetan pirates, who tend to ask questions over your lifeless form and then use your blood as an amusing table wine. Also, shrimp.

SCARRAN-CONTROLLED TERRITORIES

Unless you are a Scarran, one of their few allies or have a wish to meet your ancestors after a great deal of painful screaming, we suggest you plot a course *away* from the Scarrans. The Peacekeepers, while clearly not the life of anyone's party, are nevertheless the soul of kindness and hospitality when compared to the Scarrans, who regularly consume their enemies with a flavorful, full-bodied bottle of *flarg* wine.

TRANSPORTATION: You won't be going to Scarran territory unless you are a Scarran, a Scarran ally or a Scarran slave. In any case, your transportation will obviously be included.
   Ease of Transportation: ★★★★★ *(you just won't like where you're going)*

ACCOMMODATIONS: See *Transportation,* and note that what Scarran architecture lacks in comfort it makes up for in toxicity. If you schedule (or are scheduled for) a stay in a Scarran facility, please leave a note in advance with instructions for disposal of your personal assets.
   Comfort: ★★★★★ *if Scarran (and only if Scarran)*

DINING: You will not need to worry as you will, in fact, *be* the dinner.
   Cuisine: rate yourself

SPECIAL FEATURE

Are You a Hostage or a Guest?
Five Ways to Tell the Difference

When you're traveling through largely unpopular destinations like the Uncharted Territories, cultural norms and etiquette may be unclear. Take this quick, informative quiz to see if you know the difference between a friendly meal and a life-or-death negotiation. . . .

1. Your Sebacean host refers to you as "hot-blooded." Does this mean:
   a. Your host thinks you have a terrible temper, and finds it sexy.
   b. Your host thinks you are sick, and is offering to summon a Medicant.
   c. Your host commonly drinks blood, and thinks you look tasty.
   d. Your host is a reptile, and mammals are his/her mortal enemies.

   ANSWER: *(b) Sebaceans don't respond well to heat. Don't mention that you do. Peacekeepers would view it as evidence of Scarran sympathies.*

2. A Hynerian, seeming genial, offers you the first taste of the common dish. Do you:
   a. Eat. He/she is testing to see if you've poisoned it.
   b. Don't eat. He/she HAS poisoned it.
   c. Don't eat. It's polite to offer, but rude to accept.
   d. Eat. If you wait, there won't be a damn thing left.

   ANSWER: *(b) Hynerians can stomach nearly anything, are never polite and would kill you for hogging the plate.*

3. A Delvian mystic asks you to join her Seek. Do you:
   a. Tell her thanks, but you already have a life mate.
   b. Tell her you don't play Quidditch.
   c. Grab the body oils and announce you're ready for enlightenment.
   d. Tell her to join you on the Dark Side.

   ANSWER: *(c) A Seek is the Delvian equivalent of a religious community, and you'd be wise to go if asked. Reports are that the enlightment is . . . considerably mind-expanding. Never mention the words "Dark Side" to a Delvian. They get positively unhappy.*

4. A Scarran proposes a generous and equitable trade agreement between your homeworld and the Empire over a sumptuous dinner. Do you:
   a. Shoot him/her instantly dead, because it's obviously a trap.
   b. Shoot yourself, because you're obviously under Scarran influence and suffering from induced hallucinations.

c. Wait until dessert to see if it's chocolate mousse.

d. Counterpropose a devious plan to undermine the Peacekeepers.

ANSWER: *(a) Scarrans aren't generous, aren't equitable, don't trade and don't care about your homeworld except as something to conquer or destroy. And they don't cook. Ever.*

5. You are offered Jelifan paste as an appetizer. Do you:

a. Ask for the recipe and open a Jelifan paste kiosk back home.

b. Use it on crackers.

c. Suspect your host is trying to turn you into a living bomb.

d. Offer it to your host's pet kwalthack.

ANSWER: *(c) Jelifan paste commonly reacts to heat and creates a violent explosion. Your host is definitely not hospitable.*

If you got any of these questions wrong, we urge you to locate a copy of our companion volume, *Fatal Beauty: Underestimating Alien Cultures* (available in fine vid kiosks everywhere).

ENTERTAINMENT: Oddly, the Scarrans have quite a thriving artistic community. Granted, their paintings are usually drawn in the bodily fluids of captives, and their dances all seem to have a resemblance to the grotesque flailing of torture victims, but they do practice the gentler arts. Also the more martial ones. When the Scarrans put on a tragic play, it is, in fact, *tragic*. Usually for the actors and the audience.

LEISURE ACTIVITIES: ★

CULTURAL VALUE: ★★ *(but only if you are an academic with a death wish)*

SIGHTSEEING: No one but John Crichton and his companions ever glimpsed it, but the Sacred Garden of the Scarran royalty was said to be quite boring, actually. And it doesn't matter, as it was blown up. Very few Scarran landmarks are worth noting, as they are generally composed of the piled corpses of their conquered foes, and so are not enduring. Or particularly fragrant.

LANDMARKS AND POINTS OF INTEREST: ★

GRATUITIES: It is unlikely you will be able to bribe a Scarran to stop torturing you, but you could attempt it. On the bright side, it's unlikely to drive him/her to hurt you any worse.

THINGS TO AVOID: You *have* read this section, have you not? *Everything*. Obviously.

TORMENTED SPACE

Really, we despair. You *want* to go to Tormented Space? Have you not read the warnings that clearly say YOU WILL SUFFER FROM MADNESS IF YOU VENTURE WITHIN?

Fine. Don't say we didn't warn you. And we're not bothering with rating it with stars, either. ZERO STARS. Just take it as given.

TRANSPORTATION: Nobody will take you. You might as well fling yourself out of an airlock. Death by vacuum would be quicker and easier.

ACCOMMODATIONS: See *Transportation.* Buy a burial container. Something small. You'll be little more than a puddle of goo before it's over.

DINING: The dead don't eat much.

ENTERTAINMENT: No doubt the swirling majesty of the galaxy has its own brilliant and unknowable message, but in fact, as you will be watching this while *floating cold and dead in space,* it really doesn't matter.

SIGHTSEEING: Someone may spot your pitiful, freeze-dried corpse drifting along, but they will be in the grip of Space Madness and will likely consider you just another wretched hallucination.

GRATUITIES: As you will be dead, you won't need your money. Please bequeath it to someone needier and saner than yourself. We have several investment opportunities available, should you need assistance.

THINGS TO AVOID: We will studiously avoid *you* from now on for even *thinking* of venturing into this area of the galaxy. And yes, we know, Moya the Leviathan and her crew went and survived the experience. We are not such godlike beings, and there is considerable evidence that these famed adventurers were, in fact, frelled up in the heads before ever approaching Tormented Space.

SPECIAL FEATURE

Insanity: Making It Work as an Interesting Party Trick

- Whenever possible, declare yourself as being from a completely un-known planet, even if you look exactly like a Sebacean.
- Make up nonsensical expressions from this "planet" such as "Great Googly Moogly!" and "Holy Bad Guys, Batman!" to confuse everyone around you.
- When asked your name, say, "I am not Kirk, Spock, Luke, Buck, Flash or Arthur frelling Dent. I am Dorothy Gale from Kansas and you are going to do as I say." Chicks dig a man with a sense of mystery.
- Drink two shots of tequila, find a big long light tube to carry, and start introducing yourself to anybody who walks by as Luke Skywalker, Jedi Knight. Ask if they've seen Darth Vader hanging around. When you find someone willing to play along, announce that your name is Inigo Montoya, he killed your father, prepare to die.
- Announce that your particular brand of insanity makes it necessary that you frell the prettiest girl at the party or you're going to die.
- Tell your host that Earth customs require them to give you all their credits as a hospitality gift, or you'll feel obligated to *open up a worm-hole that will swallow the entire galaxy*.

(It's amazing how often those last two will bring results.)

EARTH

Earth's visitor's brochure says, "Earth intrigues, provokes and overwhelms. It is the apex of artistic expression, culinary daring and historical pageantry. The planet's palette is vivid and variegated: the glow of stained glass in the penumbra of the Barri Gòtic of Barcelona; Pompeii's mosaic-encrusted ruins; the majestic grace and broad-shouldered sweep of mighty New York City. Obsessed with playful and radical interpretations of everything from painting to theater to urban design and development, this planet consistently surprises itself in its constant quest for emotion and self-renewal. Discover us today!"

We disagree. The art is pedestrian, the food mostly tasteless and its "historical pageantry" is a litany of death and destruction interrupted by brief, senseless bursts of peace. The architecture is quite nice, however.

A former Peacekeeper, whose name is being withheld for security reasons (OUR security), does not recommend visiting. "The place is frelled," she said grimly. "It's hot, it's cold, it's wet, it's dry. It can't decide what it is. The people smell odd. The food is terrible, except for the candy. Although the television is under research by several alien races as a potential offensive weapon."

However, should you feel compelled, here is the required visitor information:

TRANSPORTATION: Pack your space sickness bags. The only way to reach Earth is through a wormhole—not the universe's most pleasant form of transportation, and of course, there is an even chance your pilot, who would have to be insane, will crash and kill you all.

EASE OF TRANSPORTATION: ★

ACCOMMODATIONS: Surprisingly, Earth offers lovely accommodations at its finer establishments, with lush, comfortable rooms and hospitable servitors. However, they are decidedly *not* accommodating of requests for common things such as Dentics and *tora*-root soup, and we do not recommend the substitutes they offered (a *toothbrush* and *chicken soup* simply do not meet galactic standards).

COMFORT: ★★★ *(if you don't mind roughing it in some respects)*

DINING: Earth has a surprisingly wide range of cuisines to choose from—dishes range from bland to spicy, offering everything from the safely pedestrian to live food to be devoured at the table, fried silkworms or vipers boiled in blood. Even a Scarran palate might find something to taste.

CUISINE: ★★★★★

ENTERTAINMENT: Hoomans have a wonderful and thriving entertainment industry. In fact, this often seems to be the *only* thing that Hoomans do. If you can adapt to the rapid cultural shifts that seem to occur with dizzying speed on this world, as well as the wide variety of indigenous languages and nations, you might well have a very good time. Note: *Television* is particularly addictive.

LEISURE ACTIVITIES: ★★★★
CULTURAL VALUE: ★★★

SIGHTSEEING: Hoomans simply don't seem to have a signature style. This makes for a dizzying array of sightseeing opportunities, from mud huts to soaring majestic temples. Oddly, we discovered echoes of virtually every galactic culture on Earth. Interesting, no?

LANDMARKS AND POINTS OF INTEREST: ★★★★★

GRATUITIES: We could never figure it out. Something about 15 percent, but with exchange rates and inconsistent currency, we just gave them shiny stones and gold. They seemed happy.

THINGS TO AVOID: Um…traffic is hell. And cows. We didn't like cows.

IN SUMMARY

Action, adventure, danger. New species. New worlds and galactic vistas waiting to unfold before the outward-looking traveler with the credits and the mivonks to take the journey. We've done it…or at least interviewed those who've survived.

But all in all?

Our recommendation is: **just stay home.**

It's dangerous out there. And we have satellite vid links, after all.

> *Roxanne Longstreet Conrad writes under a number of pseudonyms, the most well-known being Rachel Caine. She has contributed to a number of BenBella anthologies and continues to be surprised that they come back for more…apparently, the book she picked up on* Mind Control for Fun and Profit *really works. She's published fifteen novels and lives in Arlington, Texas, with her artist husband R. Cat Conrad, two iguanas who remind her of the Scarrans, a Mali Uromastyx who reminds her of Scorpius and a leopard tortoise who reminds her of Pilot. But only when she's gone without her medication.*

STARSHIPS DON'T JUST HAPPEN

THOMAS EASTON

So you want to build your own Leviathan? Well, you've come to the right place. Some of the science is a little bit tricky, but we'll outline the basics here. I'm sure you can manage the rest on your own.

FARSCAPE'S MOYA FASCINATES ME. The reason is simple: I'm a biologist, and she's a living starship that looks a bit like a horseshoe crab. She's got loads of room inside, all quite well designed for human occupancy. And she—or her species, the Leviathans—must have a history. Where did the Leviathans come from? What were Leviathans before they became starships? *How* did they become starships?

That we can ask such questions is a sign that *Farscape*'s creators did an excellent job. Science fiction writers, critics, reviewers and fans have long argued over just what it is that distinguishes good science fiction from bad. My own position has been that good sf is, in part, like Rufo's luggage (see Robert A. Heinlein, *Glory Road*), which looks like a steamer trunk but opens up hyperdimensionally to reveal something more like a warehouse. That is, it is larger on the inside than on the outside. Good sf invites us to wonder about the pieces of the story: Where did they come from? Where are they going? How do they connect to things outside the story? How could they let the story be extended?

Historians, political scientists, sociologists and more could all ask such questions about the components of the *Farscape* galaxy. But I'm a biologist who has committed a number of sf novels dealing with what might someday be done with genetic engineering. My attention focuses on Moya, the living starship, and for answers to my questions, I want much more than Pilot told us. He said that the Leviathans were made by the Builders as "biomechanoid" devices, partly biological and partly mechanical. When the Builders saw that their creations were developing intelligence, they set them free to roam the galaxy and multiply, which they did well enough to become appealing prey. Other species began to capture and enslave Leviathans for their own purposes. Moya, a fifth-generation Leviathan, was a Peacekeeper prison transport until D'Argo, Rygel and Zhaan freed both her and themselves.

To go further, I must play the game of deduction and extrapolation. For instance, how long ago did the Leviathan Pilot symbiosis take place? Since Pilot's people exist to be plugged into Leviathans as symbiotic communications and control interfaces, the Builders must have genetically engineered them to that specific function. Since Pilot did not mention this, the details must have faded from history, and we can estimate that the process must have been finished several thousand years ago.

With such time spans involved, it is no surprise that the details of Leviathan history are scarce. But the basic questions—Where did the Leviathans come from? What were Leviathans before they became starships? *How* did they become starships?—can be answered from basic principles. We can begin with that basic principle of evolution called "preadaptation." It says that evolution doesn't invent. It tweaks. New creatures do not just pop into existence. Old creatures do not produce new abilities or new structures all of a sudden. Creatures, structures and abilities have precursors.

One of the classic examples is the bird's wing. The oldest wing fossils we have show something shaped like a wing, but not so well shaped that their owners could fly. They had feathers, but the feathers didn't form an airfoil the way modern wing feathers do. They had muscles, but they weren't large enough or strong enough for flying. And the accompanying breastbone did not have the deep keel a modern bird uses to anchor its large flight muscles.

So what were those first wings for? No one knows for sure. Suggestions include gliding from branches to the ground, trapping insects in the feathers for lunch and even running up trees. That's right: it has been noted that when chickens flap their wings, they can run up steep slopes, even tree trunks. And of course, if a creature is running up trees, it would be nice for it to be able to glide down again.

The point is that pre-wings existed. They had some legitimate function in their early form, and relatively minor changes in form led to major changes in function. The minor changes included stronger muscles, a breastbone keel and sleeker feathers. These were enough to enable at least short-distance flying. With the addition of lighter, hollow bones such as we see in modern birds, flying became possible.

Why did such changes happen? Well, they inevitably do; one of the observations on which Darwin based his famous theory is that variation happens. Variations that aid survival get passed on to a creature's off-spring. If our pre-bird is chasing insects, flapping its wings to net them in its feathers, it's likely to find itself in the air as soon as it runs fast enough, and improved gliding ability could lead to better bug-catching and better-fed babies. Being able to run up a tree could mean being able to keep a nest safe from predators. And once the predators figure out where you are, being able to get further up the tree, or even over to the next tree, is a plus.

Where did the pre-wing come from? I like the bug-catching idea, for it makes a sequence easy to imagine. The early reptiles that gave rise to birds appear to have had something very like feathers, according to their fossil remains. Some early reptile was running around on its hind legs, trying to catch bugs with its front paws. It got some, but those of its kids with longer, skinnier, more feathery fingers (variation, remember) got more. And their kids, whose fingers had even more or longer feathers, got still more. Eventually, the forelimbs became pre-wings, and then true wings. And there you are: start with something sorta-kinda what you're after, and tweak the heck out of it. Mother Nature does it all the time, all in the interests of adjusting Her creatures to survive in their environments. Bear in mind, however, that Mother Nature has no end in view. The tweaking is quite random. Good tweaks, the ones that aid survival, are chosen by natural selection.

Genetic engineers, who so far (on Earth) are just learning their trade, will use the same basic approach, but with purpose in mind. For instance, if they ever want to produce an animal that would keep the streets clean of litter, they will surely start with an animal, such as a magpie, that has a built-in tendency to pick things up. A magpie prefers small shiny things (such as the diamond ring you left on the window sill), but a few tweaks could enlarge the bird and make it want to pick up anything that contrasts with the ground (soda cans, beer bottles, cigarette packs and butts, hubcaps, burger boxes, candy wrappers . . .), and maybe even nest in dumpsters.

What did the Builders start with to make the Leviathans? One might imagine horseshoe crabs, or whales, or some other familiar creature. But moving a planet-bound creature into space is a major step—one that would require adding a vacuum-proof hull, a propulsion system and a great deal more. It would be better to begin with a creature already adapted to the space environment.

Consider this basic principle of astronomy: An important stage in the evolution of star systems is the pre-planetary stage, when the star is surrounded by a disk of gas, dust and gravel. This is a temporary stage, for in many cases (and perhaps in all) the material in the disk will either coalesce into larger masses (asteroids, moons and planets) or be swept away by the stellar wind. But it is also a stage rich with resources. There is water, at least in the form of gas and probably also as ice. There are organic materials, enough so that some astronomers think the Earth could have received from space the raw materials for the origin of life. There is energy, pouring from a hot young star. These are conditions in which, if life could just get started, it could develop and evolve, just as it has on Earth.

The study of such extraterrestrial life falls to the field of exobiology or astrobiology, which is much richer in theory than in data. It begins as we have begun here, with basic principles and conditions. It says, "Let us suppose that life begins in a particular environment. Given what we know of chemistry and physics and evolution, what form or forms might that life take in order to survive?" In that vein, let us consider a young star system, rich in dust, water, organic materials and energy. We have already found such systems with Earth-based telescopes. If we could visit, we might find life, distinguished by some familiar abilities:

- The ability to absorb energy from the local star; on Earth, plants do this, but animals don't.
- The ability to obtain minerals as building materials; on Earth, plants extract minerals from soil. They also synthesize carbon-containing building materials such as cellulose.
- The ability to consume other creatures to obtain energy and material resources; on Earth, elk treat plants in this way, while wolves consume the elk.
- The ability to reproduce.
- The ability to move from place to place in search of food or energy, to escape predators or to find mates.

Even on Earth, methods vary. In our stellar dust cloud, we might find plant-equivalents in the form of huge sheets of sticky black tissue.

As sheets, they would offer maximum surface area to the flow of stellar energy. Because they are black, they would maximize the amount of energy they could absorb. Because they are sticky, the dust particles that bump into them would stick and could be processed for minerals. If they have some control over their movement, perhaps by flexing the sheet to tack across the stellar wind, they would be able to home in on larger rocks. Reproduction might be no more than a matter of breaking into pieces, either when hit by passing rocks or when chewed on by predators.

The predators would be more interesting, for they would have to have much more control over their movements. They would have to be able to locate and chase down plant-equivalents and other predators. This would call for some intelligence as well as some sort of drive mechanism, such as an ion drive. Ion drives expel small amounts of material at high speed and require electrical energy, which is not at all inconceivable for a living thing; even on Earth there are fish and eels that can deliver nasty shocks. If such a drive indeed did use electrical energy, then the necessary communication system for coordinating pack hunts, finding mates and calling children home to supper would surely be radio. Of course, there would also have to be a mouth, as well as internal cavities where the material of the creature's prey could be stored and processed. Each pre-Leviathan would also be likely to have a population of parasites and symbiotes. Moya has their descendants—the Hodian trill bats that seal hull cracks, and perhaps others as well.

The predators would also need to be able to reproduce. Judging from the large number of Leviathans produced in only five generations, according to Pilot, they must be able to produce a great many offspring. Since they live for many centuries, they may accomplish their prolificity by producing just one or two offspring at a time for many years. The same would surely be true for pre-Leviathans.

What else can we say about the raw material for Leviathans? The most highly evolved members of this dusty stellar ecosystem would have developed some emergency escape method capable of moving them rapidly (ion drives accelerate only slowly) out of harm's way. Given what we know of Moya's capabilities, I imagine them as having a "spasm" drive that would jump its possessor thousands of kilometers away from the danger zone. If the direction and distance of the jump were predictable, savvy predators might lie in wait while their partners provoked the jump. Thus an ideal spasm drive would produce jumps of random length and direction.

I said these stellar situations are temporary. Dust clouds either co-alesce into bigger rocks or are blown away on the stellar wind. Either way, the local creatures would have a problem. In most cases, surely, they would die out. Some would have mastered the art of sending spores or seeds randomly into the galaxy, to sprout and flourish when they encountered a new young star and dust cloud. Some might be able to choose a target and fire up their ion drives for as long as their fuel lasted. A million years or so later, they would have a new home. If any had developed a stronger spasm drive, they might have been able to leap blindly into the galaxy and arrive at least some of the time near a suit-able new home. But these methods would work only for individual crea-tures. If the ecosystem is to move as a whole, its various members would need to come together to form a single multipart mass—a "Migration Beast"—able to use the collective space drives of all its parts. If they also shared their nervous systems and thus constructed a group intelligence capable of controlling the direction and length of spasm drive jumps, they would be able to find a new home quite promptly.

Now, the pre-Leviathans I've just described are not starships. Cer-tainly they aren't ready for Crichton and friends to move in. But they have in embryonic sorta-kinda form many of the features—even the starburst drive—we see in Moya. The next step needs help, so let us suppose that long ago and far away some space-going species—the Builders—stumbled upon an ecosystem such as I have just described. They saw the potential for the bio part of a biomechanoid starship, and their genetic engineers went to work. Selective breeding alone might have been enough to enlarge the pre-Leviathans to Leviathan size, en-large the internal cavities and strengthen the starburst drive. Genetic tweaking would have been needed to strengthen the electrical systems (already there for radio communication) to support lighting systems and other "mechanoid" features, including control consoles, screens and Diagnostic Repair Drones (DRDs). More genetic tweaking would have been needed to give Moya the ability to produce portable comms for the crew.

As we have seen here on Earth, when the wolf became the domesti-cated dog, it gained a reliable food supply, protection against predators and a buddy. It had to work for its living, and it had to put up with being tweaked to do various jobs, but the relationship was not one-sided. The same would be true for the new Leviathans. They would be fed well, protected against predators and equipped with navigation systems. Like dogs, they would bond with their masters. A life of service might well seem natural to them, to the extent that, when given their freedom, they would still seek out companions to serve as crews.

At the same time, the Builders would have been designing Pilot's people as a solution to (among other things) the inherent randomness of the starburst drive. But it is only the final product of that engineering effort that could be plugged into a Leviathan's flesh as a navigational and systems control symbiote. There must have been earlier stages in the relationship. Even now, with Moya, we know that the controls can be operated manually. Were there earlier versions of Leviathans that did not have Pilots? Were there earlier versions of Pilots that could not be plugged into Leviathans?

Clearly, the *Farscape* series has by no means exhausted its material. Its galaxy is a complex social construct with a history far deeper than the hints dropped *in medias res* reveal. But the implications of the hints—the questions they lead us to ask—could provide enough episodes for whole seasons of the show.

Tom Easton is professor of science at Thomas College in Waterville, Maine. He holds a doctorate in theoretical biology from the University of Chicago. His work on scientific and futuristic issues has appeared in many magazines, from Astronomy *to* Consumer Reports *and* Robotics Age. *His latest nonfiction books are* Taking Sides: Clashing Views on Controversial Issues in Science, Technology, and Society *(McGraw-Hill Dushkin, 6th ed., 2004) and* Taking Sides: Clashing Views on Controversial Environmental Issues *(11th ed., 2005). His latest novels are* Firefight *(Betancourt, 2003) and* The Great Flying Saucer Conspiracy *(Wildside, 2002).*

JOURNEY TO THE FEMININE

THE GODDESS RELIGION ON *FARSCAPE*

KELLEY WALTERS

From the secular patriarchy of the Federation hierarchy to the self-righteous priesthood of the Jedi, men are unselfconsciously dominant in most media sf. Not so much in Farscape, *though. Aeryn demonstrated her physical dominance over Crichton in the very first episode, and if anyone was the leader of Moya in the early seasons, it was Zhaan. And that was just where they started out. Theologist Kelley Walters gives us a look at* Farscape *through the eyes of the Goddess.*

Out in the Uncharted Territories, away from the "stubbornly patriarchal"[1] system of humankind, the Goddess rules. From living ships like Moya who embody the Mother aspect of the Divine Feminine to Wiccan-style priestesses like Pa'u Zotoh Zhaan, the Great Mother's presence echoes throughout the universe.

Fate's hand stripped *Farscape*'s characters from overtly patriarchal lives and forced them to take refuge on Moya, putting them into direct contact with the Divine Feminine and giving each of them the opportunity to develop themselves into more fully actualized beings.

---

[1] Flinders, Carol Lee, *Enduring Grace* (New York: HarperSanFrancisco, 1993), 4.

Zhaan must face her inner darkness to find light; Aeryn must die as a child to be reborn a mother; Chiana must lose before she can love. Even the men are affected: John, the passivist, learns to fight for his family; D'Argo integrates the two halves of himself, the peaceful farmer and the fierce warrior; Rygel learns to look outward and care for others. Even Crais and Scorpius soften in Her presence.

As the three faces of the Goddess, the Crone, the Mother and the Maiden represent the three phases of life. This passing of power echoes what happens in our own lives as men and women: we each start as the adolescent or Maiden, change to parent or Mother (even those of us who can't or don't bear children find ways to parent) and eventually find our feet in our older years as Crones.

Passing from one phase to the next can happen as a benediction between mother and daughter, as it did between my mother and me when she was dying. Or it can happen naturally as we age.

In *Farscape*, all three phases are played out subtly in the interwoven relationships between the women. Noranti acts out the role of the Crone. Zhaan plays the Mother's role. And Aeryn, an emotional innocent, begins the tale as the Maiden.

THE CRONE: UTU-NORANTI PRALATONG

NORANTI: Peace can only be maintained if there is sacrifice.
—"What Was Lost, Part One: Sacrifice" (4-2)

Like most Crones, Utu-Noranti Pralatong is a mystery. She boarded Moya unexpectedly with a group seeking refuge from Scorpius' Command Carrier after Crais and Talyn committed heroic suicide to save Moya's crew.

Noranti was a 293-cycles-old Traskan who yielded her power with chaotic glee, able to draw upon everything she had learned, from seduction techniques to spells. John called her Granny or Old Woman, and like many crones, she drew on wisdom and humor to teach. She embodied the Crone as Trickster, seeming to cause harm and yet freeing her pupils from traditional restraints and forcing them to internalize their lessons.

Being a Crone is the ultimate freedom. Bound by neither beauty nor youth, the Crone can act as she pleases, delighting in the pleasures of her body and in the scope of her wide experience.

In "Lava's a Many Splendored Thing" (4-4), Noranti cast a spell over the Tarkans with the chant, "I am the flower, you are the bee. I am the pod, you are the pea. I am the target, you are the gun! I am the woman, you are the man!" It worked, distracting the guards and getting John and D'Argo a little closer toward the goal of breaking the crew out of their lava-bound hell.

Like Zhaan, Noranti was a cook and herbalist; unlike Zhaan, her food was painfully inedible and her potions as likely to bring sickness as health. As SciFi.com puts it, "She's a teacher whose lessons usually are clouded in riddles and hallucinogenic dust."[2]

When Noranti saw John's misery over Aeryn in the episode "John Quixote" (4-7), she offered him Distillate of Laka. "One whiff," she said, "and the pain is gone...for a time."

What she didn't say was that Distillate of Laka was addictive, and that while it was possible for John to shut down his feelings for Aeryn temporarily, he was only creating a bigger problem in the process.

Noranti had lived long enough to see the big picture. She was willing to sacrifice the few for the good of the many. In "What Was Lost, Part One: Sacrifice," as John was being led against his will into a sexual encounter with Grayza, Noranti chanted, "Peace can only be maintained if there is sacrifice." She knew that allowing Grayza to have her way with John would most likely save the rest of the crew, and might even help them find freedom. She was willing to sacrifice John's dignity and safety for the good of the group.

We naturally progress from the self-centeredness of youth, through the family-centered life of middle age, into a life focused on bettering society. The Crone doesn't have to be nice. Free from the tyranny of romance and childbirth, she can offer her wisdom in any form she deems best.

This is the Crone's prerogative: to teach Socratically. The Crone will give you what you ask for and let you decide if the consequences were worth it. Her role is not to see you as a romantic partner or to foster you like a mother does a child, but to present you with the hard lessons of life and let you work through them.

---

[2] SciFi.com, Farscape Characters, January 28, 2005. www.scifi.com/farscape/characters/noranti.html.

168 FARSCAPE FOREVER!

THE MOTHER: PA'U ZOTOH ZHAAN

D'ARGO: Zhaan, you're needed here.
ZHAAN: At one time I believe I was, but then a family was born.
D'ARGO: You birthed it.
   —"Self-Inflicted Wounds, Part Two: Wait for the Wheel" (3-4)

Before her death in season three, Zhaan took on many faces of the Goddess for the burgeoning Springer-style family on Moya: lover, confessor, priestess and healer. But primarily Zhaan was their mother.

In the pilot episode, Zhaan meditated quietly, sitting nude, her blue back gleaming in Moya's golden light. She was the picture of peace, the calm at the eye of the storm.

This calm, grounding energy drew the crew to her. Like children who test the world and come running back to mama, this peace-loving diplomat gave each "child" a maternal home. Zhaan embodied the qualities of mystics like Mother Theresa, living humbly and compassionately and encouraging her family to find the deeper good within themselves.

She fought to reach this level of inner peace and lived it so fully that she would not even help Aeryn name Moya's child, claiming that "Christening a warship is out of my purview" ("Family Ties," 1-22).

But Zhaan also had her demons to face. During Unity, the blending of minds and spirits, Zhaan had deliberately killed her lover to keep the balance of power in her Delvian order. In doing so Zhaan embodied the energy of the Goddess Kali Ma, the Dark Mother, who is not just the giver of life, but also the taker.[3]

". . . It should not be forgotten [that this] is an image not only of the Feminine but particularly and specifically of the Maternal," says *The Women's Encyclopedia of Myths and Secrets.* "For in a profound way life and birth are always bound up with death and destruction."[4]

Even though her act was rooted in the desire to protect her beloved order, Zhaan could not make peace with the fact that she had committed murder.

So in "Rhapsody in Blue" (1-12), Zhaan agreed to take Unity with

[3] Editor's Note: For a longer discussion of Zhaan and Kali, see Sherman, "Zhaan: Plant, Priest, Archetype," page 119 in this volume.

[4] Walker, Barbara G., *The Women's Encyclopedia of Myths and Secrets* (San Francisco: Harper & Row, 1983), 488.

the priestess, Tahleen, and in doing so, all of the old pain—and her repressed darkness—came rushing back to the surface.

Tahleen, embodying her own darkness, tried to steal Zhaan's knowledge and ultimately stripped her of her control, setting her many steps back on her path.

What finally brought her back on track was her gestating family. Like the placenta that nourishes us, Zhaan's family—and Moya—gave her the vessel she needed to reclaim her inner peace. But the placenta must break away from the womb in preparation for birth. While Zhaan's family gave her a foundation and a purpose, her task ultimately was to separate from them.

It was the "birth" of Aeryn, in which Zhaan gave her own life to bring Aeryn back from death, that allowed separation—and peace—to finally occur.

> ZHAAN: For the longest time I feared physical demise, because my spiritual essence was suspect, but now I know I'm worthy. Now I know the transgressions have melted from my soul. Now I know I shall meet my Goddess, and be accepted to her bosom. Sensitive D'Argo...exuberant Chiana...wise Rygel...selfless Aeryn...innocent Crichton.... My children. My teachers, my loves. There is no guilt. There is no blame. Only what is meant to be. Grow through your mistakes, and know that if patient, redemption will find you. ("Self-Inflicted Wounds, Part Two: Wait for the Wheel")

Zhaan's decision to give Aeryn life wasn't rooted in self-sacrifice but in the belief that all life is an expression of divinity. Zhaan's sacrifice not only allowed Aeryn to live, it gave Zhaan the courage she needed to move into the next phase of her own existence.

In doing so she "cut the cord" from her family on Moya and left them to do what *Mother-Daughter Wisdom* author Christiane Northrup says we all must learn to do: mother ourselves.[5]

THE MAIDEN: AERYN SUN

> ZHAAN: Aeryn Sun will surely harvest favor. Her life was a series of strides toward enlightenment. Casting off the chains of prejudice

---

[5] *Mother-Daughter Wisdom*, Georgia Public Broadcasting, Chattanooga, TN, 19 March 2005.

and hatred, reaching beyond violence and bigotry, she sought a
balance of lasting inner peace.
—from the prayer at Aeryn's funeral in "Die Me, Dichotomy" (2-22)

Change is the hallmark of all three phases of the Maiden-Mother-
Crone journey, but perhaps more than any other phase, the Maiden embodies it. The Maiden must abandon innocence for wisdom, self-centeredness for compassion and prejudice for tolerance. In accomplishing
these tasks she crosses the bridge from child to adult.

The Peacekeeper who landed on Moya was the prototypical Maiden.
Aeryn Sun exemplified the self-contained virgin warrior, the adolescent
who was waiting for her life to unfold. (Here "virgin" refers not to holding oneself physically apart, but to emotional isolation.)

Aeryn's spiritual youth became apparent when she found herself
forced to make a new life on Moya. She was selfish, lacking in compassion and isolated to the point of being self-destructive.

She had good reason for being this way. The Peacekeeper system was
the ultimate patriarchal order, reducing its members to faceless cannon
fodder, happy with them only as long as they loyally and unquestion-
ingly served a purpose. Children like Aeryn were raised without paren-
tal love to better focus on their duties as warriors. Until she came to
Moya she could not even define love.

Aeryn's evolution began as early as "PK Tech Girl" (1-7), when she
clumsily admitted her attraction for John. Later, in "DNA Mad Scientist" (1-9), she challenged the crew's mob-like decision to cut off one
of Pilot's arms. In this episode D'Argo questioned her: "Compassion?
From a Peacekeeper?" She assured him it was only compassion for a
comrade—and yet, it was compassion. The shell around her was soften-
ing.

In the very next episode, "They've Got a Secret" (1-10), Aeryn made
huge strides. In it we found out that D'Argo had been married to a Sebacean woman, with whom he had a son.

D'ARGO: Does it surprise you that such a Sebacean woman would love
me?
AERYN: D'argo, it's ingrained in Peacekeepers from birth that we must
keep the bloodlines pure. That such unions are evil.
D'ARGO: Do you therefore think that my son is evil?
AERYN: No. Because in his eyes...I see you. D'Argo, no matter what
happens to us...I will never tell anyone about your son.

The Aeryn who first came to Moya would never have been able to see past her prejudice and show this kind of acceptance for a person of another race, much less the child of an interracial marriage.

In "Mind the Baby" (2-1), Aeryn took another big step when she assumed the "mother" role, calling Zhaan to action on behalf of their family:

> ZHAAN: I love all living beings. The Seek has reopened my eyes to the wonder of the spirit. I am now going to devote my life to enlightenment.
>
> AERYN: Well, I think that's really selfish, actually. You know, before you bliss off completely into oblivion, you may want to have a little look around you, because Moya and Talyn are in danger.

The maiden's journey is a journey of change, and once Aeryn began changing, she couldn't stop the process, even when it terrified her. What frightened her most wasn't friendship but romantic love.

She resisted her growing affection for Crichton, often treating him cruelly (the opening scene of "Look at the Princess, Part One: A Kiss is But a Kiss," 2-11, for example). When she finally did give herself fully to him, he died, fulfilling the nightmares of abandonment she'd grown up with due to never knowing her parents.

After John Crichton's death in "Infinite Possibilities, Part Two: Icarus Abides" (3-15), a broken Aeryn went to a planet of seers to try to contact John. In the process she met her mother, who had been sent to capture or kill her.

Here we began to truly see how far Aeryn had evolved beyond the Maiden archetype, how she now valued connection over isolation, love over loneliness.

"You know," Aeryn said, "We Peacekeepers think that we are so remarkable. Soldiers without...equal. Precise tacticians. Purebloods. But, I've realized, we're not remarkable. We do nothing for love. Not one thing."

Aeryn's life mirrored Zhaan's, an upward spiral that took her new places but forced her also to revisit the old. Despite what Aeryn learned, she reclaimed her Maiden status when she returned to Moya, resuming the stark clothes, severe hairstyle and emotional distance of earlier days.

And like Zhaan, it was the foundation offered by her family that allowed Aeryn to not only heal but move to the next phase, Motherhood.

When Zhaan gave Aeryn her life back, it was as if it supercharged Aeryn's purpose. With Zhaan gone Aeryn moved fully into the next phase. She became the crew's compassionate leader, offering her own brand of strength and comfort.

Her journey through the Maiden archetype was nearly complete when, in season four, Aeryn revealed that she was pregnant with Crichton's child.

If, in psychological terms, the Maiden represents the developing ego, the Aeryn we met in the pilot held only the seeds of potential—but the Aeryn of *The Peacekeeeper Wars* had fully bloomed.

"You did it, John," she said. "All fighting has stopped. There's no more dying. And all of a sudden three is not such a scary number. But no matter how wonderful this is, I will not accept it as a trade-off for losing you."

But becoming a mother doesn't mean giving up the strength of youth. Even in the midst of labor, Aeryn was still a warrior, exchanging fire with the enemy and claiming, "Shooting makes me feel better." She was able to retain the pieces of her Maidenhood that gave her power and made her Aeryn Sun.

Aeryn's emotional journey was epic, from the closed-off Maiden in season one, to the Mother in the miniseries who had committed herself wholeheartedly to her family.

Each of these women, Noranti, Zhaan and Aeryn, embodied aspects of our lives. Not just women, but men, share phases like these—moving from adolescence to adulthood to old age. These characters represented what is good and bad, easy and difficult about our journeys and, I believe, offer role models for personal change.

Looking at them through the Goddess archetype shows Noranti, Zhaan and Aeryn as fully developing individuals, on a journey toward wholeness and peace.

In *The Song of Eve*, Manuela Dunn Mascetti writes, "[The Goddess'] is the voice that affirms us in our infinite variety: the attitude of tolerance born of endless creation and destruction and recreation.... Furthermore, the Goddess bestows upon us the gift of transformation.... Embodying Her, we become Her."[6]

Like the characters on *Farscape*, once you come into contact with Her, you cannot remain unchanged.

---

[6] Mascetti, Manuela Dunn, *The Song of Eve* (New York: Fireside, 1990), 6.

Kelley Walters earned a double BA in technical writing and psychology from the University of Tennessee, Knoxville, in 1989, and an MA in spirituality from Holy Names College in Oakland, California, in 1996. There she studied with well-known spiritual writers such as Matthew Fox, Carol Lee Flinders, Thomas Berry and Joanna Macy. She is a features writer for the alternative newsweekly Chattanooga Pulse *and is on the Board of Directors of the Chattanooga Writers Guild. Kelley lives with her husband, Michael Kull, and their pets Coco, Clare and Grace, in Chattanooga, Tennessee.*

The author would like to thank Nancy Ogilvie for her assistance and support in the writing of this essay.

REALIZED UNREALITIES™

OR, THE FANTASTIC ADVENTURES OF JOHN QUIXOTE

K. STODDARD HAYES

From the moment he was unceremoniously dumped into the other side of the galaxy, Crichton was faced with a series of bad choices. It was so easy to identify with Crichton as he struggled to choose between bad option number one, very bad option number two and extremely crappy option number three. K. Stoddard Hayes takes it one step further.

WELCOME, INTREPID GAMER, to Realized Unrealities™, the game of mental mayhem. You'll be playing the part of our hero, John Crichton, a.k.a. John Quixote, as he travels across magical, maddening landscapes of the mind, always confused, always looking for his princess, always trying to figure out what's real, what's someone else's mind game and what's just his fevered imagination.

Your goal at each level is to sort out reality from fantasy until you confront the Game Master and discover why he's playing games with you. You win the game by bringing Crichton safely home to—wherever home turns out to be.

But wait! Before you begin, ponder the wise words of the Level 4 Game Book:

In farthest space beyond the knowing charts
The horrid human and his band appear,

175

And though they play today at different parts,
The core of subtle truth beneath is clear. ("John Quixote," 4-7)

The "subtle truth" is that at every level of play, you are making decisions and taking actions that might play out in reality (whatever reality means in a television universe). The catch: you won't know which of those game decisions will become a "Realized Unreality"™ until you complete each level and total up your score.

With that cheery thought in mind, play on!

LEVEL 1 - "A HUMAN REACTION"

AVATAR: Astronaut Crichton

Scientist, lost boy, average John. You have no special powers except those funky translator microbes and some alien modifications to your module. You just want to find your way home.

SCENARIO: A wormhole opens off Moya's bow, and at the far end is a shiny blue planet—Earth.

Your choices:
1. Play it safe—if you call it "safe" to skip a chance you've been waiting for since you joined Moya—and just study the wormhole.
2. Jump in your module and fly home as quick as you can.

The clock's ticking, the wormhole's destabilizing; what are you afraid of? You've already taken much bigger chances out in this big universe than flying down a wormhole. So something else must be stopping you—like maybe wondering what you might find at home after so many months away? Or is it the thought of leaving some alien critters you've started to care about?

Finally, you choose number two and fly down the rabbit hole.

You're expecting happy landings, hugs from Dad, maybe a parade and a medal and the front cover of *Time* or *People* (which, by the way, is over seven months old).

Are you kidding? That would be Game Over—or at least your current fantasy of what Game Over should look like. This is only Level 1, lost boy. You wake up in a military lab, with doctors taking translator microbe tissue samples and technicians crawling all over your alien-enhanced module. Your friends from Moya drop down the wormhole looking for you, and before you know it, they've joined you in this pre-9/11 dress rehearsal for how to treat suspected enemy aliens.

Your choices:
   1. Rescue your friends from the bad guys before someone gets hurt.
   2. Tell your friends that everything's going to be okay. After all, this is home, right? And Wilson's not a bad guy, he's just a little overzealous. Right?

You choose number two, and everything's kinda okay until they show you Rygel's dissected little body. Wait! Regular characters aren't supposed to die. Are they? D'Argo has been taken away for more experiments, and they're coming for Aeryn next.

Your choices:
   1. Be a good all-American patriotic boy, protect your own ass, and let Wilson have the aliens.
   2. Try to save the last friend you have, Aeryn.

You choose number two. Saving Aeryn is a no-brainer, though it will cost you Dad and home and your career.

You and Aeryn are on your way, when you notice that nothing is real. You open the ladies' room door and meet Ancient Jack, the alien Dad, who stole the whole scenario out of your mind to find out how Earth might treat aliens. Now you both know the Ugly Truth.

Congratulations! You've completed Level 1. You're nowhere near Earth; your friends are all safe, even Rygel, and it's time to add up the Realized Unrealities™ for this level.

LEVEL 1 SCORE

Realization #1: The Dominar dissection is your first clue that in this universe, you are going to lose people you care about—and most of the time, they're going to die because of you, John Crichton. No reset buttons allowed here, and only a couple of trades. You're going to have to accept real losses—if there's any way to accept losing Aeryn, Zhaan, Crais and Talyn, the Ancient Jack, Jool, both of your best friends and one of your own lives.

Realization #2: You chose your loyalty to Moya's crew over your loyalty to Earth. You'll make that choice for real and for good when you collapse Earth's wormhole to keep your enemies away from home and decide to stay on the far end of it. By then, Earth is no place like home, not for you. Home is where your friends are, and above all, where Aeryn is (see the final score for Levels 3 and 5).

LEVEL ONE BONUS: You impressed Game Master Jack so much that you win the Extra Super Secret Bonus Power: wormhole knowledge. You won't be able to use it until at least Level 5, but don't worry. It's going to get you in plenty of trouble long before then. In fact, starting right now:

LEVEL 2 - "WON'T GET FOOLED AGAIN"

AVATAR: Mental-as-Anything Crichton
You've survived the Aurora Chair, T'raltixx and two rounds with Maldis, so you're a pro at mental games. And you've got a secret weapon that even you don't know about: Harvey the neural clone.

SCENARIO: You wake up in a hospital on Earth, with Dad telling you that you crashed your module during the test flight last week.

Your choices:
1. Dismiss all the weird stuff that's happened in the past year and a half as a crash-induced nightmare, and let Dad welcome you home.
2. Strangle Dad and start looking for a way out of this mind game.

You choose number two, because you think you're back in Level 1, where you already know someone is messing with your head. In Level 1, Game Master Jack tried to convince you everything was real. But here, you meet the Aerily beautiful Dr. Bettina Fairchild and a psychiatrist who, despite her pinstripe suit, is a beautiful blue-assed bitch. Surprise! This Game Master doesn't care whether you think this is real, and you, Jack and Leslie Crichton's little boy, are definitely not in Level 1 anymore.

Your choices:
1. Play along with the scenario to see if you can find out what's really going down.
2. Push the envelope, refuse to play, try to find the limits of the game.

You choose number two. You drive right into an oncoming truck at ninety miles per hour, shoot Dad, D. K., Doc Betty and the blue shrink, and throw the new boss' tiny shiny heiny off a parking garage. It's easy to be kick-ass Crichton when everyone's trying to make you be a good boy. It's not so easy when Mom shows up with her cancer lesions, and when D'Argo and all the girls, including Mom, start to hit on you. Scorpius—the one at the bar—says the Game Master is a Scarran who's trying to break you by driving you mad.

Your choices:
1. Trust Scorpius' advice.
2. Follow your first guess that he's the Game Master who's messing with your mind.

You choose number one, because Scorpius is the only one making any sense here. When dream Aeryn comes along to rescue you, you refuse to be rescued. Harvey distracts the Scarran; you wake up and blow his ugly head off.

Congratulations! You've completed Level 2, and you can keep Level 2's Extra Super Secret Bonus Power, Harvey. Too bad you won't remember he's around until he takes over and screws you and all your friends.

LEVEL 2 SCORE

Realization #3: All that down-the-rabbit-hole craziness doesn't shake you; it just makes you more contrary and kick-ass. In reality, you'll react the same way whenever someone starts pushing you around, whether Crais, Maldis, Scorpius, the Nebari, Grayza, the Scarrans or anyone else. "Hey, you bastards, John Crichton was here!" What makes you crazy is remembering your mom's death, or having all the chicks, including Mom, come on to you. In the real world, love hurts you more than torture—whether it's Zhaan dying because of you, or Aeryn leaving you because she can't stand how much love hurts.

Realization #4: You trusted Scorpius. Are you out of your mind? Well, yeah...but in a twisted Harvey way, you actually can trust Scorpius— sometimes. He's trying to keep you and the wormhole knowledge from the Scarrans, so when it's time to save the wormhole bacon from the bad guys, he'll be an indispensable ally. On the flip side—guess who's to blame for getting you into Level 2? Scorpius' obsession with you tipped off the Scarrans that you might be valuable. And to get your wormhole knowledge for the Peacekeepers, he'll hang you out to dry in a hundred different ways, including subjecting you to the Aurora Chair and a neural chip, killing Aeryn and having Harvey trick you into saving him from the Scarrans.

Realization #5: You killed all your friends (twice!) to prove the scenario wasn't real. So where in the real world will you draw the line at taking risks to make things go your way? Nowhere. You're going to do much crazier things, like jump out of a spaceship without an EVA suit, use a wormhole to blow up a star and a Scarran dreadnought and walk into a Scarran base wearing a nuclear necklace.

LEVEL 3 - "REVENGING ANGEL"

AVATAR: Cartoon Crichton

Human. Astronut. Natural-born Loser. With the combined powers of Bugs Bunny and the Road Runner, you can fly through painted wormholes, turn all your friends into cartoons and set off any number of booby traps.

SCENARIO: Angry D'Argo put you in a coma. To wake yourself up, you need to make up with the D'Argo in your mind, and find something to live for.

Your choices:
1. Pay attention to your own "Letterman list" of reasons to live: "Earth. Dad. Pizza. Sex. Cold beer. Fast cars. Sex. Aeryn. Love."
2. Take Harvey's advice, and focus on D'Argo and revenge.

You choose neither. Instead, you try everything that all your other friends suggest, from reasoning with D'Argo to running away into Cartoonland! Only Aeryn doesn't give you advice. She just walks into your coma and embodies all your dreams. Are you paying attention? Nope, you're listening to everyone else, and running out of options. D'Argo's still enraged, you're still in a coma, and Harvey still won't shut up.

Your choices:
1. Try Harvey's way and take revenge.
2. Try your way, how you really feel.

You choose number one. Harvey's way. What's up, D'Argo? Luxan surprise. But you're still in a coma. So you choose number two. You love Aeryn. And you wake up.

Congratulations! You've completed Level 3. What took you so long?

LEVEL 3 SCORE

Realization #6: You told Harvey that revenge wasn't your way. And in reality, you wouldn't dream of taking revenge on D'Argo, nor even on Scorpius. When Grayza offers him to you, humiliated and slobbering on a leash, and tells you to do whatever you want, you can't even stand to watch. You, John Crichton, won't take revenge on your worst enemy.

Realization #7: In the game, you tried every option your friends suggested. You could have saved yourself a lot of time and trouble by just going for what you knew all along was right for you: John Crichton loves Aeryn. So drop the first half of the Letterman list and keep the half that matters: "Sex. Aeryn. Love." Down the road, on the edge of wormhole annihilation, that's all you're going to care about. After three years of bitter struggle to keep the wormhole secrets away from Scorpius, you'll offer him the whole package just to get Aeryn back. And you'll give up your own world to stay with her in hers.

LEVEL 4 - "JOHN QUIXOTE"

AVATAR: John Quixote

Questing knight in Spanish armor, a.k.a. "the most notorious criminal in the universe," you have your trusty sword, your trusty sidekick Chiana and three little question vouchers to help you.

SCENARIO: You and Chiana are caught in a malfunctioning virtual reality game, while back on Moya, there's a problem with Scorpius. Game Master Stark says you can get out if you kiss the princess or go through a green door.

Your choices:
1. Play through the game and accept the mission of John Headroom: "Journey to the source of evil, discover the darkness."
2. Find a quick way out so you can deal with Scorpius.

You choose number two. You're worried about Scorpy, so you take the first green door and head back to Moya. And there's a problem. In the middle of your worst nightmare, where Scorpius has control of everyone, including Aeryn, you find a voucher ball in your pocket, and realize that you're still in the game. Stark tells you you're too evil to be allowed to run free in the universe, and you're back to those same

Two choices:
1. Play through the game and figure out why so much of it is about you.
2. Take the quickest way out.

You choose number two. Again. For a smart guy, you're a mighty slow learner, Señor Quixote! You and Chiana climb all the way to the tower, fight the ogre, kiss the princess—and nothing happens. Now you're starting to pay attention. If this game is about you and Stark, who do you have to kiss to get out? Stark's game, Stark's princess. Zhaan.

Your choices:
1. Climb back down the tower until you find what passes for Zhaan in this scenario.
2. Take a shortcut through the game reset protocol. Assuming it still works in a damaged game that might cause brain damage or death.

You choose number two and take a suicide dive off the castle to reset the game. It takes you back to the fat blue guy, your trusty sword frees the real Zhaan inside him, and she gives you a kiss.

Congratulations! You've completed Level 4, and you have a new mission—to figure out whether all this death you're causing is a waste or a worthwhile sacrifice.

LEVEL 4 SCORE

Realization #8: You let your fear of Scorpius distract you from what really mattered in the game. Funny how often that happens. Like making Scorpy wear the I-Yensch bracelet, when it's Grayza you need to keep your eye on. And putting more stock in your fear of Scorpius than in your trust of Aeryn, who says he saved her life.

Realization #9: You dove off a castle tower to reset the game. Sure, it's only a game death, but the game is a perfect virtual environment that you experience as real—and besides, it's broken, so who says you can't get hurt? Taking a hundred-foot dive in those circumstances looks pretty suicidal. Almost as suicidal as a "game reset" that involves a wormhole weapon and total annihilation of yourself, your wife and baby and all your friends and enemies, just to stop a pesky little war.

Realization #10 is Zhaan's question: how many more will die because they love you? Your friends keep trying to leave you and return to their own lives, but somehow, they always come back to follow you—down a wormhole to Earth, onto a Peacekeeper Command Carrier to get the wormhole knowledge away from Scorpius or into a Scarran base to rescue Scorpius himself—all because you say that's how it has to be. So be careful, John Crichton, that what you're asking is the right thing for everyone, not just for you. A lesson we'll take up in

LEVEL 5 - "DOG WITH TWO BONES"

AVATAR: Bridegroom Crichton

A romantic softie, you have the power to imagine the perfect wedding to the Princess of your dreams. But do you have the power to make your dreams fit all your friends?

SCENARIO: You're on Earth, with your Dad and friends, and all the gang from Moya, getting ready to live happily ever after with Aeryn. Who says you can't have your wedding cake and eat it, too? Chiana, D'Argo, Rygel, Pilot, Aeryn, that's who! They're not adjusting well to life on Earth—or maybe it's you that's not adjusting to having them there, buying slaves, blowing up fish and boning Dad. Are you sure it always has to be your plan?

Your choices:
1. Keep trying to make all your friends fit into your dreams of home and happiness.
2. Follow your dreams to their logical end, and find out what's wrong.

You choose number two, and ask the Game Master, Noranti, to show you the whole thing again. This time, the wedding is perfect—the ceremony, the dancing, the bouquet and the garter, the toasts—until the Peacekeepers show up and shoot everyone in sight, leaving you alone with Aeryn dead in your arms. And you know that you can't have both dreams: life with Aeryn, and life on Earth.

Your choices:
1. Accept that it's too late to go home or to stop your friends from leaving you.
2. Go after the dream you really want.

You choose number two, and head out to stop Aeryn from walking out of your life.

Congratulations! You've completed Level 5, and you finally know what, or *who*, you want more than anything in the universe. And again—what took you so long?

LEVEL 5 SCORE

Realization #11: You thought you wanted that picture-perfect Earth wedding, but as D'Argo says, no one on Moya ever gets what they want. What you want isn't perfection, it's Aeryn. Your real wedding happens in a ruined fountain with weapons hot, a baby coming and Stark providing the shortest wedding service in history. Followed by the perfect honeymoon, shooting your way out of a Scarran siege. What could be more romantic? Besides, it will make a great bedtime story the first time "Little D" asks you where he came from!

Realization #12: In the game, bringing your friends to Earth keeps turning into a nightmare. In the real world, when you bring your alien buddies home to meet the folks, they're not the only ones who accept your invitation. Grayza's assassin Skreeth attacks your family and kills your best friend and his wife. And if Scorpy and Grayza can follow a wormhole to Earth, so can the Scarrans. To save Earth from all of them, you have to blow up the wormhole that leads to it, so no one, not even you, can go home again.

LEVEL 6 - "UNREALIZED REALITY"

AVATAR: Einstein's Pupil Crichton

You've almost mastered advanced wormhole knowledge, and you have five levels' experience in the game. As a special bonus, once again, you already know the identity of the Game Master.

SCENARIO: Home Base is Einstein's floating iceberg. From there, he sends you on wormhole journeys to different places in space/time— unrealized realities that could become real.

Your choices:
1. Play along with the role given to you in each scenario.
2. Try to change the scenarios based on your past experiences and how you think the world should be.

You choose number two every time, because you find it almost impossible to just play along. You can't act like you don't know Aeryn; you can't help trying to save Sikozu; you can't let all your friends be massacred by the Peacekeepers—even though they're not quite your friends, and you clearly aren't theirs in this reality. Trying to change things is a disaster every time. You get killed, your friends get killed, you turn into someone you absolutely don't want to be. Einstein calls you back and tells you that the next place he sends you will become your reality.

Your choices:
1. Let him send you to the next disaster and take your chances.
2. Stop playing while you still can.

You choose number two and tell Einstein to leave you there, so your wormhole knowledge can't accidentally make a mess as big as the one you just left.

Congratulations! Fear of your power is the correct answer, and you've completed Level 6 and mastered the wormhole. But have you won the game? It's time for the final reckoning.

LEVEL 6 SCORE

Realization #13: Why are you, John Crichton, the guy that everyone's after, the guy whose mind goes in and out of all these unrealities? Because you've got the power. That's where this game started, back on Level 1, and that's where it ends, beyond Level 6. You have the power to locate wormholes, navigate them, blow them up, use them to unravel the past and even turn them into galaxy-eating doomsday weapons. You have it because Ancient Jack thought that maybe, just maybe, you might grow smart enough, and wise enough, to put this power to good use.

Was he right? You've seen people die for your power and you've fought and died and sacrificed friends to keep the power away from the bad guys. Some, like Stark and John Headroom, the Scarrans and the Peacekeepers, might argue that you're a bad guy yourself, with your attacks on dreadnoughts, Command Carriers, shadow depositories. And who is bad enough and crazy enough to actually use the weapon? Not

Scorpius, not Grayza, not the Scarrans. You. John Crichton. To make peace, you'll force the Scarrans and the Peacekeepers to stand on the brink of the abyss they've made you live in for four years, and you'll put Aeryn, your baby and all your friends (not to mention two huge fleets of warships) in the path of total destruction. That makes you, John Crichton, the most insanely dangerous man in the universe. And the only hero brave enough and desperate enough to play the game so that everybody wins. Thanks to you, the war is over and the universe is your playground. Welcome home, John.

A sci-fi TV junkie since the first season of the original Star Trek, *K. Stoddard Hayes finally validated her addiction when she sold her first article to* Babylon 5 *magazine. Since then, she has written about many genre series, including* Stargate SG-1, Buffy *and* Angel, Star Trek *and, of course,* Farscape. *She is also the author of* Xena, Warrior Princess: The Complete Illustrated Companion. *She recently contributed five articles on classic television series to* The Greenwood Encyclopedia of Science Fiction and Fantasy, *including the* Farscape *entry. When not programming her VCR to catch the latest episodes of current TV series, she likes to take her family to the beach or the movies, read comic books and plot to overthrow the male domination of screenwriting.*

FARSCAPE VILLAINS I'VE KNOWN AND LOVED

P. N. ELROD

Who's your favorite villain? There are so many good ones to choose from, and a few surprising options as well.

THERE IS NO DOUBT ABOUT IT, John Crichton is the one man in the whole frelling universe who knows with absolute certainty that it is, indeed, out to get him.

It's not like he's a bad person. He's got some major mojo going for him with his brash boyish charm, brains and a butt that looks great encased in leather, qualities that worked quite well for him until a wormhole and a fatal fender bender in space turned his life to dren. He ended up in a part of the galaxy where his assets were completely unappreciated save by a rare few.

For the most part he's the quintessential catalyst; harmless when left alone, but Dren Happens when you mess with him. In his brief sojourn into *Farscape* space he racked up an impressive list of enemies, and the survivors would take much delight in hanging his mivonks on a hook.

Here's a few of the ones that caught my eye.

BIALAR CRAIS: MAD, BAD AND DANGEROUS TO FRELL

John's first real enemy was the deliciously dark Peacekeeper captain, Bialar Crais, who was justifiably PO'd about the death of his little brother, Tauvo, who was in the wrong place at the right time. He was our reminder that each of those little ships blowing up in such a visually exciting manner meant that a *life* was being snuffed out, and that others would grieve for that loss, some more than most.

Although Crais' debut seemed to place him firmly in the one-dimensional evil guys file, our bad lad Bialar refused to submit to the limits of such categorization. Nazi boots and black uniform aside, through the course of the series he proved to be well above that sort of thing, stirring up a loyal cadre of fans and even getting some respect out of Crichton toward the end. Not that it mattered much to Crais, who was usually busy with more important things—like trying to keep the rebellious Talyn in line. Nothing like an angry, teenaged Leviathan with big guns and an eagerness to shoot them to change your outlook. I wonder if he bore some resemblance to the lost Tauvo, since Crais seemed to have a good instinct about how to handle the kid. Well, *sometimes* handle the kid. Theirs was a perilously rocky rapport…except when they both agreed on shooting something. Family outings must have been a barrel of laughs with those two.

Crichton's relationship with Crais grew slightly less contentious and more complicated with every new encounter. I've heard some speculation that they might have been best buds had they not gotten off on the wrong foot, but I doubt it. Crais didn't unbend; he had the whole inborn Sebacean superiority 'tude, and that was just too easy a target for the egalitarian, 100% American beef who is Crichton to resist. Potshots, whether verbal or using pulse pistols, were inevitable.

Eventually Crais gave up his revenge motif in favor of playing the rogue captain, motivated by his link to Talyn and having gotten enough time away from Peacekeeper propaganda to become thoroughly corrupted by a taste of freedom. Of course, having his Command Carrier stolen out from under him, along with some sessions in the infamous Aurora Chair, could have had something to do with it. The poor guy just needed a break and the love of a good Leviathan gunship to give him some perspective.

After linking to Talyn, Crais' attitude did undergo what for him must have been a sweeping alteration. Though we did not notice anything like a kinder, gentler fellow running around blowing things up, we *did* get to peek at some of his well-hidden emotional vulnerabilities. He was frustrated by his life situation, by chaos intruding and ripping away his once comfortable black-and-white, regulations-for-everything world. Whatever plans he had for his future as a Peacekeeper officer were never going to materialize. He ended up making the best of what he did possess, but the anger he felt for the lost might-have-beens must have run very deep indeed. Mix that in with fear of reprisals (like the Aurora Chair) should he be caught, and the awful ache of wanting a woman who wouldn't have him, and you end up with not a villain, but an anti-hero with whom we can sympathize and identify.

This is unheard of: he morphed from a standard snarling black-hat-at-large into a three-dimensional, shades-of-gray *person*, doing his best to survive in a harsh, crazy and unpredictable universe... just like the rest of us.

That *is* unheard of—and really, *really* cool.

From being the model soldier who carried out unforgiving Peacekeeper policy to a self-sacrificing hero who saved everyone's bacon at the cost of his life and that of his foster child, Talyn, Crais wrote his own page right up to the end.

Way to go, dude.

MALDIS: STOP IN FOR A SPELL

Whether disguised as a fool, ancient wizard, or oddball shopkeeper in drag, or taking sinister form in the elegant pseudo-Jacobean threads, Maldis made and left an impression, and not a nice one. He appeared in only two episodes, but Crichton warily referred to him in a third, so the psychic scars from their clashes clearly ran deep in Our Hero.

Crichton called Maldis a vampire, and for want of a better term it works, though I think the entity might have proved a bit more complicated than that had we been allowed additional visits with him. Such are the limits of forty-page scripts, however tightly packed they are with neat stuff. He was also described as a wizard, which is pretty accurate considering the funky things he was able to do. Happily we were spared scientific explanations of his powers. When it's done well, I don't mind a bit of magic in my sci-fi. (Hats off to you, Arthur C. Clarke. I know you're right; now let me get back to my suspension of belief.[1])

Considering the books I write, I have to admit that my own soft spot for vampires in their many forms (especially the imperious ones with piercing eyes and perfect diction) is one of the reasons why this dude hit my "include" button. Instead of blood—*lots* of that in the *Farscape*

---

[1] "Any sufficiently advanced technology is indistinguishable from magic."

universe—Maldis fed upon fresh-from-the-soul negative emotions, delighting the most in fear. I've rarely encountered anyone who enjoyed his meals so much. Now, had Maldis *really* wanted to gorge, he should have used his wizardly powers to set himself up as a tax auditor. He'd have been forced to go on a diet within a week.

His first encounter with Crichton also served to intensify the conflict with Crais, who was thoughtfully chosen to share the honor of being the main course. Have to admit Maldis knew what he was doing on that dish. Nothing like combining matches and gasoline to produce a negativity soufflé with a side order of death *a la carte*.

Too bad for Maldis that Crichton had seen enough movies to figure it out and attempt to calm things down. It didn't work, but hey, he tried.

Maldis was eventually defeated, but returned for a rematch in an attempt to get his life back. He was even nastier than before—that calculated walk he took over Zhaan's body had me cringing and roaring for his blood. Oh, yeah, he's *really* bad to have dragged that level of reaction from me. But I respect him for being able to inspire such rage. I was very relieved when our heroes made their escape and left him well behind.

All things considered, two episodes worth of Maldis were plenty. I'd hate to think what he'd have done to raise the bar for a third round.

NATIRA: IS THAT HER OUTFIT OR IS SHE REALLY NAKED?

Any guys out there with an H. R. Giger fetish? Have we got the babe for you! The trouble is the exotically dangerous Natira used to be Scorpy's main squeeze, and how do you follow an act like that? Better have plenty of currency mixed with lots of power and influence or you won't impress her. She only respects strength equal to or exceeding her own. Be very, very careful. She's deadly serious about her pleasures.

Natira does have a hobby: collecting eyeballs, especially blue ones. Ew.

In her part of the universe she had absolute authority and held it tight; she was very aware of how quickly that kind of control could vanish. She was careful and smart, but all it took was a short stopover by the crew of the Moya to send her spiraling into failure and on to Scorpius' dren list.

That is known as a Very Bad Place. Just ask Crichton.

THE SCARRANS: YOU'RE GONNA NEED A BIGGER GUN

Okay, these guys were just not-so-plain over the top. Nightmare looks, dang near bullet (or little yellow bolts of light) proof, fatally strong, equipped with that Heat Thing, smart if not always clever, inflexible to any ideas outside of their own, and the winners of the gold medal for possessing the nastiest bad breath in the galaxy. They're aptly named, being just plain scary!

Fortunately we didn't see too many of them throughout the run of the show, though they were referred to often enough. They were best served in small but highly effective doses, kind of like Tabasco sauce for those of us with wimpy palates. (I know people who can drink that stuff down like soda on a hot day, and they frighten me, they really do.) When I see a Scarran emerging from some dark lair I just want to hide behind the couch. Not that it will do much good. I *have* to look, to see what they're up to, kind of like not being able to turn away from an imminent train wreck.

How might galactic history have been different had some distant Scarran ancestor with the munchies not sampled the pretty flowers?

A Scarran with brains. We're so frelled.

GRAYZA: MAE WEST'S E-VUL SISTER

What a babe. Fantastic features, hypnotic eyes and the ability to turn men into instant love machines whether they liked it or not. She was bad and beautiful, but rather too single-minded in the pursuit of her goals. Whatever The Plan, it dang well better have been *her* idea or it wasn't gonna happen.

When thwarted—watch out. She didn't take failure, much less humiliation from her boy toys, at all well. Scorpius got on her bad side and only escaped by the skin of his fangs. I'm surprised Crichton survived her amorous embraces, though he had an ace in the hole thanks to a little assist from Granny Noranti's medicine cabinet. With a gal like Grayza you need all the help you can get, plus a good set of legs to run like hell—providing she hasn't cut you off at the knees.

BRACA: CUTE, BUT HIS HEART (AND OTHER VITAL ORGANS) BELONGS TO DADDY

It was those big expressive eyes and that rarely seen smile that got to me. I *know* he was working with the bad guys, but gosh-oh-golly, I bet he was *fun* on his day off.

Braca's a Company Man, through and through, first following Scorpius, then Grayza, then back again with his half-breed daddy. In his heart he never really left. Theirs was an oddball combo, rightly compared to *The Simpsons'* Mr. Burns and Smithers. (*Feel* the love!)

Braca achieved the unparalleled position of being someone that Scorpius could trust and depend upon, and he even inspired a portion of affection from the dude. That could be a very scary thing, but Braca seemed to take it all in stride. His chief quality was unswerving loyalty no matter what; he chose not to have a life beyond the aims of those he served. He helped Scorpy progress his goals even when playing the game meant shooting the boss in the back.

Not all of us are that lucky.

HARVEY: BAD GUY, GOOD GUY AND ALL-ROUND PAIN IN THE FEK

Haven't we all got a Voice in our head? You know, the one that nags us constantly, is never satisfied with anything we do and reproaches us for every fault, whether real or imagined. Unchecked, that Voice can eat through the skull like boiling sulphuric acid.

Well, this one was *worse*, and no amount of therapy could shut him the frell up.

Harvey was real, first a chip, then an echo of a chip, inside Crichton's head, and he was dang near impossible to lose. And he looked like Scorpius. Nice. What a companion for your nightmares, daymares and various unscheduled subconscious zone-outs.

Sometimes he was useful, since Crichton would occasionally call on him for help in making tricky decisions involving Scorpius, but at his worst Harvey was a right bastard, as bad as his old man. He got his fangs pulled in a big way when Scorpius removed the chip from Crichton's brain, but like grape juice on a white carpet, you never can quite get the stain out no matter how strong the bleach. Harvey just kept oozing back to the surface.

And yet I liked him. He was just trying to survive. And maybe he was driving Crichton crazy because—being trapped within the confines of another's memory and experience—he'd gone a whole lot fahrbot himself.

MOYA'S CREW: "WE HAVE MET THE ENEMY AND HE IS US." —WALT KELLY

Crichton's best friends supported him, saved his life, drove him nuts and, on occasion, did their level best to kill him and each other. Now, the latter brand of violence was usually because they were under the influence of some Alien Thing that was messing about with their normal—such as it was—behavior, but Moya's inhabitants were the ultimate in motley crews of misfits, so anarchy could be expected with or without outside interference. Here are my favorite standouts:

D'ARGO: SOMEONE GET THE THORAZINE, QUICK!

Ka D'Argo was the first of the lot to actually strike Our Hero, unless you want to count the DRD assault that injected John with the translator microbes. (Hey—ow!) The Luxan warrior had a lot on his plate what with trying to escape the Peacekeepers, and was in no mood to deal with yet another problem, but he was cranky at the best of times. The sheer number of assaults he committed on Crichton and the rest of the crew must have equaled or exceeded those executed by all the guest villains put together. One would hope that D'Argo would be considerate enough to take an anger management course to more constructively deal with his Luxan hyper-rage glitch. He never did, though Scorpius did make an effort to coalesce the group by enrolling all the guys in that mystical retreat course. (Who'd have thought it?)

It worked. Sort of. For that episode.

The truth is we *liked* it when D'Argo was cranky.

He's just so *good* at it.

AERYN: GETTING TO KNOW YOU, ESPECIALLY THE KILL ZONES

Crichton's dream girl? Zangblats, Our Hero needs therapy then, as this lady was a hair-trigger killing machine. The first time they met she beat the dren out of him, and he just didn't take the hint. (Or perhaps he *liked* that sort of thing. Yow.) The woman was a walking tommy gun and thus best employed when pointed away from one's vulnerable parts, but he patiently kept at her, and finally, crazily, she *did* come around to his side. To the point of having his *baby*. Hard to believe, but it did happen. We saw it.

Still, there were times when she relapsed. Don't get between her and crackers, or you might live to regret it.

Then again, you might not.

RYGEL: TOAD IN THE HOLE... WITH A PULSE PISTOL

In his worldview, it wasn't selling out, it was cashing in, and heaven help you if you got in his way. You could only ever trust Rygel to lead you merrily into death and destruction, all the while assuring you that he was in control and had your best interests at heart. Out of all the crew he was the most obviously dangerous in terms of fraxing you over, and the first to vote for leaving longtime companions to certain doom if it made him a profit or saved his Hynerian hiney.

Yet for all that they kept him aboard. I think it was a Size Thing. We tolerate a lot of outrageous dren from small children, the kind of behavior that would land a full-sized adult in jail, so perhaps the same attitude applied here. It's hard to take such bluster seriously when it's coming from so diminutive a body. But it paid to be aware: he was usually armed and dangerous. It wasn't just because he was a Dominar that you should never let him see your back. Given the right circs, he'd just as soon stick a knife in it—or a fork, should you prove to be edible.

I'd be curious to learn whether his negative qualities were his alone or endemic to all Hynerians. If the latter is true, then how the frell did they ever survive as a species?

STARK: SEE ABOVE NOTE ABOUT THORAZINE

I'd really hate to have to live inside this fahrbot's head. He had only short bouts of sanity, and the rest of the time he was either staring and too quiet in a corner or froth-mouth hyperactive. His relationship with Zhaan helped calm him down for a time, and when truly needed to help in an emergency, he'd rise to the occasion, but the guy was a decidedly loose plasma cannon in need of restraint.

Still, he was likeble if you didn't mind the "my-side-your-side" kink, and he tried very hard to reclaim mental normalcy, though those attempts had been known to be badly misdirected. After Zhaan, Crichton was the one person who best understood Stark, having been in the Aurora Chair himself. His was only a brief taste of the torture; poor Stark had to endure countless sessions, so it's clear John saw what might well have been his *own* fate manifested in the man.

Yikes.

SCORPIUS: OH. OH! OH, MY!

In our very first glimpse of Scorpius all he did was just *stand* there, a still, dark figure, mostly in silhouette. He didn't say a word, but it was enough.

We knew. This one was *special*.

The reaction of all the tough guys looking his way tipped us off that he was scaring the dren out of them. Some species would rather have bitten off their own mivonks than have to deal with him. Crichton picked up on this vibe and knew to show some caution, but it wasn't enough, not nearly enough. Scorpius was a whole new class of bad, raising the bar for everyone.

As a villain, Scorpius worked so well and perfectly on so many levels one could devote whole books to him. Poor John had no idea what he was in for with the guy. Just when he thought he'd gotten ahead, the circs changed, and Our Hero was flat on his face with a boot on his neck. Or strapped to the Aurora Chair, or to any number of other unpleasant furnishings with or without the top of his skull in place. Scorpy did seem to have a penchant for the Bondage Thing, and he was way too good at it.

Like with Crais, the relationship Crichton had with Scorpius was a hate-is-a-many-splendored and highly complex thing, but to an even greater degree. It developed from just another good guy/bad guy conflict into a creepy mutual-necessity partnership, involving lots of torture, yelling, shooting, hitting each other with large heavy objects and blowing up big, expensive places. Much more of it and they'd have been on the red-eye to Vegas for a Chapel-O'-Love quickie.

Scorpius was not one of nature's beauties, but undeniably charismatic. Like the James Bond song said, when he walked in a room you could feel the heat. That was his Scarran blood making you sweat. He worked hard to keep it under control, literally trying to keep his cool. His great asset was that beautiful, light-touch velvet voice of his, so persuasive it was almost hypnotic, especially when he was purring. But you had to be ready to duck when the rough lower tones surfaced, which they did whenever Crichton did something disagreeable, like breathing. Scorpy in a rage was not a pretty sight.

One of the few who ever really succeeded getting under that tough Scarran hide in an effective way was Crais—who finally got his revenge for various issues. Crais had things good, more or less, until Scorpius usurped his Command Carrier out from under him and treated him to a ride in the Aurora Chair. That would be enough to send anyone around the twist, but Crais was the wrong man to pick on. He was not as forgiving as Crichton, nor did he have a Harvey in his head to keep him distracted and under control.

Crais' revenge, blowing up the Command Carrier from the inside out, cost him his life, but it also left Scorpius in a very bad place. That incredible sight of him on the stairs with the water flooding down and destruction everywhere he looked said it all.

I don't envy Scorpius, who had the ultimate in bad childhoods, which explains much about his outlook on life.

I wouldn't want to meet him (too dangerous).

But oh, man, he's so frelling *fascinating*.

Dren, I'm so fraxed over this dude it ain't funny.

JOHN CRICHTON: BUREAUCRACY'S WORST NIGHTMARE—CATASTROPHIC CHANGE

Yes, it had to come to this: the truth is that Johnny-boy is his own worst enemy. He learned from the best. Dealing with experts in badness like Crais and Scorpius, having Harvey popping up at the worst possible moments to put in his two cents and getting tortured and shot at on an almost daily basis, not to mention dealing with a touchy girlfriend and various homicidal shipmates. Some of it just had to rub off.

From the point of view of the Peacekeepers, and countless others in the Uncharted Territories and Tormented Space, our good-guy *hero* was a mass-murdering psycho who should have been put down yesterday, if not sooner. It's true; just look at things from their viewpoint. When John appeared on your event horizon, you ran and didn't look back.

How many deaths could we lay at his feet? I'm sure there's a Web site somewhere that's made a rough calculation for the totals. All I can say for sure is that it was a LOT, starting with Tauvo's accidental offing and ending—for the moment—with the uncounted lives swallowed up by the giant wormhole weapon he activated. From the time of his arrival in the *Farscape* side of the galaxy, John was an unstoppable death factory.

Okay, granted, some of the things he had to deal with more often than not deserved to be taken out. Not a few of them qualified for the "why'd you wait so long?" category, but innocent victims aplenty were left fallen and bleeding on the paths he trod. In some cases, by allowing a bad guy to survive, he certainly cost others their lives.

But John was aware of (most) of his actions, and the horror of it caught up with him now and then. No wonder he had bouts of insanity, whether drug- or Harvey-induced, or faked. No wonder, on an extended stop on Earth, he was unable to tell his family and friends about his adventures. How could he possibly have revealed that dark side of himself to them? Better that they assume he was still the nice, brave, brainy guy they knew and loved than let them find out about the rivers of blood he'd waded through in his short but spectacularly violent sojourn on the other side of the galaxy.

But—it wasn't his fault. He was mostly a victim of circumstance, and to survive he chose to defend himself with the same amount of force that was inflicted upon him. Crichton gave as good as he got. He didn't like it, but he did rise to meet the challenge.

Oh, yeah, he's *baaaaaad*.

The one thing that saves his soul from total destruction is that, given the *choice*, he preferred not to go medieval on anyone's ass. He would walk away if he could, only it wasn't always an option. The beings and places he encountered were unconscionably violent, for this was a section of an aggressive universe where nearly everyone had an agenda, and no one had a problem stealing the butter off the other guy's fritter.

If there's anything we've learned, it's that, truly, the universe *is* out to get him, and just as truly, he ain't gonna let that happen.

And don't we love him for it?

You betcha!

P. N. Elrod is the print-published author of over twenty novels and twenty short stories, and is best known for her ongoing hard-boiled noir series, The Vampire Files. She has cowritten three novels with actor/writer Nigel Bennett. She's edited three collections, including coediting Stepping Through the Stargate *for BenBella Books, and is work-*

ing on a fourth, and writing, writing, writing. Her Web site is www.vampwriter.com. She would love to buy Harvey a drink and talk about Crichton's lesser-traveled subconscious paths, especially if it includes dish on where he got those leather pants.

(Reprinted from last cycle's third-quarter issue of *Intergalactic Imperium and Hegemony Illustrated: News for Effective Empire Builders, King-Makers, and Power Brokers*)

SUPERIOR VILLAINY

SIX SECRETS OF THE PROS

CHARLENE BRUSSO

Being a good villain is not simple, as any James Bond fan knows. The first rule—so simple yet so rarely followed—is to kill your enemy now! Don't put him in a fiendishly clever device that will kill him in a few hours, and, above all, don't rush off to celebrate your victory because he is "as good as dead." This is an obvious one, I admit. For more subtle insights we need to turn from James Bond to Farscape, *and from me to* Farscape *columnist Charlene Brusso.*

Hatred between the Peacekeepers and the Scarran Empire has provided fertile ground for dark deeds and blood-fueled skirmishes for hundreds of cycles. Couple this with the recent and appalling devastation of a region on the border between Tormented Space and the Uncharted Territories by a directed wormhole weapon, and it's no surprise we're seeing a renewed interest in contemporary villains. The lifestyle is a seductive one, encompassing vast wealth, influence and power. But one shouldn't jump onto such a career path without first taking time for careful consideration.

Let's be realistic: less than one villain in a thousand has the mivonks to make a successful career out of it. (This does not include the banal evil of petty bureaucrats elected or appointed to public office, or those allowed seats on any corporate board of directors.) A life of treachery demands intelligence as well as ruthless daring. A skilled villain must be able to think on her feet; she must be capable of assessing risks, taking chances and deftly removing obstacles from her path.

It is our hope that by following this step-by-step outline, you will learn the fundamentals necessary to lead a fruitful and satisfying life of duplicity, intimidation and ultimate power.

AMBITION AND COMMITMENT

When it comes to villainous characteristics, ambition and commitment are at the top of the list. You must know exactly what you want, and you must want it so badly you will do anything to get it, whether you hunger for pure knowledge or superior technology, wealth beyond avarice, political power or simply revenge.

A celebrated recent case of revenge—and, some say, precursor to all the other events which precipitated the current uneasy stalemate between the Peacekeepers and the Scarrans—involved the renegade Peacekeeper Captain Bialar Crais. A decorated officer, well respected and seemingly assured of an illustrious military career, Crais threw it all away to hunt down the human John Crichton, whom he held responsible for the death of his younger brother Tauvo. Whether Crichton deliberately brought about Tauvo's death is beside the point. Within a cycle Crais' obsession had cost him his commission as well as his ship and left him tragically, irreversibly contaminated, thus destroying any hope he might have had of returning to his former life.

Rejected by the PK hierarchy to which he'd previously dedicated his life, Crais then allied with Crichton and the other renegades aboard the Leviathan Moya. He gained his final revenge by using a defective Leviathan offspring to commit suicide while destroying an entire Command Carrier—and doing so under the very noses of two PK officials who should have known better: wormhole scientist Scorpius and Commandant Grayza. Though Crais is no longer with us to provide insight into his actions, it seems clear that his PK background allowed him to accurately predict Grayza's overconfidence in the carrier's security and the skills of her own spies. With Scorpius removed from command by Grayza and distracted by Crichton's addition to his wormhole research, Crais had a clear path to his goal.

Crais' grand mania illustrates the deep focus which separates mere crime from true darkness. A professional villain lets nothing, not even previous failure, stand in his way. Anything which does must be annihilated in an appropriately dramatic manner.

Recall the ever-widening path of destruction left in John Crichton's wake as the human strove to solve the puzzle of wormholes. En route to his goal, he blithely assisted in the destruction of not one but *two* very expensive wormhole research facilities. He destroyed the highly secure and secret Scarran base known as Katratzi with a primitive fission device, and eventually escalated his attacks with the annihilation of several PK Command Carriers and Scarran dreadnoughts in an uncontrolled demonstration of a working wormhole weapon.

Crichton's commitment—and amazing success—is especially noteworthy considering his homeworld's isolation and his complete lack of experience with other intelligent species. With hindsight it seems as if any number of people should have had the opportunity to stop this lone human, but in a universe where Peacekeepers and Scarrans vied for supremacy, the wormhole knowledge hidden in Crichton's brain by the cryptic Ancients made him too valuable to kill. And Crichton took full advantage of this fact. With a little luck and an impressive ability to manipulate individuals to support his cause, he won against immense odds. While it is certainly possible that all humans are not as duplicitous and single-minded as Crichton, if they are as adaptable as he, the intelligent species of Known Space would do well to avoid Earth.

We cannot depart this topic without pointing out the commitment of half-breed Scarran/Sebacean scientist Scorpius. Despite setbacks that would have overwhelmed most others—from his half-breed status to the loss of a sturdy Gammak Base unfortunately situated on an oil-covered moon, as well as direct interference from a superior officer that led to the loss of a PK Command Carrier, a cycle's worth of valuable research and his own position within the PK hierarchy—Scorpius refused to give up his quest to defeat the Scarrans. Having lost everything, he rose to the occasion and before long had manipulated his way aboard the Leviathan Moya, forcing Crichton to accept him, however tenuously, as an ally. As PK Officer Braca, Scorpius' most valued assistant, has said, the thing about Scorpius is that, "He survives. He always survives" ("Incubator," 3-11).

APPEARANCE

A villain is a creature of extremes, a point you should to take into account when selecting a "look." Nowhere is appearance more important than in the way you present yourself to allies, enemies and victims.

Certain wardrobe rules appear universal. Black is, and always has been, the traditional color of villainy. Both slimming and dramatic, one can't help but seem more self-contained and in control when wearing the color of deep space. Consider Peacekeeper uniforms and armor: tight black, black, and more black, relieved only by a startling red, the color of Sebacean (and human) blood. Remember how quickly Crichton replaced his sloppy Earth clothing with more businesslike Peacekeeper garb? Baggy orange IASA jumpsuits may have their purposes on Earth, but they get you no respect in the Uncharted Territories.

Scarrans are also drawn toward scarlet and ebony, particularly at higher castes; but while the PK uniform is generally streamlined and efficient no matter the wearer's rank, high-level Scarrans wear jaggedly ornamental clothing. Emperor Staleek's long-skirted scarlet uniform of layered diagonals and razor-sharp edges suggests a weapon covered with blood, a resonant image in a culture where one advances by killing one's superiors. War Minister Akhna's funereal black is equally imposing, but her ornate headpiece has been known to destroy the effect outside Scarran society—as noted by the iconoclastic Crichton.

For sheer drama, it's hard to beat Nebari such as Varla, whose monochromatic features, supporting homogeneity at home, make them stand out all the more outside Nebari Prime. Their stark appearance—white hair, gray-white skin and austere gray and black clothing—resonates with the grim Nebari ideals of social discipline and spiritual denial.

Some villains, such as Peacekeeper Commandant Grayza, fancy intimidating others with a striking, even decadent, appearance. Grayza accomplishes this with dramatic makeup and sumptuous black fabrics tailored to show curves in all the right places. This style is most useful when dealing with members of the opposite sexual orientation, particularly those from a very sober social background. It won't accomplish everything, however, and you should never expect it to. Unless you enjoy such nicknames as "Commandant Cleavage," you may invite more scorn than submissive attention by choosing this route.

Many villains find extreme ugliness or just plain bizarre features to be more useful than beauty. Such a look is usually less trouble to maintain and tends to be more memorable than mere physical attractiveness. With her impressive bulk swaddled in mechanic's coveralls, Furlow is no beauty, but her keen wit and wide vocabulary of invective make her unforgettable. While her clothing is well suited to her lifestyle and work, it also telegraphs that she is a serious businesswoman with a preference for multitasking and little time for foolishness.

Consider the genetics researcher Namtar, who used his own body as an experimental specimen—so much so that no one could have guessed his original species. Namtar's ambitions, including his disdain for any kind of "natural order," are made perfectly clear by his jumbled appearance. Unfortunately, such genetic enhancements are unstable and prone to failure without careful maintenance.

Scorpius, with his lanky yet graceful body and sunken features, carries himself as a sadomasochistic dandy in formfitting black leather and tails worthy of a ballroom dancer. His stylish armor has absolutely nothing to do with scientific research, but in a military setting it has everything to do with claiming resources and power. Scorpius' taste was probably influenced by his sometime lover and ally Natira, a grotesque beauty with a flair for fetish and the cash to buy the best.

The very nature and independence of villains gives them a great deal of latitude in the choice and design of a signature outfit. In the end, whether one chooses to appear colorful or serious, theatrical or disarmingly utilitarian, the goal should always be the same: *be memorable.*

SECRETS: RUMOR AND REPUTATION

Long before others meet you, they will form a mental image of you based on stories they've heard. Can you picture a Scarran agent carrying out an interrogation without imagining the fetid and painful heat of its scorching breath? What about the impossible task of returning fire when ambushed by Kalish renegades who shoot from cover, exploiting their ability to alter their personal gravity, standing sideways on a wall or upside down on a ceiling?

Rumors can be powerful, and it's well worth the effort to pay attention to the ones circulating about you. If there are none, you might consider starting some. Rumors precede you, introduce you and set the foundation for your working relationship with every new acquaintance.

Maldis, a self-proclaimed sorcerer, possessed the ability to enslave minds with hallucinations to feed his hunger for pain and other strong

emotions. He billed himself as "all-powerful," and such was his reputation that he managed to hold the entire population of a planet in
thrall until the Delvian mystic Zhaan drove him from that world. Maldis proved resilient, but instead of claiming some other world, he went
hunting Zhaan to avenge his defeat—and was destroyed. Although it
is tempting to regret his loss, it's unlikely Maldis could ever have been
a large-scale success. How can you hope to control others if you don't
know when to hold yourself in check?

The most successful professional villains recommend cultivating an
aura of mystery as well as menace. Never let all your secrets, or all your
abilities, be known. This tactic hides weaknesses as well as strengths
from your enemies. It is also an inexpensive way to increase your intimidation factor. Nothing trumps pure imagination when it comes to an
otherwise rational being's ability to think the worst of somebody else.

This tactic certainly assisted Commandant Grayza as she manipulated and schemed her way up through the Peacekeeper Command structure. Universally acknowledged as a tough officer, she held secret what
she considered her strongest asset: a special gland installed in her throat
which manufactures a powerful pheromone. This compound, a powerful sexual attractant, left males of more than one species subservient
and desperate for her attention.

Unfortunately Grayza failed to anticipate, firstly, the existence of an antidote to the pheromone—one which enabled Crichton to withstand her
manipulation. Secondly, she mistakenly assumed that a man exposed to the
compound on multiple occasions would remain loyal even when free of its
effects. As Braca's betrayal demonstrated, this was far from the case. Without the personal charisma or strength of character necessary to reinforce the
pheromone's effect, Grayza's ability to sway others was greatly reduced.

Grayza's example makes clear that the best equipment means little
when the villain doesn't have the sheer presence needed to back it up. A
Peacekeeper scientist known primarily for his half-Scarran heritage and
calculated brutality, Scorpius commanded the PK troops at his research
facilities through fear as much as respect. Little did they—or Peacekeeper Command—suspect exactly what drove him so obsessively, nor
what his half-breed biology demanded in exchange for the abilities he
possessed. Thanks to the internal cooling system designed in secret by
Diagnosan Tocot, Scorpius not only survived but thrived. The problem
with secrets, however, is that they have a way of leaking out. In this
case, it was sheer bad luck that Crichton learned about it and devised a
scheme which nearly killed his nemesis.

Such vulnerabilities are present in even the most powerful villains, a challenge to survival as well as success. Secrecy and trustworthy assistants (see **Toadies and Sycophants**, below) are a must.

Villains are, of course, expected to be accomplished liars, but you must also know when to tell the truth. If someone asks you point-blank whether you were the Scarran commander responsible for exterminating a newly established Sebacean colony, or whether, like the infamous Selto Durka, you ordered the torture of prisoners in your care for no reason other than your own entertainment, you should calmly admit your part in the action. Such admissions can only add to your reputation, as well as creating a false expectation that you will also tell the truth about other, more important, things.

As a corollary, be certain never to kill *all* your enemies during any given operation. Always leave someone alive to spread—and exaggerate—the story of your deeds.

ALLIANCES AND BARGAINS

In a perfect world, every villain would be born into a life of wealth and privilege, guaranteeing each the resources needed to bribe the greedy and intimidate the weak-willed. In our less-than-ideal world, one should never discount the value of simple blackmail, theft, murder and strategic alliance.

Alliance arises from the promise of mutual gain, a concept which carries weight with all races across the galaxy no matter what their form or provenance. Journal entries by the pilot of the Leviathan Moya describe a being named Mu-Quillus, a possibly unique humanoid with claws, a skull crested with horny protuberances and crusty skin with the approximate texture and color of cooling lava. Mu-Quillus possessed the unique ability to change state at will—from a physical body to pure energy and back again. Discovered living within a distant star's corona, he had been hired by salvagers to lure Leviathans toward the star, where they would be killed and their equipment cannibalized.

By most accounts, money is the most universal incentive, whether in Known Space or the Uncharted Territories. Even the most dangerous jobs can be made to seem reasonable if the price is right. Consider the motley crew of mercenaries contracted by Crichton and his cohort to help break into a notorious shadow depository: a Vorcarian Blood Tracker, a fire-belching Sheyang, a Tavlek and a crew of Zenetan pirates. As you might expect, such a team of misfits could not exist for long before one faction betrayed the others. Keep in mind: the more beings involved, the shorter your scheme's life span, and the less likely your plan is to succeed.

Good working alliances are more valuable than Borinium ingots—and more dangerous than an uncontrolled wormhole. Allies know what you want, and where you may be vulnerable. Should your relationship with them become too expensive, they will not hesitate to sell you out to the highest bidder. Neither should you.

Consider the crafty mechanic and engineer Furlow, a low-key figure well below the radar of most power structures. One look around her run-down shop at the backwater world called Dam-Ba-Da Depot might convince you that she could never be a threat to anyone. Yet give her a copy of Crichton's early wormhole data and within a few cycles she's solved some major puzzles, including the space stabilizer problem which stymied Scorpius—and arranged to sell her knowledge: first to the Charrids, then the Scarrans, then the Peacekeepers, and finally to whoever would pay the most.

Even long-term alliances with old friends must be subject to constant reevaluation. Natira, administrator of the shadow depository mentioned previously, had no qualms about double-crossing her old lover Scorpius for mere money. Ironically she failed to predict Scorpius' plan to sacrifice her in order to gain Crichton's knowledge of wormholes. That each would turn on the other at the same time is more amusing than surprising. Old friends are a treasure, but no successful villain puts them before his business.

This precarious style of alliance is particularly notable in Scarran culture, where blackmail and assassination for political advancement are considered everyday activities. Lower-caste warrior Sastaretski Cargn schemed to plant a puppet king on the throne of the independent Sebacean Breakaway Colonies, a tactic he gambled would give him control of the Colonies, which occupy a valuable position between Peacekeeper space and the Imperium. Cargn's plan crumbled for two reasons: first, his chosen puppet was too weak to be useful, and second, he failed to anticipate covert interference from the Peacekeepers, who had an agent in place with orders to do whatever was necessary to keep his puppet off the throne.

Swinging in the opposite direction, the Scarran official Jenek was too cautious in his planning when Crichton's lover Aeryn Sun accidentally fell into his hands. Learning she was pregnant, Jenek saw a sure route to Imperial favor. If the fetus was indeed Crichton's, then its DNA would contain the same wormhole information encoded in Crichton's DNA. Unfortunately Jenek lost the advantage by failing to remove the fetus and sample its DNA when he had the chance. Had he done so, he would have been able to extract the necessary data after Crichton rescued Sun. His hesitation left the advantage to Crichton, and undoubtedly cost the Scarrans an early victory against the Peacekeepers.

One of the most curious—and intimate—alliances on record involves Crichton, Scorpius and a neural clone on a chip which Scorpius implanted in Crichton's brain to uncover his wormhole knowledge. Although Scorpius removed the chip a cycle or so later, the clone "Harvey" was left behind in Crichton's mind, subject to Crichton's displeasure. Betrayed by his creator, Harvey became a somewhat annoying ally, most useful when he altered the human's energy signature, enabling him to lie to Scorpius about his willingness to help build a wormhole weapon. At last report, however, the clone had displayed yet another layer in its mission programming, revealing itself as something of a "sleeper agent" who continues to work for Scorpius.

TOADIES AND SYCOPHANTS

Part ally, part assistant and part cheering section, a sycophant is far more than simply a trustworthy employee who handles the details. In the ideal villain/toady partnership, it is understood that the loyal sycophant will rise in prestige and wealth in the villain's wake. If you're considering the idea of genetically altering some wayward race in order to create a convenient and eager servant class, you would do well to consider the example of ro-NA, obsequious Jakench servant to the Royal Family of the Sebacean Breakaway Colonies. Bred to serve—and to prize her employer's rewards—her loyalty proved to be too easily purchased, perpetually vulnerable to a better offer.

At best, some believe the villain/toady relationship can approach actual friendship. There does seem to be something in this theory. Consider the relationship between Scorpius and his Peacekeeper aide Braca. Braca cut his teeth as a toady, so to speak, while serving under Bialar Crais, where he rose in rank by helping to distract PK Command from the fact that Crais had, against their orders, abandoned his responsibilities to pursue John Crichton. After Crais was falsely implicated as Crichton's ally, Braca was swept into Scorpius' employ and rewarded with command of Crais' ship while Scorpius reestablished his laboratory there and continued the pursuit. Then Commandant Grayza shut down Scorpius' research and made Braca an offer he couldn't refuse.

Forced by Grayza to shoot Scorpius in what was meant to be an execution, Braca truly began to regret joining Grayza's side. She treated him like a convenience rather than an officer, and he abhorred her plans to build a peace with the Scarrans. Biding his time, he was perfectly placed to take advantage of Grayza's bumbling at Katratzi and quite legally remove her from command when her so-called peace talks fell apart. Then he learned that Scorpius was still alive. After Katratzi, one of his first acts as commander of Grayza's old ship was to find Scorpius and give him sanctuary, reestablishing their relationship and allowing the scientist to once again pursue his dream of a wormhole weapon which would defeat the Scarrans once and for all.

This kind of loyalty is rare enough between officers. Between sycophant and master, it is truly beautiful, and an example to which we can all strive.

FINAL THOUGHTS: VILLAINS AND HEROES

We would be remiss if we ignored one final topic: the deep bond between long-term heroes and villains. If you stay in the business long enough, you will eventually find yourself opposed by the same do-gooder again and again. At some point you may be forced to work together toward a mutual goal. Over time you will come to know each other well. You may even find a surprisingly mutual respect growing between you and your nemesis. And one day you may even need to kill him.

This will be the most difficult thing you've ever done. It's not unusual to respect your most virulent opposition, but some villains over time actually come to like, even love, their nemeses. The game can be titillating, but *beware*. Heroes in their deepest hearts *must* oppose you and your goals, or they cannot stay heroes. And unless you can completely seduce them to your side, your hero—if a true hero—will oppose you unto death.

It is the nature of villains and heroes to fascinate each other. Dark and light, each is the other's doppelgänger, contorted images of beauty and ugliness reflected by fate.

But you must know when to look away. Become mesmerized and you will lose everything: all that you've worked for, everything for which you've sacrificed. Worst of all, you will lose yourself.

"Don't be a hero, John," wily Furlow once advised Crichton. "Always be the one to walk away" ("Infinite Possibilities, Part Two: Icarus Abides," 3-15).

A villain is more than just a criminal, far more than a mere breaker of laws. Dedicated villains aspire to greatness. The best become legends.

Charlene Brusso is a science fiction author and science writer with a B.S. in physics and astronomy from the University of Rochester. She has written for an array of magazines and venues, from Amazon.com and InQuest Gamer *to Publishers Weekly and Playgirl. For a time, she was the* Farscape *columnist at SPACE.com. She is also a founding member of the Neural Clone Anti-Defamation League.*

MASKS OF TRANSFORMATION

KEVIN ANDREW MURPHY

It actually worked. We complained and we protested. We wrote and we called. And it happened. We got season five, in the form of a brilliant, action-packed and heart-breaking miniseries. The series—always intended to run for five seasons—was allowed to reach its natural conclusion. We can revel in our triumph. Now...how about a feature film?

"Crichton, whenever we cross paths, I leave the encounter transformed, and none more so than on this occasion." —Stark, *The Peacekeeper Wars*

THERE'S A CURIOUS THING about masks: they at once hide and transform, can be used both to deceive and to reveal the inner self. Take up a mask and you're one person, assuming that role. Relinquish it and you're another, though not necessarily the same as you were when you began, since to wear a mask is to live another's life, and it is very hard to live without being changed by the experience. As in a quest, the wearer is thrust into an unexpected role he is forced to live up to. Think of Dorothy, the small and meek, trying to get to the Emerald City to ask the Great and Powerful Oz to send her back to Kansas, only to find herself thrust into the role of the heroine, having to face down wicked witches and steal their broomsticks. Or Oz, the charlatan hiding behind the mask of the great and powerful wizard only to find, after his unmasking, that he was not such a bad wizard after all.

The story of *Farscape: The Peacekeeper Wars* was all about transformations, revelations and admissions, the beginning of some quests and the conclusion of many more. And along the way, there were no small number of masks, not to mention more than a few references to *The Wizard of Oz*.

At the beginning of the tale, after a hellish vision of interstellar war and flaming starships done in the black and red hues of a Brueghel apocalypse, the scene switches to the placid pale green and aqua of a tranquil underwater scene, serene as the bottom of a goldfish bowl. There we find Rygel—proud, selfish, egotistical Rygel—swimming about the ocean floor of a water planet. This, however, is not for his own pleasure—though he does find a moment to suck up a passing fish—but to find and gather all the crystalized bits of John Crichton and Aeryn Sun, transformed to this state at the end of the last episode of season four. The mask of pride he usually wears on his face has slipped aside for a moment, allowing us to see below the surface to his inner core of care and concern, though once he comes back to the water's surface his protective mask of pride and indignation is firmly back in place; he complains both about the bits of Aeryn and Crichton he's been carrying in his stomachs and about having ruined his manicure as he scoured the bottom for their pieces.

The next mask is set aside as Moya arrives and the Eidolons order the concealment canopy lowered, a veil of invisibility that hides their society from the outside world—much like the spell of invisibility which Glinda placed on Oz in the later Oz books, and with an identical function. The invisible canopy, like the helm of Hades long before in Greek myth, allowed them to operate unseen by the outside world, to be as the dead (over whom Hades ruled). The Eidolons are the last of a race of Peacemakers, hunted to near extinction, and the name "Eidolon" itself—though not mentioned in the course of the show—is the term for an enlightened spirit or benevolent ghost, one who comes back to aid the living. An apt name, for their power, aided by their inner sight, was once to sense others' needs and desires and foster reason in their minds, so that all could come to agreement without need for war.

The faces of the Eidolons are almost masks themselves, initially appearing the same as a human's or Sebacean's except for where the face is divided by raised seams that come to a star in the center of the forehead. When they will it, however, they can open up their faces in the exact same manner as a sacred Haida or Kwakiutl transformation mask, one face splitting apart to reveal another beneath. With the Eidolons, the hidden face is the mystic third eye of Eastern legend, flanked by two smaller eyes on either side so as to not be quite so obvious, questing about to sense the desires of the universe.

The next transformation as the story progresses is that from death—or at least death for all practical purposes—to life. The remains of Aeryn and Crichton are restored to the moment they were crystalized two months before, as they announce that their separate lives will be one. In short, John yells, "Hey, we're gonna get married!"—another transformation of life and another rite of passage. But with their restoration, another transformation of life has occurred—Aeryn feels somewhat different than before. Before crystalization, she had been pregnant, and now she suddenly isn't. After the initial shock and grief, they realize that their offspring might still be in inside Rygel—which it is. However, the child has implanted in Rygel and, due to its fragility, can't be transplanted back to Aeryn yet.

Instead they proceed with the wedding. The High Priestess of the Eidolons begins their marriage ceremony, but the festivities are interrupted by Scorpius and Sikozu's arrival via a troop carrier, Scorpius still after the wormhole knowledge locked in Crichton's head. While hiding from the arriving ship, Noranti sees an ancient symbol—a star, bearing a strong resemblance to the star in the center the Eidolon's foreheads—and puts this together with her own knowledge to realize that the Eidolons they know are in fact descendants of the ancient Eidolons, some of whom the crew had brought out of a temporal suspension sometime prior. She reveals this knowledge to the Eidolons: both that she knows who they are, and that their ancestors exist once more—the same ancestors who possess the crucial knowledge they have lost regarding how to use their inner sight to bring about peace.

We see here, in rapid succession, the transformative power of knowledge: the desire for it, the possession of it, the revelation of it. The Eidolons are at once stripped bare of their protective anonymity and handed news of their greatest hope, as well as knowledge of their ancient culture. By the same token, Noranti goes from being viewed as a crazy old woman, ranting about arcana and esoterica that no one cares about anymore, to being a revered teacher and herald of wonderful news. Even Crichton wonders if the world is going mad, for the crazy lady, who he'd just been calling "Witchy-Poo" scant minutes before, is suddenly making sense.

It's resolved to have two Eidolons come aboard Moya and be taken to see their ancestors, to learn the knowledge which they might then use to negotiate peace between the Peacekeepers and the Scarrans. Scorpius insinuates himself into the group, still desiring to learn Crichton's secret knowledge, and Noranti stays behind to instruct the Eidolons, having found a place where her arcane knowledge is needed and useful, and thus comes to the end of her quest.

Onboard Moya, Rygel begins to perform the postponed marriage ceremony when suddenly a harpoon breaks through the ceiling like a giant iron chandelier, heralding an invasion by the Peacekeepers and some hired mercenaries. During the firefight, D'Argo remarks that he didn't think Aeryn had wanted children, to which she responds, showing her true emotions, "He wants it so badly. So I do." But this strips aside her mask for only a brief moment before it is back to battle and business. A more significant bit of unmasking comes with Crichton, who, when stressed, speaks in the terms of Earth and refers to the shaggy mercenary aliens as "The Electric Mayhem," the shaggy creatures that made up the band for *The Muppet Show*—like *Farscape*, a Henson creation, but more than that, part of Crichton and the audience's shared cultural knowledge of Earth. Crichton recognizes them as what they are, even if they don't understand his terms, and that recognition gives him insight in how to deal with them.

This is even more true after they arrive at the planet of the Eidolons, and after meeting with their old comrade, Jool, go to see the ancient Eidolons...where they are blown off with requests for time to go meditate. Hierarch Yondalao even mistakes Crichton for a Peacekeeper and asks him to clear the temple. Crichton, deciding to take up this role for a moment, jams the clip into his gun improperly and accidentally discharges the weapon, causing the hierarch to ask, "Are you assassin?" to which Crichton responds, "No, I'm just the guy without a brain." He then gestures to Stark, "The lion here would like some courage," then to Scorpius, "Tin man, he needs a heart," then to Rygel, "Toto here just wants an easy birth," and then to Pikal, the young Eidolon supplicant they've brought with them, "And Dorothy here, she is just looking for a way home." He shoves the young Eidolon forward and tells the hierarch, "Now, we're not going to be here tomorrow, so I suggest you take a long hard look at our broomstick. He is your heir, an Eidolon."

Crichton has the gift to see through masks to the heart of the situation. He likens himself to the Scarecrow, wise yet foolish at the same time, notes Stark's cowardice mixed with his core of bravery, Scorpius' coldness tinged with passion, Rygel's tendency for both being in danger and good at escape and Pikal's role as the ingenue who's trying to get back to his roots while at the same time serving as the prize which they have fetched at great danger to themselves to bring to the wizard who can solve all their problems.

Jool has come to the end of her quest and found her place among the ancient Eidolons and their temple, but after Crichton and company leave, the Scarrans bomb it. However, Crichton's skill at seeing to the heart of such matters continues with another *Wizard of Oz* reference. Captured by Emperor Staleek, locked in a chamber and told they will die if they don't turn over the wormhole technology, Crichton lists all the perils facing them, concluding with, "and the sand is trickling through the hourglass," a direct reference to the scene where Dorothy has been trapped by the Wicked Witch of the West, who wishes to get the all-powerful magic of the ruby slippers.

This, in fact, is key to understanding the story, since everyone wants the wormhole technology, just as everyone wants the ruby slippers—or at least enough powerful and dangerous people want it to make it the same difference. The writing in the sky is not *Surrender Dorothy* but *Surrender Crichton*.

Revelations continue. Chiana, using her new eyes in a more psychic sense than Crichton, sees into the hull of the Scarran ship so that D'Argo will know the vulnerable points to target. Meanwhile, Aeryn speaks with Hierarch Yondalao, who reveals a secret long wondered about: not only are the Peacekeepers ancient creations and bodyguards of the Eidolons, created to ensure the peace after it had been negotiated, but so as to not be partisan, the Eidolons chose a species from the far side of the galaxy to breed and modify. Sebaceans have the same ancestry as humans, and Aeryn finds that Crichton is less different from her than she had thought.

Then the Scarran war minister Akhna discovers D'Argo and Chiana's ship flying cloaked and has it destroyed. Meanwhile, Crichton takes Emperor Staleek into a wormhole to introduce him to the being known as Einstein and explains to him the futility and danger of creating a wormhole weapon via an Earth catchphrase. Crichton picks up a snowball and says, "This is your universe." He then crumbles it in his fist. "This is your universe on wormholes. You mess with the natural order, you destroy multiple timelines."

It is a warning, and an omen of what is to come. The emperor returns, angry, but then speaks with Hierarch Yondalao, who reveals his desires and has begun to steer him toward a plan for peace before War Minister Akhna comes in and blasts the hierarch. Before Hierarch Yondalao dies, however, Crichton and Aeryn force Stark to unmask and help the hierarch pass over, taking the knowledge of the ancient Eidolons so that it can be preserved. Meanwhile, Chiana and D'Argo are rescued by Jothee, who's been following in a cloaked ship. Then, at that moment in the emperor's ship, the sands in the hourglass run out and embalming gas is pumped into the chamber as part one of *The Peacekeeper Wars* comes to a close, and in John's dream fugue, he lists the perils facing him and Aeryn, closing with the episode's last reference to *The Wizard of Oz*: "and the lions and tigers and bears."

Oh my. Yes, John Crichton knows what he's up against, even if no one else recognizes all the perils for what they are. He is Dorothy in the Wicked Witch of the West's castle, waiting for rescue and trying desperately to escape. War Minister Akhna's headdress even bears a strong resemblance to the witch's black hat, while Emperor Staleek, in his overelaborate armor, is reminiscent of an extremely overgrown flying monkey.

Part two continues with a dramatic reversal: Crichton finds that the embalming gas is flammable and has "Zippo girl," Sikozu, use her fire-starting powers to ignite a blast, freeing them. D'Argo then gets in contact, revealing that he and Chiana are not dead, and break into the ship to rescue them, just as Dorothy's comrades come to rescue her.

As if that weren't enough, Rygel is not doing well with his pregnancy, so the baby is transferred back into Aeryn. John Crichton then goes into the wormhole to find out how to build the coveted wormhole weapon, which he hopes to use to negotiate a peace, his explanation to Aeryn of the threats facing them an echo of his "lions and tigers and bears" from the end of part one.

More transformations occur, transformations of the mind and emotions. Rygel is reduced to tears by the hormonal imbalance of post-partum depression while Stark vacillates between utter madness and complete lucidity from having the burden of Hierarch Yondalao's mind within his own. Crichton reveals the plans for the wormhole weapon to Pilot and Moya, but they refuse to build it. Stark is taken to see the Eidolons, who are currently under attack by the Scarrans, with the Peacekeepers fighting there as well. Crichton continues his insights, seeing the parallel between himself and Stark as he says, "Stark, I know what you're feeling. You've got something in your head that everybody wants. Something that never should have been there in the first place."

Meanwhile, on the emperor's ship, Staleek proposes a familiar bargain to Akhna: bring him the head of John Crichton, and he will make her Empress when he goes on to rule the galaxy. She descends to the planet to go after the required broomstick.

Another revelation: there is a spy among Crichton's company. It is revealed to be Sikozu, spying for Akhna, but there are greater matters at hand: Aeryn's water has broken, and Stark has begun the transfer of Hierarch Yondalao's knowledge to the Eidolon High Priestess. However, the baby is turned and the doctor has died in the firefight, so Crichton asks Chiana to use her skill to turn the baby, and Aeryn finally allows Crichton to take over cover-fire for them, forced to transform from warrior to mother, at least for the moment.

The breathless transformations here are those of war and chaos. Roles are reversed rapidly. Scorpius and Sikozu go from lovers to enemies. The Priestess has gone from leader and administrator to truly enlightened. Aeryn is about to change from warrior to mother, and Akhna has taken on her own twisted role as Dorothy with Crichton as the witch.

Aeryn then demands for Stark to come to her—yet not to take her pain, but to marry her and Crichton. Rygel provides the lost ring, and after the third attempt, the two are finally married.

While these transformations are those of wartime and pain, mixed in there is an omen for peace. A scant minute after the marriage, Aeryn gives birth. Aeryn asks for John to do her a favor: get them out of there. Though obviously not forever, Aeryn has taken the role of wife, and accepted the protection, or at least aid, of her husband.

In the battle to escape, D'Argo is fatally wounded saving Chiana, but Aeryn saves John from death at Akhna's hands, killing her. She's thus stepped back into her role as warrior, but remains both wife and mother as well, protecting her husband and her baby—and becomes more than a bit of Dorothy, killing the witch.

D'Argo takes some pulse rifles and stays to cover everyone's retreat, giving his sword to Chiana to give it to his son, Jothee. And Rygel steps into a role somewhere between godfather and surrogate mother to the baby as he tells Aeryn to let him carry the boy, since Rygel is hovering and when they leap into Moya's net the baby will be safer.

Once back on Moya, they find that she and Pilot have changed their minds and built the wormhole weapon. Then comes the final and terrible revelation: the wormhole weapon is the ultimate weapon because it starts a wormhole which rips wider and wider, continually doubling, until it destroys the universe. Crichton gives an ultimatum to Scarran Emperor Staleek and Peacekeeper Commandant Grayza: stop fighting and swear peace, with the Eidolons present, or the universe ends—the ultimate transformation, not from war to peace, but from life to nothingness and oblivion.

Grayza is first to capitulate, extremely pregnant and first to think about her children and future generations, but even Staleek sees the futility of his present course. John stops the wormhole and peace is sworn. But in the process, he lapses into a coma.

The omens of peace, however, continue. Stark has made peace with himself from holding the mind of the Eidolon hierarch, and leaves his mask with the unconscious John, the side of his face it previously covered no longer radiating light and his soul but showing only a healed-over scar. Chiana gives Jothee his father's sword, her first step toward coming to grips with her own grief.

Then, in John Crichton's comatose mind, the neural clone of Scorpius John has carried tells him that as all his knowledge of the wormhole technology has been removed from his mind, the clone is dying as well, appearing as Scorpius dying in bed.

Aeryn speaks to her comatose husband, coming to grips with her own motherhood but refusing to give up on him. Yet he awakes, speaking to the baby who's been left beside him, and life goes on. He and Aeryn name their son D'Argo, son of Crichton, and tell him that the universe is his playground.

The end of *The Peacekeeper Wars* is a phantasmagoria of wild action, but as with *The Wizard of Oz*, everything finally falls into place. The Cowardly Lion—Stark—has found his courage. The Tin Man—Scorpius—has realized the futility of his quest, and must go on to find other meaning for his life, perhaps love with Sikozu. Rygel will go off to rule his homeworld, as a Dominar should. D'Argo has died in battle, as he wished to eventually, but passes his sword on to his son and his name to John and Aeryn's child.

And John and Aeryn find that there's no place like home, which they already knew, but for them, home is Moya and a new peaceful universe. The masks have been set aside and they are allowed to be themselves, with no other roles than those they choose, with the same promise for their son.

Somewhere over the rainbow has transformed into somewhere through the wormhole.

> *Kevin Andrew Murphy is the author of various science fiction, fantasy and horror novels, including* House of Secrets, Penny Dreadful, Drum into Silence *and* Fathom: The World Below. *He's also published many short stories and novellas, a number in the* World of Darkness *and* Wild Cards *anthologies, as well as formal poetry and, of course, essays. He lives in California with three whippets and tries to keep up with them. He thinks they may have knowledge of wormholes.*

Printed in the United States
by Baker & Taylor Publisher Services